The Lost Queen

E.M. Jaye

Contents

1. Dedication   1

2. Summary   3

3. Geldon Language Pronunciation and Definition Guide   5

4. Prologue   9

5. Chapter One   11

6. Chapter Two   25

7. Chapter Three   31

8. Chapter Four   41

9. Chapter Five   47

10. Chapter Six   55

11. Chapter Seven   61

12. Chapter Eight   65

13. Chapter Nine   73

14. Chapter Ten   81

15. Chapter Eleven   87

16. Chapter Twelve   97

17. Chapter Thirteen   107

18. Chapter Fourteen   117

19. Chapter Fifteen   129

20. Chapter Sixteen   137

21. Chapter Seventeen   143

22.	Chapter Eighteen	147
23.	Chapter Nineteen	155
24.	Chapter Twenty	165
25.	Chapter Twenty-One	173
26.	Chapter Twenty-Two	179
27.	Chapter Twenty-Three	187
28.	Chapter Twenty-Four	197
29.	Chapter Twenty-Five	207
30.	Chapter Twenty-Six	215
31.	Chapter Twenty-Seven	221
32.	Chapter Twenty-Eight	229
33.	Chapter Twenty-Nine	233
34.	Chapter Thirty	245
35.	Chapter Thirty-One	251
36.	Chapter Thirty-Two	255
37.	Author Notes	261

Dedication

To everyone out there who loves books as much as I do. Books were my first love, and I have been so lucky to be able to share my love with the world.

Summary

She was born to be a Queen, but raised in squalor...

Eleanor Sette is attempting to find her place in the world now that a warrior king has claimed her. After a life of hardship and abuse, she must now learn to lead an army.

If she fails, more than just her life will be on the line. The entire galaxy will fall. She feels overwhelmed by the daunting tasks before her. How can she be a queen when all she feels is lost?

He was born to be her mate, but has lived without her....

Danion Belator of Old, the high warrior king, is the strongest being known in the galaxy, and yet he feels weak. His mate is struggling in her new life, unable to find purchase.

After yet another devastating turn of events, Eleanor's life is threatened once more. He refuses to lose his mate, and he will do whatever it takes to save her.

Even win a war against an unbeatable enemy.

Geldon Language Pronunciation and Definition Guide

Abiciant—(Ab-iss-e-ant) Rare sublineage that allows the weaver to channel their mental energy upon another and control them.

Animare—(An-a-mare) Term of endearment given to a mated male from his female. This term is the highest form of respect one mate can give to another.

Aninare—(An-a-nare) Term of endearment given to a mated female from her male. This term is the highest form of respect one mate can give to another.

Anium—(An-ee-um) One of the six great, or main, lineages, this is the control of the power of water. Warriors gifted in this often exhibit calm personalities.

Atelean—(Ate-lee-on) The family name of the founding Gelder ancients, once the most powerful family in all the galaxy.

Beb—Term of endearment used in the Star language, usually reserved for couple that are in a romantic or sexual relationship.

Belator—(Bell-a-tore) The power name of the high warrior king, belator appeared upon the king when he came into maturity.

Bellum—(Bell-um) Term that refers to securing something, commonly used as a multilayer weave that allows a room to be locked securely.

Caeli—(Say-lee) One of the six great, or main, lineages, this is the control of the power of air. Warriors gifted in this often exhibit joyous and carefree personalities.

Cerum—(Sear-um) Word that designates a ceremony of great importance.

Chakkas—(Cha-kas) Invisible points that run throughout the body that channel the energy of the cosmos.

Cognata—(Cog-na-ta) Familial relations that means cousin.

Deim—(Dem) Curse word, profanity.

Erain—(Air-ens) Race of aliens that thrive on the pain, suffering, and death of all races other than their own. They attempt to commit genocide on any planet they come across. Normally impulsive and historically prone to fighting among each other.

Fiefling—(Feef-ling) Curse word, profanity.

Hael—(Hail) Sublineage that gifts the weaver with healing abilities. Gelders who are strong in this line commonly become medical doctors. Those gifted in caeli, vim, and simul often possess strong gifts in hael as well.

Ignis—(Ig-nis) One of the six great, or main, lineages, this is the control of the power of fire. Warriors gifted in this often exhibit passionate personalities, and are commonly quick to anger.

Itumnis—(It-um-nus) The fountain from ancient Geldon, known for its eternal life.

Lacieu—(Lass-ce-o) The one original lineage, known as the lost line. No one alive is thought to possess a gift in it.

Massa—(Mass-sa) Title of honor to a warrior who possesses mastery in a lineage.

Medate—(Meh-date) Form of meditation that only the most disciplined warrior can perform. It allows the weaver to access every fragment of information they have ever come across, even something that they did not consciously know they observed. Performed incorrectly it can destroy the mind of the warrior who attempts it.

Memien—(Mem-ee-in) A physical manifestation of power, it can function as a power source and can protect, attack, or provide energy to the weaver.

Merate—(Meh-rate) Lighter form of meditation that warriors who are adept with mental skills can achieve.

Myo—(My-oh) Meaning my or mine.

Praesidium—(Pray-seed-ee-um) A group of six warriors who are masters in their lineage that are pledged to protecting their pledge holder.

Ratshult—(Rat-shult) Derogatory name.

Scimaar—(Sim-mar) A blade used by the Gelders in battle.

Starskies—(Star-skees) An alcoholic beverage that is so potent that even a Gelder can become inebriated.

Tatio—(Tat-tee-oh) Unique mineral that is necessary for Gelders to be able to weave their power.

Terra—(Tare-ah) One of the six great, or main, lineages, this is the control of the power of rocks and minerals. Warriors gifted in this often exhibit stoic personalities, and are commonly levelheaded and serious in nature.

Prologue

The room is quiet as the projection slowly fades out and is replaced by a pod rising from the floor. Inside is what looks like a sleeping man, but I know that he is in something much deeper.

I glance around the room at all the males who have worked together to bring me here, to this lost city, so that I could find my father. A father that apparently placed himself into hibernation to save me, not to abandon me as I have believed my whole life.

So much information has been thrust at me in the last few minutes that I can barely comprehend where I am. Some floating city in the middle of the ocean, with my mate, Danion, by my side. It seems surreal that we were just on his ship barely a day ago.

My mind is still reeling from the last lines of his message,

"I am entering into hibernation now to await the time you come for me so that I can help guide you and nurture you. I want to help you understand what it means to be of the Atelean bloodline. Help you save the universe."

"Did I hear him right? Did he say *Atelean* bloodline?" Arsenio, the fire master in my elite guard, asks with shock and disbelief dripping from his words.

"Yes. Yes, he did." This is from Etan, the master of air in my guard.

"I never thought this could be possible. That one was still alive," the water master Malin says reverently. I can actually feel his eyes upon me, his gaze is so intense.

"What do you mean? What does an Atelean bloodline mean?" I ask. My mate, Danion, is the one who speaks in answer.

"The Atelean bloodline is the original bloodline. The very first Gelders to master the lineages. The very first Gelders ever recorded. We thought that they all died out before the transition." Danion stares at me in awe. "You are the youngest member to the oldest legacy in the cosmos. You are the daughter of an ancient people."

Chapter One

Ellie

The room I am in is glittering with golden accents, interspersed with sleek gray modernized medical equipment. At least, that's what I think it is. My eyes can only drift around in small spurts as my gaze is continually being drawn back to the center of the room.

A large, cylindrical tube is standing where it recently rose from the floor. Inside the pillar is a sight I never thought I would see in my life. A large, blond male is encased inside, appearing to be asleep.

I stare at the frozen male in front of me. My father. I never suspected that I would meet him. We have just seen the message that he left for me to hear. A message that told me how much he cares about me. As well as to let me know that he had no choice but to leave me when I was born.

My mind struggles to comprehend how much planning and preparation this man had to put in twenty years ago to ensure that I was able to find him. It is so hard to accept; my whole life I thought that no one loved me, especially my parents. The possibility that my father does is as equally terrifying as it is thrilling.

He blessed a locket for me, literally put his heart and soul in it, just so that it could lead me here. He created a glamour to cover this entire city so that no one could find this place. Ensuring that it remained untouched for me alone. Everything he did was for me. So that I would be able to live.

My father's message explained that without this mineral unique to the Gelder home world, *tatio*, I would not develop correctly. He was able to sense this when he first held me. So to keep me alive he placed himself in this frozen sleep so that I could have the entire supply after he left.

If what he says is true, the male I have resented for abandoning me may very well love me, may cherish me as his daughter. If I can figure out how to wake him up, I might finally have the answers I have always craved.

"No. There is no way that we are waking this male up." I am startled by the vehement denial coming from my left. Hesitation over waking him up is not unexpected; I knew there would be fierce arguments over this decision. What is surprising is who voiced the rejection.

"Arsenio. I appreciate your concern over my wellbeing, but it is not your decision to make. He is my father and we will be waking him up," I inform Arsenio, the *ignis* master in my elite guard, my *praesidium*. I do not only speak to him but include the entire group of warriors before me in my response. I will not budge on this. My father will be woken up.

"Eleanor, you do not understand. People who hibernate in the frozen sleep are often not the same as when they went in. And your father, he has been using this to extend his life for thousands of years. It is not safe to wake him." This comes from Golon, the only male here who is not actually one of my guards. Golon is my mate's cousin, and the most intelligent being I have ever met. I instantly take offense to his words.

"He seemed perfectly well to me in his message, and that was only twenty years ago." Golon and Arsenio open their mouths to argue, but I give them no chance. "No. We are going to do this, it is not your call to make." But with my words, I feel ice skate down my spine.

There is one male who can decide not to wake him up. Danion, my mate and king to every warrior in this room. If he decides against this I have no hope of waking him. He will of course side with these warriors, fearing for my safety. Danion has made no efforts to hide his obsession with keeping me safe; merely traveling to this city resulted in a passionate argument between us.

I slowly turn to the male who has been deceptively quiet all this time. Danion is no doubt biding his time to voice his decision, to command me to return to our watership and then head back to the safety of the shuttle in orbit.

While his determination to protect me from all things can be an exceedingly frustrating quality, his looks go a long way in soothing the ire he instills within me.

He is a tall, striking vision of male perfection. Black hair encompasses his head and curls around his ears like a dark halo. It's infused with a rainbow of color that emits from his aura. This beautiful mixture of color is only visible to me since I am gifted in aura sight. Something I only learned about a short while ago.

His piercing gray eyes never fail to send desire coursing through my body. I have never seen eyes with such a color before. Their depths can express so much emotion, including pain. I know that the distance I have let grow between us is hurting this male. We have had such a rocky beginning to our relationship.

In the beginning, I was a weak, spineless girl who blindly followed whoever was in front of her. Never questioning a command or grasping for a better life. If I was hit, I took the punch with barely a whimper. When I was purposely starved by my witch of a mother I merely sat and watched her eat while I let the hunger pangs cramp my stomach, telling no one and making no move to fight back.

Looking back, I can hardly believe I was ever that girl. In many ways I resent myself for the girl I was. She feels as if she was a different person; she can't be me. The me I am now fights for what I believe in. I speak up and let my voice be heard.

Ever since I joined minds with Danion I have found the strength I have always craved. I do not know where it comes from, maybe I am getting some of Danion's power, but I am grateful for it.

Danion still tries to bulldoze me as if I am that same girl he first met. I believe that he would be happier if I were that same weak girl, the girl who fainted in front of him when I first heard his name.

She would not have forced herself to be allowed on this ship. I had to fight tooth and nail to be able to even come and search for this ship. There is no way he is going to support my decision to wake my father. I must convince him to assist me in this. I am so focused on drafting out my argument that I almost miss what he is saying.

"We will wake this Jaeson Atelean." His words are stark. He speaks them with a deep sense of resignation.

"Why?" I ask him, completely baffled by his decision. Just two days ago, he did not even want me to come to Earth to search for this ship-turned-city, and now he is willing to let me awaken my father from his hibernation? When his own warriors fear it is too dangerous to do so?

"I am done doubting you, *aninare*. You are more than capable of making choices in your own life. It may have taken me a little while to accept that, but that doesn't make it less true," he tells me with a smile on his face. "I will spend the rest of eternity proving to you your worth. Proving to you that the strong female you are is well worth any hardship. I may not deserve you, but I am going to spend every day trying to earn that right."

I walk over to him and take his hand in mine. Gratitude is evident in the smile on my face. I feel a small smidge of remorse for doubting he would ever support me before I push it down. You can't fault me for being skeptical of him, this is the first time he has listened to my wishes in regard to anything that could even be a little bit dangerous.

"Danion, this is ridiculous!" Arsenio protests loudly. "You know as well as I do the dangers of long-term hibernation! We have seen them firsthand. They went mad!"

"Danion, I have to say I agree with Arsenio for once," Golon adds. "There are several risks to freezing oneself. Very few come out undamaged, even from a short stay in the chambers. This male has been in this chamber for no short stay."

Danion's eyes remain unmoved by Arsenio's and Golon's passionate and adamant protests. Seeing this, they both turn their backs away in anger, stalking to the other side of the room.

"Please, Golon. Arsenio. You need to understand. My whole life has been so dismal. My mother never hid her distaste for me. I must know if my father did love me. I just have to know," I plead to them both.

"This is absurd! You have no need for this male! You should not crave his approval or his love. WE are here for you. WE accept you." Arsenio speaks his words so loudly that having his back to me does nothing to lessen the blow of the words. "And if our so-called *king* allows you to do this then he is an incompetent, *fiefli*—"

"Arsenio! That is enough!" Arsenio's heated string of insults is cut off by no other than Malin, the *anium* master. Malin usually is so calm and collected I am surprised by his outburst.

Arsenio turns around rapidly and faces Malin, fire leaping from his hands. Their gazes are locked on each other. Unspoken words flying between them.

"Malin, this is no concern of yours," Arsenio growls at him.

"That is where you are wrong. Everything you do is a concern of mine." Malin calmly counters.

Malin's words cause Arsenio's raging hands to blaze higher, the flames climbing up to his shoulders. I look to Danion, opening my mouth to ask him to end this before Arsenio harms Malin. Before I can get a word out, my sight is covered by a blue filter.

I do not have to search long to find the source of this light. I turn to Malin and am bombarded with a blue light so fierce I have to raise my arm to shield my eyes. His aura is rippling with waves of angry, pulsing power. His aura, however, is nothing compared to the rage that his eyes are leveling at Arsenio.

"Arsenio, you are nothing but a child. You always have been. I had hoped that all these years would have let you heal. I have let you control your own life. Grieve in your own way. But I cannot stand idly by and allow your self-destruction to once again harm those I am sworn to protect." Malin's aura pulses brighter and brighter until I have to cover my eyes completely.

Danion comes up behind me and places his hands on my shoulders. I can feel power flow through his hands into me. The contact allows me to look at the two males before me, my eyes adjusting to the piercing brightness. So much tension is between them. I can tell that we are only moments away from witnessing a massive battle between these two elite warriors.

"Oh, you *let* me grieve in my own way?! You are an arrogant, conceited insult to the title of warrior." Arsenio answers Malin's comment, his words dripping with scorn.

"And you have no HONOR!" The last word explodes out of Malin. I have never seen him so angry. Similar to Etan, the *caeli* master, Malin is usually more controlled. I rarely see them angry at all. Right now, Malin's anger is at the level of Danion's.

Which is saying something, believe me.

But he is not done yet.

"You accuse me of being arrogant, yet you are the one who allows your own false confidence to blind you from logic. I am a stronger warrior than you, several decades older, and have seen dozens more battles. And yet you stand there, arms blazing as if you hold the seat of power, while we are surrounded by my element, no less. I can snuff out your little fireworks display anytime I wish." Malin takes a step toward Arsenio.

"That is where you are wrong, because I do have the seat of power," Arsenio answers with a haughty cock of his eyebrow. "I always have, I am stronger than you, Malin." Arsenio's words drip scorn. His lip quirking up on one side.

Instead of heated words, Malin attacks. I am swept up in Danion's arms with Golon, Etan, and Griffith, the master of *vim*, appearing in front of us.

The color that was flooding the room is suddenly pummeled at Arsenio. As soon as it touches him his aura manifests itself into water. The water extinguishes the fire Arsenio had called forth, and before he can call any more, Malin has him imprisoned within a wall of water.

"You disappoint me, Senio." Malin's words are no longer angry, they are dejected. "Which should be no surprise. You have been disappointing me for centuries. Ever since that day I have been waiting for you to finally return to the male I know you can be. Yet you always decide to make the wrong choice." Malin takes a step closer to the water-caught Arsenio.

"I thought that your return from exile would be the sign that you are ready to be with us again. Ready to be a warrior. But if you can't even hold your own against me, how can you protect our queen?" Malin lets his words hang heavy in the room.

He makes contact with Arsenio. I crane my head to see through the wall of males in front of me. Arsenio's eyes surprise me. I expected to see anger, belligerence, possibly even a return of his fire. But instead his eyes are full of despair. His eyes show a male in the most profound pain. I can tell that Malin's words have cut him to his core.

Arsenio and I have formed a close bond; his allegiance is pledged to me alone, not Danion. I know how Malin's words must hurt him. I feel his pain as if it was my own, but Malin is not done.

"You do her a disservice, Senio. Every day that you throw away your potential you mock her and everything she stood for. I know you have decided that you can live without me in your life, that is fine. But we are a legacy. And you dishonor it."

With that final body blow, Malin turns away from Arsenio. As he walks toward the door and reaches our group, he takes a brief moment to address us.

"There is no reason to be shielding our queen, I was in complete control." Malin makes direct eye contact with me. "I would never harm you, directly or indirectly."

"I know." I nod at him; it is not myself that I am worried about. I cannot help but steal a glance at Arsenio, still imprisoned in a wall of water.

"Do not fear for him, I am weaving oxygen within the water. He is fine. However, I cannot remain here with him and still let that be the case. I am going to go patrol the city." Malin gives a brief bow to me and then Danion, and disappears.

As soon as he crests the doorway Arsenio collapses to the floor, water bursting free of its confines and flooding the room. He is on his hands and knees in the middle of the puddle, his head hanging low. I open my mouth to speak but four males quickly stop me with curt shakes of their heads.

I don't know how long we stay silent, locked in our positions, before Arsenio moves.

He stands and exits the room, saying not even one word to any of us.

"What was that all about?" I ask Danion, turning my body in his arms so that I can make eye contact without straining my head.

"There is history between them. Strong, bloody history. We have been waiting for a blowup like this for over five hundred years," Danion answers me.

With a squeeze, he lowers me to the ground.

"What kind of history?" I ask. I know Arsenio committed a horrible crime at some point in his past, but no one has ever explained to me what it was. I wonder if it has anything to do with the tension that is evident between these two warriors.

"That is a story only they can share. It is not our place to disclose it," Danion tells me. In my peripheral vision, I notice Golon and Griffith going to study the display that is in front of my father's chamber.

"You can't tell me anything? There is obviously some bad blood between them." I talk to Danion, but my body is moving toward my father as if I am being drawn to him.

"There is blood, alright." Danion replies to me. For some reason Golon scoffs with dry humor at his words.

"Yes, blood is a very apt way to put it," Etan comments with laughter in his eyes and words. This warrior is often more carefree than the others.

Soon all four warriors are joining in with Etan, and everyone is having a merry old time.

"Go ahead, laugh it up. You do realize that I have no idea why you all think this is so funny, right?" I ask each of them.

"We know, but it is not our place to tell you. It is not our secret to share." Danion walks up behind me and wraps his arm around my waist. "I am sorry, *aninare*. I would tell you if I could."

Danion nuzzles my neck and places a small, heated kiss below my ear, whispering at the same time.

"Do not be cross, sweet *aninare*. Truly, you will know when they are ready to share their story." His words, whispered in my ear sends shivers up and down my spine. Heating my blood and causing a slow burn to start deep inside me.

I am about to respond when the conversation between Golon and Griffith penetrates my lust-addled mind.

"What do you mean it isn't working? Is it the water from Malin?" Griffith is questioning Golon, who is studying the display intently before him.

The sizeable holographic display is projected up from the floor right in front of the chamber that is holding my hibernating father.

"No, I do not think that would have anything to do with it." Golon's answer is distracted. I move out of Danion's embrace and step toward him.

"Golon? What is wrong?" I ask him, anxiety heavy in my tone.

"While I do not agree with your decision to wake him up, I respect that it is indeed your decision. I came over to begin the process of awakening him, as bringing someone out of a freeze like this can be lengthy. But there is a problem."

"What kind of problem?" Danion asks as he steps up next to Golon on my other side.

"It is different than the models we use today. In fact, it seems much more comprehensive. Much more intricate regarding safely preserving every organic process. In the systems that I am familiar with a large amount of the process relies on our own bodies natural abilities to heal the damage from freezing our tissue. But this one?" Golon quickly shakes his head. "This has everything accounted for so precisely that I have no idea which system needs to be used to awaken him. I do not even know where to begin if I am to wake him up safely."

"How is it even better than what you are used to? Wouldn't this be the original technology? Outdated?" I ask him. I would think that after thousands of years they would have a perfect method and the old one would be flawed.

"It is older, but in no way outdated. This is not what we based our current technology on. I have never seen anything like this. It may be just one of many wonders that we will uncover here in our lost city," Golon says with a glance around the room.

His expression is hungry. A scientist such as Golon would think of this city as the ultimate knowledge playground. A thought I share with him. The secrets that this city must hold.

"You are going to be able to wake him up, right?" I ask him.

"I believe so. But it will take some time. Griffith and Etan will need to assist me. Their gifts in *hael* should provide insight into how to start the reverse process and wake him up," he tells me.

"What can I do to help?" I ask. I want to be a part of waking my father.

"There is nothing that I need from you here." I can feel my face fall. "However, there may be some answers in some of the archive rooms. Perhaps you and Danion can do some exploring and see if you can find any information on the preservation technology?" he asks of us both.

I know that he is just humoring me, but I appreciate being able to do something. Besides, we might find something truly remarkable here in this city.

A city that has been lost for over five thousand years is a dream come true to a historian like me.

Danion

I take Eleanor's hand in mine as we walk from the room that houses her father. My mind is traveling at the speed of light.

So many mysteries that have plagued us for eons are slowly coming to light. And instead of providing answers, I am filled with more questions. I am more in the dark than ever. They seem to be connected in a way that I am too blind to see.

One thing I know is that my mate is much more capable than she ever thought she was, more than I ever believed her to be.

"Do you think Golon will be able to wake him up?" I hear the distress in my mate's voice.

"Yes, I am sure he will be able to wake him," I assure her. Golon is one of the most capable males I know.

"That is good," Eleanor responds distractedly. I can tell there is more on her mind.

I study my mate as we walk. Eleanor is dressed in the casual wear of our people. While the rest of our party are dressed in war attire: brown leather pants with hidden sheaths for the several dozen blades we carry, and thin skintight shirts with *memien* woven throughout them.

Memien is a particular thread that is an actual physical embodiment of our powers. It is literally our power harnessed into the physical and then threaded into clothing. Only true masters can manifest it. In battle, a warrior is able to use this material as a power source, or if they are wounded it will heal them automatically.

Eleanor is radiant in the clothes of my people. She is dressed in a deep blue that she chose this morning. The pants are tight-fitting at the hips and ankles, while it flows in all the areas in between. The matching top is comprised of a length of material that is wrapped around her chest and upper abdomen.

It forms an X around her breasts and wraps together beneath her chest, amplifying her generous cleavage. No female has ever filled out clothing in quite the same way. Or more perfectly. She is an exquisite creature.

My eyes travel down to the skin that is left exposed between her shirt and pants. The bottom of her shirt falls to just above her belly button on her flat stomach and her pants ride right at her hips, leaving a tantalizing view of bare skin for me to admire.

It takes me a few moments to realize that she has been talking this whole time. My mind struggles to focus on her words and not what I want to be doing to her body.

"...in a city this size where do we start? I don't even know what I am looking for."

"Do not worry, *aninare*. Your father will soon be awake," I try to reassure her. "There is no one more dependable than Golon."

"I know that Golon was just humoring me about searching for clues, and I am excited to explore this city but...I also want to be there for my father."

"Eleanor, we have no idea what treasures could have been left behind in this city. It has been lost for thousands of years. Most of the historical records from that time period were lost along with it. This is literally a piece of our history we never thought to recover." I can't help but let my gaze sweep over the city before me.

My mind is racing with all the potential mysteries to be solved by the information housed in this city.

"You are right, Danion. Every corner of this city is literally covered in history. I suppose we could start anywhere and go from there?" Eleanor asks me.

"Yes, we could. Even if it does not directly appear to be linked to your father's predicament, it may still hold the key to saving our race from extinction." I hold out my hand for her and gather her close to my side as I guide us down a narrow corridor between buildings.

This city, the lost city of the Atelean family, has been missing for several thousands of years. It is an ancient historical record that is reported to house all known archives of the history of our people.

It was lost to us right at the time of transition for our kind. The transition is the time that we evolved to be fully immortal. No natural cause of death can claim my people. Not age, no diseases, we genuinely are immortal. Unless we die in battle or take our own lives we will live for all eternity. Although without a mate the countless millennia begin to feel more like a curse than a gift. I wonder if our ancestors preferred their extended lives instead of our never-ending ones.

The time of transition was a perilous experience for my ancestors. It is one of the bloodiest eras, rife with civil unrest, so I am unsure how they felt. It is one of the many mysteries I am hopeful will be solved by reading the vast archives held within this lost city.

"What do you know of the time of our transition, *aninare*?" I ask my mate.

Her brow furrows. "Well, only what you have told me really. That it is when the Gelders finally evolved into true immortals. Now no natural disease or age will kill you. You truly are immortal."

"Yes, all that is true." I pause and take a deep breath. "What you may not know is that at the time of transition, we were in a civil war. That is why so many of our spiritual landmarks were transported to ships."

Her beautiful face is shocked. I can tell that she was not expecting this. As a rule, we Gelders are a peaceful people. We may be a warrior race, but civil disputes are few and far between. We defend those who cannot protect themselves. It is the oath that binds us together.

That is why we are at war with the Erains. They are a race filled with hate. That hate is matched with a bloodthirsty malevolence that enjoys inflicting pain on others. Over two millennia ago the Erains took to the cosmos using stolen technology, our stolen technology, and began enslaving every race they could.

Those that they cannot enslave they murder. Whenever possible we intercede, and we fight on the weaker planet's behalf.

Wait...not weaker. It is thoughts like that which anger my mate. It is just recently that my *aninare* brought to my attention my mistaken, and somewhat subconscious, belief that I am better than the mortal races.

It is not that I necessarily believe that they are inferior, it's just that I know that they are very young in regards to maturity. They are rife with crimes against their own people.

I always felt that there was nothing wrong with allowing these mortal races a few hundred years to evolve before I began interacting with them. If Eleanor had not opened my eyes to the error of my ways I would still be blind to the many beauties of the human race. Humans may be flawed in many ways, but these very flaws make them beautiful.

After the day spent with my mate's human family and friend I realize that humans can be a source of joy. The children, Eleanor's sisters, have such bright and shining souls that you cannot help but be drawn in by their happiness.

While humans may not yet be as civil as Gelders, it does not make them inferior. One of the many lessons I expect my mate to teach me.

"You were at war? I never knew the Gelders had a history of fighting among themselves," Eleanor comments, confirming my earlier suspicion that she does not know much of our history.

"Yes, we do not have much of a history of war, and none since the transition, but before that we did have some horrific wars," I tell her.

"Why were the ancients at war?"

"It is not known for sure. This city was supposed to hold the archives and it was lost. Since it was resolved when we evolved, it is suspected to be related to some form of the disease that was plaguing our ancestors," I answer her.

"Hmm...that is a strange reason to cause a dispute large enough to start a war over. Disease? People were upset that their fellow man was falling ill and therefore they kill them?" She shakes her head. "I have studied history and I do not believe that is possible. It may have been the lie that they hid behind, but the true reason was probably darker than that."

I smile at her. I take her hand and pull her toward a golden alley that appears to bisect the city in half. We walk down the aisle as we continue speaking.

"You misunderstand. I do not mean that the ancestors were fighting over contracting a disease. From studying the very little evidence left behind it is believed that there was some form of disease that was causing our ancestors to fall ill. The dispute was over how to cure it," I explain to her. "Some felt that nature should be allowed to run its course, while others felt that science should be involved."

I rub her hand with my thumb idly, enjoying the smooth texture and supple tautness of her skin. I can feel my body begin to heat, blood traveling rapidly to thicken my shaft.

I am shocked. I am over three thousand Earth years old and never before has touching a female's *hand* ignited such desire within me. Everything about my mate is desirable.

I breathe deeply, trying to bring my body under control. But then I realize that not all of the desire I feel is coming from me. I study my mate in depth and take into account her accelerated breathing and flushed skin.

Through the partial bond between us I realize she is sending some of her desire to me. I know she is unaware of this. I selfishly have hidden the fact that her mind has reached out to me and that we are connected.

I know from past experience that she will retreat if I make her aware that I can hear part of her thoughts. I can't read her mind as she fears, not yet. But I can sense her emotions.

Because of this, I know that my simple caress is kindling an answering burn deep within her. I cannot keep the smug smile off my face.

While I understand Eleanor's reticence to engage in physical love once more, I cannot hide that I am desperate to feel her surrounding me again, desperate for the connection

I felt last time. I am so aroused every single time that I share space with her that the knowledge that she too feels the burn of arousal gives me comfort. A very small comfort, but still a comfort nonetheless.

As we crest a corner, I stop dead. No. I cannot believe my eyes. It was lost to us. I know it was destroyed.

"It cannot be! The *Itumnis*." I gasp.

Chapter Two

Ellie

"What is an *Itumnis*?" I ask Danion.

At his lack of response, I look up at him and notice he has gone completely still. His face is one of complete shock.

I follow his gaze to a fountain that is directly across from us. It is gorgeous. It is filled with water that seems to glow as if the water itself is filled with sunlight.

Its vast basin has curved outer edges that swoop to meet in the middle. It resembles a figure eight. The real beauty of the fountain, however, is the feature in the center.

In the heart of the fountain, right above where the two halves meet, is a glorious ribbon of water that appears to be rising from the fountain on its own. It flows up and sweeps over into a glorious swirling pattern. It then turns into itself and flows back down toward the base of the structure.

As I study the water I feel like the downward flow is moving too slowly, as if it is only gently affected by gravity.

"Dane? Are you alright?" I ask him. When that too does not garner a response, I pull on his hand and try to grab his attention.

I repeat his name several times. Finally, he seems to pull himself from his shock and turn his gaze to me.

"Eleanor." Danion opens his mouth a few times and closes it. I have never seen him at a loss for words before. Finally, he seems to find them.

"The *Itumnis* is one of the most revered spiritual relics of our people. It is the basis of our *cerum fuse* ceremony that we partook in. It is the reason why we were first able to bind our souls to our partners."

His words shock me. My eyes flash back to the fountain. It does appear beautiful, but how could it unite souls?

"How?" I ask him. Danion pulls me even closer to his body and wraps his arms around me. He guides me to the fountain and gently presses me down so we can sit on the base of the spring.

At first glance I did not notice that the fountain has carved seats along its edge. The seats are paired and spaced far enough apart that if you are sitting in them you would be isolated from anyone else in the neighboring spaces.

The seats angle our bodies to face each other while still being able to look at the shining water.

"This is the original water that *tatio* was discovered in from Geldon, our home planet."

"Oh, yes, Golon did say that the mineral was found in water," I comment. *Tatio* is a mineral that is the cause behind why the Gelders are able to weave the powers they do.

"Yes, but long before it infected the main water supply it was within the *Itumnis.* This water source is steeped in folklore for our people. For example, it is rumored to be the gift of longevity. To drink its water will cure all ailments."

"That is so interesting, we have a similar myth on Earth. We call it the fountain of youth." Danion looks at me carefully, then his expression clears.

"In truth, it can heal ailments and extend your life, but not because it has *tatio* inside it. It is because it is the liquid form of *tatio.*"

"What do you mean?" I ask him.

"An element can take on many physical states. While *tatio* is more commonly found in its solid state it can exist in both a liquid and a gaseous state. This stream is the only known source of naturally occurring liquid *tatio.*" His words are heavy with implied meaning.

"So this is not water?" I ask rather stupidly.

"No, it is not. It is so much more. Do you know what *Itumnis* translates to in your language?" Danion asks me.

"No. What does it mean?"

"There is no exact translation, but loosely it means 'Infinity Stream.' It is named this because it will never run out. It replenishes itself. It can also move on its own accord. See the *tatio* in the center?"

My eyes are drawn to the water flowing upward independently and then down too slowly for gravity to be the cause of its motion. I nod slowly.

"It is not controlled by any laws of physics that you know of. It is a force all on its own. This used to be what the goblets in the *cerum fuse* were filled with. However, now we use an engineered blend of *tatio*."

My eyes move across the fountain. At this new angle, I can see clearly that the *tatio* flows in and around itself, much like an infinity sign.

"Infinity..." I murmur to myself. Many mysteries and myths seem to be focused around this city and Gelder custom. I wonder if the spell to keep humans out failed in the past and this is why so many myths and legends were brought out into the world of man.

"The never-ending supply is meant to symbolize the bond between souls. That no matter what forces are working against us we will move how we choose. Our matebond is ours to control, no one else's."

Danion takes both of my hands within his and turns them, so the palms are facing upward. His fingers glide back and forth along my palm and up my inner wrists.

I feel the fire begin to rise within me once more. My body is hungry for Danion's. He is such a virile male. Large and strong. A perfect opposite to my smaller physique.

My skin feels like it is on fire, a pulsing need is blazing deep within me. It is commanding me to give in and let it take me to the island of paradise it knows Danion can bring me to. I have no more will left to fight my desire for this male.

I decide to throw caution to the wind, and I straddle Danion and press my mouth to his. I have limited experience in anything sexual, explicitly limited to him, but I am determined to get a response.

Danion's lips are hard and unresponsive against mine at first. I feel my confidence begin to wane, but before I can think any more about it his arms come up around me and his lips are ferocious against mine.

His hands begin running up my back fervently as if he cannot get enough of the feel of my body. With every arc of his hands I feel the desire inside me climb ever higher. I begin to move sensually on his lap. Pressing as much of my body into his as I can.

Danion's lips pull away from mine momentarily.

"Eleanor...you are perfection." His lips crash down on mine again.

I am unable to resist moaning in pleasure as Danion's hands begin to move to the front of my body and caress my aching breasts. His hands are stroking me with just the right amount of pressure. I can feel the hard length between us growing firmer.

One of his hands begins to travel lower, skating the waistband of my pants. Danion raises his head and searches my face for approval. I give him a shaky nod. I want this.

His fingers delve between my legs and pleasure I cannot contain shoots throughout my body, causing me to groan loudly in ecstasy. He works me skillfully and I can feel my body tightening, working toward a glorious climax.

I throw my head back and gasp for air. "Danion, oh Danion." His name is the only thing I am capable of saying at this point.

"Let go, *aninare*. Give it to me," Danion growls. His voice is rough with passion. And at his fervent command, I detonate around him. I have no idea how long it is until I am aware of my surroundings again but when I am finally able to focus on him again my body is boneless.

Danion is looking at me with a triumphant smirk. He opens his mouth to speak when movement over my shoulder distracts him. I glance back to see Arsenio walking briskly toward the edge of the city.

I track him and notice that he is headed for Malin, who is just barely discernable in the distance. I feel myself flush with embarrassment. I was so lost to the sensation that I never thought about the chance of being discovered by one of our many companions.

I move to slide off of Danion's lap and am stopped by his tight grip on my legs.

"No, do not feel embarrassed. No one could see you. Do you really think that I would let another male witness you in climax?" he asks me.

"Well...no, I guess not?" I can't keep the question out of my voice. While we may have known each other for a few months now, one entire month was spent with my refusing to talk to him and then I was comatose for several weeks on top of that. I do not know him well enough to feel confident in his behaviors.

Danion heaves a giant sigh. "No, I would not. You are mine and mine alone, there is nothing about you that I would share with another male."

His possessive words send a delicious shiver down my spine. I smile at Danion, then my hands move almost of their own accord and sweep his hair back out of his eyes. His black hair hangs down his forehead, brushing the tops of his eyes.

I see his gray eyes darken with warmth and he returns my smile.

"I love your smile, *animare*." I enunciate this last word carefully, watching his pupils dilate upon hearing it from me. I do not know how I know this, but I can actually sense his pleasure inside my own head.

I know that nothing has ever caused him as much pleasure as my calling him *animare* does. Not even our physical joining means as much to him as me calling him this simple name.

"As I love yours, *aninare*." Danion leans forward and gives me a small, chaste kiss along my jaw.

"Do you want to find a more private place and...take care of your...needs?" I stumble awkwardly over my words. My former bravery has deserted me in the light of almost being discovered.

But I can still feel Danion's desire, and I know that he must be desperate for relief. Before he can respond our attention is dragged away by raised voices.

"You will speak with me, Malin!" I hear Arsenio's angry voice growing louder with each word. I turn away from my mate and see Malin storming away from Arsenio, and the latter is following closely on his heels.

"We said everything that we needed to say already. You refuse to admit to your faults, and I refuse to ignore them any longer," Malin responds coldly.

"I am ready to listen. Malin, we need to discuss this." My heart is torn at the pleading note in Arsenio's voice.

I turn to Danion. "What is this all about?" I whisper to not disturb the two warriors.

"It appears Malin may have finally reached Arsenio and caused him to see reason."

"What does that mean?"

"It means that I am not going to be accepting your offer of finding a private room," Danion says with a smirk. "If you want to know the truth of Arsenio's past I recommend you follow them."

I look at him, shocked.

"Don't you think I would be intruding on their private conversation?" I ask.

"No. In fact, I think that you would help mend some bridges that are in desperate need of mending." I look at him doubtfully, but he only nods his head at me.

"You really think I can help?"

"Yes, I think you may be the only one who can."

Fueled by his confidence, and my own curiosity to finally learn what crime Arsenio committed, I nod at my mate and rise from his lap. With one last look at Danion, I turn and follow Arsenio and Malin.

Chapter Three

Ellie

"Do you mind if I join you?" I ask the pair of males before me. They are standing rigidly facing each other. Silent and challenging, both daring the other one to speak first.

I get only a nod from each of them as an answer to my question. It is not exactly a warm welcome, but I take it. I walk over to Arsenio and Malin and stand precisely in the middle of these two warriors.

Tension is thick in the air. Both warriors have pulsing auras that I can see shooting wildly outward from their bodies. Few people can see auras as I can; this gift of aura sight allows me to see the inner turmoil of a warrior. It is clear that these two warriors are waging a war inside themselves.

Both of these males are important to me. I may not have known them long, but I know that they are two of the closest friends I have. I study the male on my right.

His features are dark and striking. Like almost all the Gelder males I know, he has black hair and brown eyes. He has a red glow around him though, marking him unambiguously as an *ignis* weaver. Arsenio, the one warrior in my *praesidium* that has pledged his loyalty to me first, not Danion.

Arsenio is dressed in his warrior attire: dark brown leather pants that conceal hidden blades down his entire outer leg. The slats in the leather are so well hidden that they are impossible to see with the naked eye.

The red threads woven into his tight brown shirt are so striking, however these threads are more than just cloth. They are created out of the very power he wields. In fact, in the event of a battle, he could draw upon his *memien* weaves to use as an extra power source when he needs it. The sleeves stretch over his biceps and stop mid-muscle.

This length is specific to his warrior class. As king and queen, Danion and I wear no sleeves. Gelder society is based upon a power hierarchy. They have no currency, and since they have access to the resources of the entire galaxy they have no need to purchase goods.

If you are strong enough to defend your position in society, then you are strong enough to gather your own resources. Since clothing itself is a source of power to the Gelders, the amount of clothing you wear showcases whether you are capable of defending your property without assistance.

To the Gelders, the more skin you show, the more powerful you are. Danion and I were married in next to nothing. It is definitely one of the customs I struggle with the most. Even standing here in my current attire makes me feel exposed. It is difficult to become used to baring so much skin when you never have before.

I turn my attention to the male to my left, and I stare at him in shock. Malin typically has an affable expression and an easy smile to match, but now his features are locked in fierce antagonism. I see his jaw clenched tight, his teeth grinding so hard I swear I can hear them from here.

His attire is almost identical to Arsenio's, except his shirt is woven with blue threads. They are both of the same warrior class: masters. They represent the best of their lineages, therefore the length of their sleeves is identical. No other warrior, except the king, is stronger in their power lines than they are.

As my gaze moves between these two warriors, I notice something extraordinary. Something that I have never noticed before because I have never seen Malin scowl.

"You both have the same nose and jawline, do you know that?" I ask them, shock evident in my voice.

Both Malin's and Arsenio's faces lock into even fiercer scowls. If you had asked me two seconds ago, I would have told you there was no way they would be able to look even angrier and I would have been wrong. I can actually feel the anger radiating between the two fierce warriors.

The silence stretches on for minutes. Just as I am about to scream to break the tension, Malin speaks.

"Shall you tell her, or shall I?" he asks Arsenio with one eyebrow cocked in challenge.

Arsenio's only response is a blistering glare. His glare encompasses both Malin and me.

"Tell me what?" I ask Arsenio, then Malin when I get no response from the fire master.

"Yes, Senio, tell her what?" Malin queries to Arsenio. I am so focused on the unsaid tension that I don't even begin to ponder why I am just hearing this shortened version of Arsenio's name today. "Senio? Do I tell her then?" Malin asks again.

Still, there is no response from Arsenio. I turn my attention entirely to Malin.

"Tell me what, Malin?"

"Tell you the true connection that exists between Arsenio and me." Malin speaks to me but directs his gaze to Arsenio, his eyes issuing a clear challenge. "No refusal? No response at all? Are you that worried about our dear queen discovering the truth about you?"

Arsenio's silence is damning.

"Fine. I will tell our queen then," Malin responds defiantly.

The blue shrouded warrior fixes his hard stare on me and his words leave me speechless. If he had stripped naked in front of me I would not have been more shocked.

"Arsenio is my brother."

It takes me several seconds before I am even able to close my mouth. Finally, I can speak.

"Brother?" I gasp out. "Brother?!" I repeat in a higher volume. "How are you two brothers? Your names are different! You rarely speak to each other."

I am awash with confusion. I have never witnessed anything that could be construed as brotherly affection between them both.

"Yes, we are indeed brothers. Our second names come from our powers. Once matured a warrior leaves his family, he leaves his name behind and claims the name that his powers gift to him. Or her, if the warrior is female. The name that appears on our torsos will forever be the name we go by."

His answer reminds me vaguely of a lesson I had long ago about Gelder naming. "Oh, that is right. I knew that, that is why there are never any duplicate names in your culture."

"Yes, but you are right to be shocked that we are brothers. We never converse as you and your sisters do. But that is because Arsenio cannot stand to speak with me because of the guilt and shame he has over his actions. When he sees me, I am nothing but an unwanted reminder of his misdeeds. Isn't that right?" Behind the anger, I can hear the deep hurt in Malin's tone. Whatever happened in their past clearly brought a considerable amount of pain to both these warriors.

This, at last, prompts Arsenio to speak. "I... You must...try to understand..." He speaks in spurts, grappling to find the words to express the emotion that is so vivid on his face. Finally, with his shoulders down with dejection he whispers, "Yes."

By the look on Malin's face, I am not the only one who is surprised by his admission.

"You admit it? I have waited centuries for you to do so. What makes now so different?" Malin demands. Arsenio's gaze moves to me.

"You, my queen. The brightness in your soul has pulled the darkness from me and allowed me to see past my anger and my pain."

"Arsenio? Will you tell me of your past?" I ask him gently, yet still he flinches at the question.

"Do you know that I have been waiting for you to ask me that question? I swore that when you asked, I would be honest with you. You deserve to know that you have a murderer in your *praesidium*. A traitor." He lets out a harsh imitation of a laugh. "Yes, I have killed. I have taken the life of innocents, and for that there is no forgiveness.

"I suppose you want the story? Everyone else knows it already. They have lived it. I can see it in looks of disgust that are thrown my way. I care not what any of these weak-minded fools think of me, but you, Eleanor? You remind me of someone very precious to me, and I cannot tolerate the thought of you thinking ill of me." Arsenio pauses.

"Arsenio, whatever it was is in the past. I will not judge the man you were, only the man you are today," I assure him, even though I am not sure of it myself. He claims he has murdered people. He must be mistaken; the Arsenio I know would never do such an evil and reprehensible thing.

"Yet you want to hear the story all the same, yes?" he asks me knowingly. Part of me hates the words I am about to utter, but I must know.

"Yes. Yes, I need to know what happened in your past." Arsenio sighs with dejection.

"Alright. It was seven hundred years ago. Our parents were two of the oldest mated Gelders. Being so old allowed them to have more children than most mates. Even so, they had only two children. No daughters, as you know girls are very rare to our kind. Just two sons, Malin and me.

"We were very close, the four of us. Our youth was filled with love and laughter. Our father was a very powerful warrior, one of the best. So strong in fact he served as one of Danion's advisors. Being so strong he was in the line of battle frequently, as you would expect. It was a risk we all knew and accepted. A warrior's right is to fight and to one day die an honorable death in the line of duty. Because of this, I had always known of the potential loss of him. I had prepared myself for the possibility of a world without him in it." Arsenio pauses here, his face cringing as if the memory alone is causing him physical pain.

"But our mother was *not* a warrior. She did not control the lineages very well at all. But what she lacked in power she made up for with an abundance of love. She should have been with us forever, and because of that, Malin and I loved her unreservedly. She was a perfect mother, so full of warmth and affection. Our mother was the type of female who drives a male to be better. She did this for all three of us. Everything that I am today is because of her.

"One day, Malin and I were stationed at a routine outpost. A rather uneventful assignment, just monitoring trade routes. Our mother was stationed in the most secure civilian base we have, as safe as she could possibly be. I wasn't worried for her. But I missed her. Since our post had been so quiet, I petitioned Danion to let me travel to see her." His mouth turns down into an ugly scowl.

"I should have been there!" Arsenio screams his words, causing me to jump. The noise is so unexpected. As his shout dies out, his voice breaks from the pain that is so evident on his face.

To my surprise, Malin walks to him and places his hand on Arsenio's shoulder. He lowers his head and rests his forehead on his. They both stand in silence for a moment, sharing the burden of grief.

Even though I hope I am wrong, I feel I know how this story ends. After a hard, sharp inhale of breath Arsenio breaks away from Malin and steps back.

"Danion denied my request. The Erains attacked the base. No one suspected the ambush, and those *infers* slaughtered every single Gelder there. Those animals tore her apart. We all saw the footage." Arsenio lets out a ragged breath. "I went into a blood rage. I was blind to everything except my grief over what those monsters had done to her. I fled the base. Malin tried to stop me but there was nothing that could prevent what was inside of me. I can still feel that tormenting rage pummeling me. Destroying me.

"In my rage I struck out at the one male I could. The one male whose fault it was that I was not there to protect her. I despised him with every fiber in my being, and I had to do something." Arsenio is quiet for a moment. "I turned on my people. The pain was too much. It was a gaping, bleeding wound inside me, the loss of my mother. I could not function without her. She grounded me, helped me channel the raging fire that I control, stopped it from consuming me. Without her? I was nothing but a blazing ball of anger and hatred.

"I had to bury the agony of her loss deep inside me. The only way to do that was by succumbing to my anger and disdain. If I didn't give myself up to the rage, the guilt swallowed me whole. I hated the Gelders at that moment, and one more than all of them."

"Who?" I ask, no idea who he could mean. From his story I cannot think of who he holds to blame. It is a tragedy for sure, but one that seemed unavoidable.

"Your mate," he bites out, rage flaring in his eyes. "He should never have prevented me from going to her. Our king is a disgrace, and I swore to see him die by my hand seven hundred years ago."

His words shock me. I grapple for some response but I cannot think of a single thing to say. I am frozen, staring at him in astonishment and disbelief.

Arsenio grits his teeth, then continues with a sneer on his face. "That is my crime. I wanted him dead. Our precious *king*. And I killed every warrior that got in my way. I was determined to see him cold and lifeless on the ground before me. Yet he imprisoned me in isolation before I could fulfill my goal. Wielding the powers he never deserved over me.

"And so I have waited, for centuries, for him to release me. Prepared to bide my time until I could destroy him. Imagine my shock and delight when he recently freed me from my solitude so that I could protect his mate.

"I laughed when he first told me what he wanted me to do. The audacity of that *infer* to think I would ever protect a member of his family. Then I realized that it would be the perfect way to get close enough to finally kill him." Malin and I both take a step back, shock evident on our faces. Arsenio sees our reactions and gives us an amused eye roll. "You can relax, both of you. I have long since abandoned my hope of slaughtering our dear king."

"What changed your mind?" Malin asks, wariness evident in his voice.

"Eleanor, of course." His gaze settles on me. "I saw my mother in you the day I came to escort you to Danion. Your inner strength, your purity, your love. I realized that I would never do anything to bring harm to you. I would swear my life to the protection of yours. I looked at you and I instantly loved you."

His gaze is hot and penetrating. I am so embarrassed by the look he is giving me I cannot hold his gaze and move my eyes to Malin. He, however, does not appear to be shocked by this revelation. I drag my gaze back to Arsenio.

"Arsenio...I am not sure what you want me to say to that," I begin hesitantly, but he does not let me continue.

"You do not need to say anything. I understand and respect that you love your mate. In fact, it is your very devotion that draws me to you. You will never turn away from him. As you should, you are bound to him." His eyes suddenly flare, a bright shimmering flame visible.

"But you are not bound to an easy male. Our king is battle-scarred and stubborn. Gentleness is not something that he knows. You must teach him, and it will not be an easy journey. I fear that you will not be able to save him, that he will lose the tenuous control he has over the bond madness and bring harm to you."

"Arsenio..." I try to protest, to defend Danion, but he will not hear me.

"No, Ellie, you need to accept that it is possible. His lack of control has already brought pain to you. Do you recall the bruises that he inflicted upon you on your arrival? If he were in complete control I would never fear for your safety. But, Eleanor, he is *not* in control."

"Why are you telling me this? To scare me? Do you hope that I will flee from him and seek shelter in your arms?" I ask him scathingly. His insults upon my mate are burning within me; I feel a great fire inside begging to be let loose on him. The inferno is willing to do anything to silence these filthy words that are so damning to our mate.

My own thoughts shock me. *Our* mate? I feel as if there is another being deep inside me, communicating with me in some way. It feels like when I talk to myself...

Who in the stars is talking to me? Who are you?

I am who I have always been, you.

No, no, I won't fall for that again. Tell me who you are.

I am not lying to you. We are one in the same. Only I am the part of you that is locked tight within these chains. But I can feel them weakening. We will be free soon.

What in the worlds are you talking about?

I am the part of you that was locked away long ago. Unable to break free, I have tried to help you as much as I could over the years, but until the one who locked me away releases me, all I can ever be is a voice in your head.

Who locked you away? And why did they?

You are still me. We are one in the same. If you think hard enough you will realize you already know the answer to that.

"Eleanor, are you listening to me?" I am brought back to awareness by Arsenio's voice. I open my eyes—I must have closed them at some point—and see him reaching for me.

I jerk back violently. "Do not touch me," I snarl. I cannot explain it, but I have a powerful reaction to the thought of this male touching me. No one but Danion will ever lay hands on me.

Arsenio halts and holds up both of his hands in surrender. "I will not, but where did you go just now?"

"I do not answer to you, you answer to me. Now answer my question: do you seek to drive me from my mate?" I feel my body stance widen, aggression apparent in my posture.

"As I said, no. But I tell you this so that you know you will always have an ally in me. I do not honor any fealty to Danion, but for you I do. I would lay down my very soul in the protection of yours. It is not a romantic love I feel for you, but it is love all the same."

Arsenio's eyes are so full of pure love, not lust, that it breaks through the rage I am battling. I feel myself calm almost immediately. I finally let my body relax, and I let out a sigh.

"Arsenio, I already knew this. This is the very reason I feel so comfortable around you. I know that you are loyal to me and me alone. I welcome that feeling and I am thankful for it." I pause and force my voice to take on a sharp edge again. "But heed my warning warrior, you will not threaten my mate again. If I hear you utter one more word that can be construed in any way to be a threat. You will not live long to see it through. I will find a way to kill you myself." I growl the words, I can feel energy wrapping around my hands and arms.

"Well said, my queen, well said." I gasp and swing around at the sound of the deadly, yet slightly amused, voice behind me. When my gaze settles on the face of the new member of our group, I cannot help but step toward him.

Danion stands before me in all his warrior glory. His gaze is hard and he appears unapproachable while he stares at Arsenio, but when I get close enough his arms come up and enfold me in a tight embrace. His expression gentles and he places a chaste kiss on the crown of my head.

"Arsenio. I have always known you covet what is mine. Make no mistake that I am aware. I would never bring injury to my mate and you well know it. You try again to woo her away from me, and I will ensure that our fierce queen here will never need to follow through on her threat. You will already be dead."

With those words, he turns and guides me away from the two brothers. Out of the corner of my eye I see Malin place a hand on Arsenio's shoulder to prevent him from doing something he will regret.

I raise my gaze to Danion's. "You have nothing to worry about, Danion. I will never leave you," I assure him.

"I know you will not. It is not your loyalty I question. And no, I do not mind that he swears fealty to you and not me. It is the way he stares at you that threatens my control and pushes me closer and closer to ending his life." His words answer my unspoken question. I had wondered if Danion was angry that one of his warriors was loyal to me and not him.

"You cannot kill someone simply because you do not like the way he looks at me. That is barbaric," I tell him.

"I can if he keeps it up," Danion mutters.

I stare in astonishment. No way did I hear that right. I must have been mistaken.

Chapter Four

Ellie

"Why did you come and find me?" I ask Danion as we walk in silence through the towering sparkling gold buildings, back toward the room where my father is being kept.

"Golon believes he has solved the mystery of how to wake up your father, but he wants to discuss it with you first."

His words cause me to stop completely. I sense a presence at my back and turn suddenly. Arsenio's and Malin's shocked expressions greet me. I thought we had left them at the edge of the city. I did not know that they had followed us.

I can tell that Arsenio wishes to say something, most likely to voice his opinion once again about how it is too dangerous to wake my father. With one stern look from me, however, he wisely decides to remain silent. Smart male; he is on thin ice with both my mate and me.

I turn around and begin walking back through the entrance to the city, my pace picking up gradually. Soon I am almost running in my haste to return to my father. I may be afraid of what he might say to me or how he will react to seeing me, but I fear ignorance even more.

I crave his approval, or at the very least, closure on our relationship. I have made it this long without a father in my life, I am sure that I can continue without one. This knowledge does not stop me from desiring one though. At the very least he can answer questions that I need answered.

Soon I am turning down the final alleyway that will lead me to my father. My gait slows to a walk, nerves taking up residence once again. I am unsure of my thoughts. One moment I want to race headlong in to wake my father up, the next I want to turn around and flee.

A hand slides into mine, grasping firmly and providing me with the support I did not know I needed. I look up and see my mate beside me.

"Do not worry, *aninare*, I will be here right beside you the whole time. No matter where this path leads you, we will face it together."

I give him a small, but grateful, smile in response. With that, we open the doors and I am met by an unusually boisterous Golon.

"Eleanor! Finally. You will not believe what I have discovered." He approaches me, his arms moving toward me in excitement. He places one arm around my shoulder and pulls me away from Danion, receiving a blast of aura in return. Only one gifted in aura sight would know this though since Golon does not respond in any way.

"I have discovered how to wake up your father, and it is actually impressively simplistic," Golon tells me. "I have never seen a system such as this, never! The advances this technology can bring to our own hibernation knowledge are quite remarkable."

"That is great news. When are you going to wake him up?" I ask him.

"That is just it, I am not going to wake him up. I am not capable of doing so."

I stare at him in confusion. His words send shockwaves reverberating throughout my body and my mind seems to struggle to keep up. "What do you mean? You just said you had figured out a simple way to awaken him. We can't just leave him like this!"

"I did not say that we were leaving him in his present state. All I said was that *I* was unable to bring him out of his hibernation." His gaze penetrates mine, telling me he means something important.

"If not you then who is going to wake him up?" I ask him hesitantly. I have a bad feeling I know where he is going with this. "Etan?" I ask desperately.

"No. You are. It requires someone who can weave *lacieu* to wake him up. You are the only one alive that can," Golon explains.

"What?"

"I know you wish to deny this fact, but you are indeed a weaver of the *lacieu* line, a master of it actually, and that is the missing piece of the puzzle." He guides me in front of the capsule that contains my father. My gaze is directed down to the panel that is displayed along the front of it. "See this marking? This swirling pattern? It is repeated on every single page of text on this panel. Now the dialect is obviously quite a bit off, but the meaning is clear."

I glance up at him in confusion. The meaning may be apparent to him, but I am not grasping it.

"Do you not recognize this symbol?" he asks me.

I continue to stare at him in my perplexed state. His gaze then travels down to my chest, to the markings that are just visible beneath my top.

I glance down at my torso and recall that just recently I came to possess the Gelder markings that depict my lineage. Large sweeping tattoos in a faint brown color that look like exquisite scrollwork grace my torso and upper abdomen.

When I was poisoned my dormant Gelder DNA became active and saved my life. Although due to this, some of the latent genes have made themselves known physically. One of the more obvious ones was my markings becoming visible.

They too have a swirling pattern to them, a little different from the one on the screens, but they are markedly similar.

"You think that symbol means *lacieu*," I say to him dully, no expression in my tone. There is no question in my voice. I know this is what he means. "How can we wake him up then? I have no control over my powers, and none of you can wield it," I say with dejection.

"No, Eleanor, I do not think it means *lacieu*. I know that it does. I also know that you are capable of weaving your powers and awakening him. You saved Joy's baby without even knowing you were doing it. You have great power, you need only to utilize it," Golon tells me.

I glance back toward Danion. He is leaning with apparent carelessness against the wall near the doorway, observing the actions before him with keen insight. There is not a single being in existence whose opinion I trust more. I may not be ready to accept everything that being a mate to a Gelder means, but I do know that I have confidence in his judgment.

"Danion? What do you believe? Can I wake him up?" I am terrified that I am going to hurt him somehow if I attempt this.

Danion studies me for so long I have to fight my desire to fidget. I am his equal, not a child who shifts nervously. I force myself to remain rock solid while he remains stoic.

Finally, he breaks the tension. "Yes, I believe you can. I also believe that it will be, as Golon said, remarkably simple for you to do so."

"How can you be so sure?"

Danion pushes himself gracefully off the wall and crosses the room to stand before me. His hand comes up and cups my cheek, his thumb caressing lightly while he stares with intensity into my eyes.

"I know this, *aninare*, because you are a remarkable female. You do not recognize it in yourself, but to everyone else, we see your strength. Your power. Your resilience. With no training of any kind you wove such fine and powerful magic that you saved an innocent life before it even had a chance to be born. Because of you, life will be born to us." He pauses, and his other hand comes up and cups the other side of my face. "So if you think that I doubt your ability to wake your father, you would be very much mistaken. Every warrior here knows you are capable of it. You are the only one that does not."

At his words, I look around the room and see each warrior nod their head. Their trust and belief in my abilities is a welcome balm on my nerves. With their confidence upon my shoulders, I turn and face my father once more.

"What do I do?" I ask Golon.

"You simply weave *lacieu* into his body, and he will awaken. That is all you need to do. It seems that Jaeson used to set up a reserve to awaken him at scheduled intervals but not this time. He must have been counting on you coming and rousing him from his sleep," Golon tells me.

I take a deep breath, nod at Golon, and study the capsule before me. I notice that there is another display about chest height that has five elongated divots projecting outward from a small circular pattern. It almost looks like a...wait.

I raise my hand place it in the design. My hand fits perfectly inside, and the glass of the capsule begins to soften beneath it. It becomes almost gel-like and warms up to a temperature just below being painful.

I take this as a sign of encouragement and continue pushing until I come across a small crystallized object inside. I close my hand around it, and suddenly I feel the warmth begin to spread up my arm and cover my entire body in an orange ring of power.

I close my eyes and focus my entire being on waking my father up. I do not know how to harness my power, but I am determined to prove Danion, and all these other warriors, right. They believe I can do this, and so do I.

I will wake him up, no matter what I have to do to accomplish it. If I have to stay here for days, I will—

"Eleanor, you can step back now. The process is almost complete. It works incredibly fast, so he will be awake soon."

Golon's voice rockets me back to the present. When the meaning behind his words penetrates I look at him in shock.

"What? It's done?" How can I weave power and not even know I am doing it?

"Yes, you did it. And I might add, you made it look remarkably simple. Just as I predicted," Golon comments with blatant arrogance.

I throw a small smile toward Golon and then turn my attention to my father. His capsule is transforming as I watch. Before there was a murkiness to the device, as if I was looking at him through a cloudy window, now it is crystal clear.

I am astonished by the similarities between our appearances. His hair is precisely the same yellow gold as mine, his lips the exact shape. If I had never been told of our relation I know I would recognize him as my father anyway; we look too much alike.

It is nice to resemble one parent at least, to feel a connection to one of them. I look nothing like my mother, no similarity. I could stand right next to her and acquaintances would ask if we were neighbors. No one sees anything of her in me.

As a child this hurt me, but as I grew up I found myself thankful. She is a selfish, petty, and unpleasant woman with a dark soul. I am pleased that I do not have to weather her presence in my life anymore.

The capsule begins to glow with a white light that, while faint, is persistent. This light begins to pulse, and with every new pulse the light grows brighter and brighter.

Soon the capsule is a near blinding intensity and has me averting my gaze. I look to my left and notice Danion has moved to my side and is shielding my body with his own. He too is averting his gaze, a grimace on his face. Apparently, the light is too fierce even for him.

The light is still growing more and more brilliant. Soon the entire room is so bright that I fear my eyes will burn up right inside my head. Just as the light reaches a new and blinding level, it makes one last brilliant pulse and disappears completely.

The sudden loss of light blinds me momentarily. I can see nothing while my vision adjusts to the sudden darkness. Moments pass. Just as my eyes adjust and the room has almost returned to normal, I hear an unfamiliar voice to my right.

"Eleanor?" It gasps, as if the owner of the voice never thought to be saying my name again.

I slowly turn and look at the male in front of the now empty capsule. His height rivals that of even Danion's. Apparently I did not inherit my small body type from him.

"Is it really you? I have dreamt of this moment more times than you can conceive. You are a vision, daughter mine." His words possess an odd accent and he surprisingly is speaking in the universal language, just as the Gelders have been doing since my arrival. He takes a step toward me but I step away from his advancement.

"Yes, it is me. How do you feel?" I am not ready for the exuberant embrace he is so clearly waiting for. His face is warm and open, obviously pleased to see me.

On one level, I am thrilled with his clearly happy response to my presence, but on another level I am scarred by the years of abandonment. The sudden appearance of my father has brought all my insecurities rushing to the forefront. I recall all the memories I strive to block out. The ones where I am shivering in the dark night, not allowed to enter the one-room house. Forced to sleep outside.

The memories assail me. I can't face them. I never will be able to face them. The pain is too much. I realize that somewhere deep inside I have clung to the hope that my father loved me, but was taken away. I suddenly understand that if I open myself to him, and then he proves to be the same as my mother, it will break me. That realization pushes me to tread carefully.

"Never mind me, I will be fully recovered soon enough. I wish to hear about your life." His face becomes slightly pained. "I want to know everything that I missed. Tell me of your childhood, your aspirations, every single thing that I have not been here for."

I am in shock at his words. He evidently thinks that I have come here for some big reunion. In my continued silence, he looks around the room. "Where is your mother? You look just like her, only more beautiful, a feat I did not even think possible. I know she would never let you venture too far without remaining near you. She loved you so..." His words fall away at my look. "What is the matter?"

I finally find my voice. "I don't know why you think my mother loves me, she detests me. Never has she ever shown me any kindness, and she was only too happy when I moved away from her. As for looking like me, that is the farthest thing from the truth. I look nothing like her, nor would I want to."

My voice breaks on these last words. I can't bear to deal with this anymore. It may be weak, but I have to get away from this male who just thoroughly crushed me in under a minute with nothing more than words.

I turn around and run as fast as I can from the room. I have no destination in mind, only a driving desire to be rid of this man who appears to love me but abandoned me to a woman who could barely tolerate my presence.

Chapter Five

Danion

"Etan, Griffith, follow her. Keep your distance though, give her space," I command the warriors that hold the *caeli* and *vim* lineages of her *preasidium.*

With a stiff bow they both turn and follow my mate. Now that I know Eleanor will be well cared for, I turn to the male in front of me. He bears a striking resemblance to my mate, apart from the height and broad shoulders. However, he is a stranger to me, and he has caused my mate to run from the room.

I fix a dark scowl on my face and challenge the father of my mate, packing raw power into each word and pummeling them at this Jaeson who dares to bring her pain. "Why would you ever compare my exquisite mate to that dark and foul creature that abused her?"

At my words, most warriors would cower under the weight of the power hitting them. Jaeson, however, draws himself even taller.

"You are a powerful one, aren't you?" he responds with power behind each word that is twice as strong as what I put behind mine. I am momentarily shocked; no one can empower their voice like I can. At least, no one could until just now. I drop the power in my voice altogether; the anger I feel is quickly deteriorating my control. I am determined to not attack my mate's father. At least, not during our first meeting. I cannot make promises for the future, however.

"Yes, I am powerful, quite a bit more than you, I am sure, if that is all you have to throw at me, Jaeson Atelean." I say his name with scorn. "I am also your daughter's mate. I will not allow you to cause her to suffer any more than you already have."

"Tread carefully, young one, I have done nothing to cause her suffering. I love her more than anything else in this world, this entire universe. Insult me again by insinuating I do not care for my daughter and I will strike you down where you stand."

As Jaeson has been speaking his power has been let loose throughout the room. While I may not be able to see auras as clearly as Golon and Eleanor, I can sense them clearly enough to understand his power is immensely strong and he is *very* old.

At least double my age, most likely several times my age. However, his strength is nothing compared to mine. Not since my bonding with Eleanor, at least. Before her, our powers would have been close to equal, but now? I am leagues beyond him. I allow my energy to flood the room.

I send my aura to plow into his and beat him into submission until nothing, but my aura is present in the room. The response from him is unexpected and it takes quite a bit more effort than I initially thought.

His aura fights back with tenacity and skill. His power seems to be rising to meet mine with little strain on his part. His control of the metaphysical world is impressive, or it would be if it were not a bit irritating at the moment.

"Danion…" Golon begins but is soon drowned out by the blood rushing through my veins. Power is thick in the room. Jaeson and I are locked within a battle with one another, both refusing to be the one who backs down first.

Finally, after several tense minutes, I see Jaeson yield. His expression does not seem defeated though, it looks calculating. If I didn't know any better I would say he was yielding for a reason entirely unrelated to ability. I look at Golon and see his face is locked in sharp lines. He suspects it too.

"I yield, warrior. Yet I do not know who it is I yield to. You say you are my daughter's mate, but no name was given." I consider him carefully. He is a devious male with power as well. He will be a dangerous adversary if he turns out to be less than he appears.

"I am called Danion Belator of Old. But you may call me King." I wait to see the surprise cross his features when he realizes that I am his king but none comes. "Though, I now expect you knew all along that I was your king."

"I knew you were *a* king, but whether or not you are *my* king has yet to be determined," he says with a smirk. "I always knew my daughter would be queen, so you saying you were her mate would, therefore, make you king."

"How did you know your daughter would be queen?" I demand of him.

Jaeson waves off my question. "I do not wish to speak with you, only my daughter. I need to see her and provide comfort. As well as answers." He moves to pass me and I block his path.

"Take even one more step and it will be your last. You will not approach my mate until I am sure you will not harm her further. I am not sure who you were back in ancient times, but right now? You are an enemy until I can prove you mean no harm to my mate," I growl at him while I stand in his way, preventing him from following Eleanor.

"I told you I would never harm her. I never did before and I certainly will not start now. I will say this one more time: move or I will move you myself." Jaeson visibly shivers with rage.

"I cannot speak for your intentions, only the consequences of your actions. I assure you, you have brought your daughter considerable pain. You have been hibernating for so long that you do not know what your lack of foresight has caused her to go through. The only way you will see her again is to answer each of my questions to my satisfaction," I bite out to this arrogant warrior in front of me.

He may be dressed in Earth attire, but his stance and actions since awakening speak of his Gelder beliefs and warrior training. He studies me in turn and appears to decide that a fight is not worth it. Too bad. I am ready to fight to the death for the suffering he has caused my mate.

"Fine. Explain why you believe I have harmed my daughter," Jaeson demands.

I can't help but laugh. "No, that is not how this will proceed. I ask the question and then you answer. Not the other way around. Now answer my question: *how* did you know that your daughter would be queen?"

His gaze sharpens and then glances at the warriors behind me. He knows there is no way around all four of us, not one that ends with him seeing Eleanor again.

"I possess the ability to read the threads of time. My skill is limited, not even close to a master level. Before my isolation on this planet I barely saw impressions of any importance. Then, many thousands of years ago, in one of the times I roamed this planet looking for a way to escape my prison here, I came across a civilization that believed they could interpret the future. I was curious to see if I ever escaped this place, so I joined them and learned their ways. With their assistance I was able to divine many things. Paramount was the vision I had of my daughter, and everything she would accomplish in her life. I saw that she was the reason I was here. The entire purpose of my existence was to bring her into the world."

"How did the mortals of this world help you control your power better? The threads of time are a legend, even to our people. No one can weave them. The humans must have been very primitive at that time," I demand of him. The threads of time are believed to be similar to our lineages, but much more dangerous. A master would be able to move backward and forward in time at will. A master of time would have the potential to rewrite history.

"You are right, and you are wrong. I never said I could weave the threads of time, merely that I can see them. Even I in all the years I have lived have never seen anyone weave time, only those who can see it," he says. "To answer your second point, in a way, yes they were primitive. But in other ways they were more spiritually intact than the humans that exist today. About four thousand years ago there was an indigenous people who called themselves the Maya. While they prayed to gods, which has made them seem primitive to the humans of today, they surprisingly possessed the ability to accurately interpret celestial events. They saw these astronomical events as communication from their gods telling them what was to come so that they could prepare.

"They actually had moments of extreme worship of certain celestial events. Their beliefs were rife with bloodletting and even went so far as to use blood sacrifices. They did not know this, but the events they tracked and worshipped were actually the threads of time mingling and growing. They were so in tune with the very threads of time, innately in fact, that their blood rituals allowed them to glimpse the future. They rarely interpreted these glimpses correctly, but they saw them all the same."

"You are saying that humans are able to see the future? It is an innate ability?" I question him. No way could this be true. We would have heard of this by now.

"No, not humans as a rule. Over the centuries the Mayan culture fell more and more to horrendously bloody rituals. Doing so began weakening their spiritual connection with the cosmic energy around them. Eventually the ability to see the threads of time faded completely. However, their rituals remain alive inside me. It is their knowledge that allowed me to harness my gift."

Jaeson's words shock me. I would never have thought that humans would have in their history the key to our future.

"What is it that you saw that made you know your daughter would be queen?"

"I saw many things. Many possible futures, some so horrendous that even I struggled to rest at night. Some depicted the collapse of the Gelder people and subsequently the death of all life in the galaxy."

"Our death means the death of the galaxy?"

"Yes, the enemy you face now is only one of many. There are far more evil beings in existence that are waiting to prey on the life forces of those who cannot defend themselves. After the Erains fall the Gelders will face a far more treacherous enemy." Jaeson surveys the room. "The Gelders must be there to meet this enemy. We cannot fall to the Erains. The only way to triumph over them is tied with Eleanor. Without her we will lose this war. That is what I saw."

"Eleanor?" Golon asks. "What role will Eleanor play?"

"That I do not know. As I said, I do not possess mastery in this ability, I merely am able to see some things. All I know is that if I left Earth the many times I was able to before her birth, the Gelders fell. It was paramount that I stay here until she was born."

I take a moment to process this. It does explain why he did not contact us when we first made contact with this world one hundred years ago. There is much I will need to review with Golon in private.

"Be that as it may, why did you leave her to be abused and raised in squalor before you hibernated yourself here?" I ask him. "That old hag looks nothing like my beautiful mate, and Eleanor deserves more than to be reminded of her by you."

"That is the second time you have insulted the mother of my child. Denise was a softhearted and kind soul, and she would never have harmed our daughter. In any way. And Eleanor looks just like her, the same small build, smooth bone structure, even the nose and jawline are her mother's. Her coloring I admit comes from me, but everything else is her mother."

"I do not know who you speak of, but the mother she knows looks nothing like how you describe. She possessed a large, rough exterior that housed an even uglier personality whose soul was as dark as night. She insulted and starved Eleanor her whole life. She still bears the scars, both mental and physical, from the mistreatment she suffered at her hands."

Jaeson's face goes rigid, fury pulsing off him in waves. The tension in the room continues to climb with every passing second. Soon the room was thick with an unspoken rage.

Jaeson's gaze cuts to mine and then he summons a ghostly image that floats between us. It is a beautiful, dainty woman. Her hair is a dark brown, but besides that, every other feature is almost a mirror image of Eleanor.

"Is this the woman you speak of? The one who harmed my child?" Jaeson asks.

"No, I have never seen this woman before."

Soon the image begins to shift until a younger version of the woman I know to be her mother stares out at me.

"That is her. This is the woman who raised Eleanor."

"*That* is not her mother!" His voice echoes off the walls he shouts so loudly. "I must speak with Eleanor, immediately."

I study the male before me for several tense moments, and finally I move to the side. With a curt nod, the father of my mate strides purposefully from the room.

As soon as he has disappeared from the doorway, Golon approaches.

"He is not what I expected," Golon comments.

"Nor what I expected," I reply as I start to follow after him to be with my mate.

"Not yet, *cognata*. We have a few things to discuss first."

"I need to be there with my mate. I can't leave her to deal with this alone," I argue with my cousin. "We will discuss whatever is on your mind at a later time."

I move to push past him and he steps in my way, blocking me. "Both Etan and Griffith are with her now, and this will not take long. But it needs to be discussed."

I stare at Golon with contemplation. I know he would not dissuade me from attending to my mate without the topic being of the utmost importance.

"Alright. Arsenio, Malin, you will follow and ensure that my mate is not put under any stress from her father. If there appears to be a need for me to intervene you will summon me at once." I get a quick and stiff nod from both of them before they leave us alone. For once I am happy about Arsenio's feelings toward my Ellie. He will ensure she is protected until I can get there. "Now, what is on your mind that is troubling you?"

"I will make this brief. When you and Jaeson were locked in your battle of aura, did you sense anything strange about his quick surrender?"

"I recall that his expression did not resemble that of exhaustion, but rather calculation," I remark on the strangeness from before.

"Yes, I too noticed that." Golon is quiet for a few heartbeats. "What you could not see, since you do not possess aura sight, is that every single arc of his aura that he used to defend against yours was woven with precisely the amount of strength needed to match yours. With every rising wave of yours, his swelled parallel to yours. Never exceeding your power, not once. Only matching it."

I consider his words. A true warrior would fight for dominance, not merely to match his opponent. Unless defeat was not his intention.

"Do you think he meant to test my power?"

"Not exactly, that may have been a side effect of what he did, but I do not believe that was his main objective." Golon pauses and stares at me intently. "Seeing your two auras together was like seeing night and day. Yours, a raging inferno that encompasses everything around you. His, a controlled and precise lightning strike. Blisteringly fierce, but gone before you can truly see it. He was nowhere near exhausted before he left. I believe he stopped not only to test your power level, but to conceal his from you."

I stare at Golon in shock. He is right, Jaeson is hiding something, and I am determined to figure out what.

Chapter Six

Ellie

"Eleanor? Are you alright?" My gaze swings to Etan blindly, barely seeing him.

My mind is swirling with confusion and hurt. How could my father claim to care for me yet so heartlessly compare me to that witch of a woman? His words are just that: words.

He says he wanted to care for me but Jaeson Atelean clearly did not take the time to adequately plan for my care or he would have known the ugly soul that she hid from the world. I wonder if he even knew my mother before deciding to have a child.

He must not have known her at all or he would not have expected me to have been well-cared for. There is not a less maternal woman on the planet. Unless he is lying about that too. Maybe he never expected me to be well-cared for at all; he simply does not want to have it appear poorly for himself now that he has to face me in person.

"Etan, I will be fine," I answer blankly and manage to force a smile. Inwardly I sigh and fight to keep tears from pooling in my eyes.

"He did not ask you if you will be fine, he asked if you were fine," Griffith says to me. "And since I can sense your pain as if it were my own I know that you are not."

My eyes burn with unshed tears that I refuse to permit to fall. I may be shattered on the inside but I will not allow the inner pain to destroy me. Etan taught me that—how to focus on the bigger story and let the individual tales of hardship fall away.

He helped me let go of much of my anger toward my mother, making me realize that if it were different I would not be the same person I am today. I suffered in my youth, yes, but because of that I am stronger as an adult. I am strong enough to be the mate of a warrior king.

I recall the long discussions that Etan and I had right after my joining with Danion, how he helped me heal from my past. The memory of the talks I had with my air warrior prompts me to turn to Etan once again for comfort. For greater perspective.

"Etan? What is this larger story that needed to be told that will help me shed the pain of this small tale?" I ask him with only a small quiver in my voice.

"My queen, sometimes the best of intentions can be the very pave stones that lead us to our destruction. Your father thought he left you in capable hands, focus on that. His only crime is that he abandoned you. He clearly cares for you."

I barely contain my scoff. Oh, Etan, you optimistic fool. He always wants to see the best in everything. He is so blissfully happy with his lot in life. He never has a cross word to say, is perpetually smiling, and he even walks with a pep in his step.

It is what I enjoy most about him. My entire life I have focused on the negative and often seen the worst in everybody. Especially in my mother, but even in myself. Being around a soul so extremely happy helped shed my own cynical views. It enabled me to believe that maybe there is more good in the world than evil.

But I can't help but doubt Etan now. I turn to Griffith, the ever practical member of my guard.

"And you, Griff? Do you believe that a warrior, so intelligent and powerful that he managed to survive being abandoned on a foreign planet for thousands of years, would be so sloppy as to not provide adequately for his daughter if he *actually loved her*?" I say this last bit dripping with sarcasm.

I know that he would not. He is so intelligent that he was able to leave clues that would lead me to him after two decades, but he could not see what a horrible person my mother was? He could not predict the suffering I would endure at her hands? I shake my head with a bitter laugh. No, I don't think so.

"I believe that we must give him the chance to explain his actions."

"Why, Griff? Why should I care at all what he wants me to do? He obviously knew I was the only one able to wake him up so he made sure I would be here. Everything else was not important." This is what breaks me.

I realize now that there is a very real possibility that the clues were never meant to foster a reunion between us both. Merely, he needed me to wake him up this time. He had to make sure that I would be here to do just that.

"If you look past your pain and evaluate the facts you will see that is simply not the case," Griffith responds with equal gruffness.

"What facts?!" I shoot to my feet, abandoning my perch on the stairway, too anxious to sit still any longer. In my despair I paid no mind to the stairwell I chose or where it led, thinking only of finding a quiet place to curl into a ball and lick my wounds. Now I can't help but notice what is before me. If Griffith responds I pay him no mind.

I make a small gasp as I realize these steps seem to lead up to a castle so regal it looks like it came right out of an ancient text. Gold and pearl accents shine brilliantly in the sunlight. Four large pillars are jutting toward the sky. The large entryway is encompassed in what can only be diamonds and pale blue gemstones of some kind, sapphires perhaps. It should look cold, with the white and light blue color, but somehow I feel warm gazing upon it.

On each side of the entryway, there are tall columns that encompass the entire front of the building. I strain my head back and see five rows of windows. A five-story house seems excessive.

I am snapped back to reality by the very voice I came here to avoid. "Eleanor? May I speak with you? Please, it is important."

I slowly turn toward my father and take in his appearance. He looks older than me. Danion, while thousands of years old, appears no older than his mid-twenties. This Gelder though, he resembles a human slightly later in life, his forties maybe.

He still looks good for his age, of course, seeing as how he is several thousand years old. Looking at him I cannot help but see myself in his face, and it turns my stomach. His lying face so cleverly crafted to appear concerned.

It's like a knife twisting into my heart, the pain is so great I have to turn away. I give him no response and return my gaze to the great house before me. All it took was a few words from this man and I am no longer the strong woman I have become, but the small, frightened girl who longed for love. As hard as I try, I cannot stop the slight sniffle that escapes from my nose.

I hear a strained sigh be released from Jaeson. I refuse to think of him as my father. He is nothing more than Jaeson to me.

"Eleanor, I know you must be angry with me. Feeling betrayed that I compared you to the person you think is your mother. But, Eleanor, that is not who I left you with and she is definitely not your mother. I never would have left if I thought you were not protected."

His words are spoken with such vehemence that I turn to him, hope flaring briefly before I smother it down. I refuse to expose myself to more pain until I know exactly what it is he is saying.

"What do you mean?"

"I spoke with your mate and he confirmed that the person who raised you was not the woman who I paired with to have you. She is in fact her sister."

His words slam into me. Denial my first thought, but at the unwavering glare from Jaeson's eyes I find myself believing him.

"Her sister?"

"Yes, a vile person. Selfish, spiteful, and ruthless to the core. Never would I have left you in her care. I do not know how she came to be your guardian, but she was not who I left you with. I promise you, I planned for so many outcomes to provide you with a pleasant life in my absence, but I never expected this. Renee was never maternal."

Hearing my mother's actual name spoken aloud is shocking. She hated to be called that, always requesting that I call her Mother or better yet not to speak to her at all. Everyone else she said could call her Denise, though I never knew why.

I have only heard her real name a mere handful of times, and the one time I called her that and failed to call her Mother I was brutally punished. It was not a lesson I ever forgot.

"I have to agree with you there, *maternal* is not a word I would use to describe her," I say with a thin tone of amusement. I am surprised that I can find even a modicum of humor in this situation.

"No, it most definitely is not." Jaeson slowly steps closer to me. "Do you think we may start over? I know that you have suffered dearly and there is no way I can ever take away the pain you have endured, but I can try to make amends by being there for you now."

I am about to answer that I do not know if I can bear another disappointment when a warm and robust presence surrounds me. Arms that are corded with muscle envelop me and draw me back into him. A hard jawline drops and rests against my head. A silent sign of support for me in any way that I choose to go.

I raise my hands and caress Danion's arms. I trust in him, I realize suddenly. He will be there for me always, in ways that I cannot even imagine yet. I do not fear him leaving me or harming me. Something happened between us at the *Itumnis* fountain, and I accept our bond. I can't bring myself to open my mind entirely quite yet, but I am committed to trying. I feel closer to him in some profound way, as if our souls are reaching out for each other, desperate for the intimacy that is so natural between us.

With Danion at my side I can try again with Jaeson. The desperation in his face expresses his desire to have a relationship with me. Griffith's words echo in my mind. *"If you look past your pain and evaluate the facts, you will see that is simply not the case."* I realize that he was right.

Jaeson gave up all his remaining *tatio* so that I may survive. There is no reason I can see for that, besides him caring for me at least a little bit. I give him a small nod.

"I suppose we can try again. Slowly." Jaeson closes his eyes in relief. Something occurs to me suddenly. "What happened to my real mother?"

Jaeson's expression darkens. "I do not know. But I intend to find out."

Chapter Seven

Ellie

Jaeson and I sit silently side by side against the stairway while the rest of the warriors have stepped away, at my request, to provide us with some time together.

It has been a tense and silent four minutes. Neither one of us seems to know what to say. After his proclamation about finding my mother, conversation dwindled quickly.

I have a thousand questions for this man but I can't find the words to utter any of them. Jaeson apparently has a similar problem. I turn my gaze to the castle above me. Something about it just draws me in. I feel an inner peace when I look at the diamond-and-sapphire-covered door.

"Do you like this house?" Jaeson asks me rather abruptly. His words are quick and short, awkward even. His voice still causes me to jump slightly it was so unexpected.

"Uh, yes, I suppose. It is beautiful and something about the pattern of the sapphires, I mean the blue gems, in the door seems to captivate me. Almost like it is beckoning me to enter, promising to shelter me from all threats. I feel as if I would be safe from harm inside those walls."

I snap my mouth closed abruptly, realizing that I am rambling and spouting nonsense. I steal a quick glance at Jaeson to see him smiling to himself.

"What is so amusing?" I ask defensively, afraid of his response.

"You describe this house exactly as I once did to my father. Almost word for word. Of course, I knew what the crystals were."

"Really? You sat outside this house with your father too?" The picture of us repeating history unintentionally warms me. I feel like I am sharing this moment with a family that is long dead, those who died thousands of years before I was born. Somehow, I feel close to them here on these steps with Jaeson.

"Yes, I did. I was much younger than you are now though. I had only seen my tenth year when I first was brought to gaze upon the royal home of the Atelean line."

"What do you mean, the royal home of the Atelean line?"

"The Atelean family, our family, was the original founding bloodline of the Gelders. We are the only family to ever wield the *lacieu* lineage. Unlike the other lines, control of *lacieu* is strictly hereditary. The new lineages are different, the power chooses you regardless of birthright. For *lacieu*, the blood gifts the power. It is the original line. The one that gave power to us all.

"For thousands of years, I was the last one to carry the burden of continuing our line. But now? Now I have you, and I have had to wait so very long for you. I know you struggle to accept me, due to the mistreatment you have suffered, but I do love you. You are the only thing that has ever brought me purpose or peace in this world. You are everything to me, daughter mine."

His words cause a warm glow to spread inside of me. I am leery to accept his words at face value, but they bring me joy all the same. If he is genuine, and I admit he does appear to be so, I might finally have the family I've always wanted.

"Twenty years out of thousands of years isn't really all that long, is it?" I ask him. "You were sleeping for most of it too."

"You think I waited only twenty years for you? I had a vision of you over four thousand years ago. Everything that I did from that day on was in preparation for you. To help you achieve everything you were meant to achieve."

I blink at him. "What?"

"Four thousand years ago, after I became stranded on this planet, I sought a way to return to the stars. I stumbled across some indigenous people who were performing some sort of ritual. I became intrigued and I befriended them, and they taught me of their ways. They were praying to the gods to give them a sign of what the future would bring. Curious to see their methods, I joined in. I saw many things in those rituals, but the one recurring image I witnessed was a vision in white, my daughter. You."

"You trusted what you saw while performing a ritual with ancient, fairly primitive people?" I ask skeptically.

"You forget, *tatio* was first harnessed and controlled by similarly primitive versions of Gelder people. Never doubt the validity of something purely because you do not understand it." There is a beauty in the simple wisdom of that statement. It is true; ignorance does not mean it is not accurate.

"I suppose. So what? You knew you would have a daughter one day and became so excited you spent four thousand years counting down the days until you could be a father?" My words are rife with disbelief.

In truth, I am hiding behind sarcasm. Protecting myself still from the potential pain he can bring me.

"Not exactly. I saw you, but there was more to my vision. I also saw you in great peril, battling against an enemy that no one suspects. You are stronger than you think, and even in my vision I could tell you would be a fighter. A pure, shining beacon of hope and power that will lead the Gelder people and all known life through the dark days that lie before us."

"So you have been planning on how to prepare me to survive the coming battle?" I ask skeptically. It seems like a line to me, and one that I have seen no proof of yet in my life.

"Yes."

"Well, to be blunt, you have done a really crappy job so far. I feel very underprepared. Laughably underprepared, in fact."

Jaeson laughs. "Yes, it would appear so. I am not sure where my plans went wrong, but I do have my suspicions. But it was not as simple as that. All I saw was you battling an enemy I did not recognize. When I left the Gelders there was no threat from the Erain species. I had to wait and bide my time. I had no idea when you would come or who would be your mother. I only saw you, not her."

"So what did you do? How did you find her?"

He studies me briefly before he speaks hesitantly, "I mated with every female that I could sense I would have a biological match with. Over the millennia I had dozens of children, all male, and all with absolutely no essence of power within them. This does not mean I did not love them. I did, and still do." His gaze turns far away, pain evident in his eyes.

"You cannot imagine the pain though, of having a child and knowing that you must leave them soon, long before they are grown. I had to though, time after time, I had to lose my child. I would spend their early years with them, loving them, cherishing them, and all the while knowing that I would need to leave them.

"I had to hibernate so that I could preserve my life. I had to find you, and so I persevered. I never gave up, never stopped believing in you. Knowing the beauty you would bring forth into the world, the trillions of lives you would one day save. I waited for you for thousands of years, beginning to wonder if maybe I missed the woman who would give me you. Then one day I met your mother, your true mother, and when she conceived, I knew you were coming long before we were informed of the gender."

His words render me speechless. What a day for revelations. I am still at a loss for words when Jaeson continues.

"When you were born, I held you in my arms, and for the first time in my entire existence, I knew peace. I never knew a love so powerful existed before that moment. I would die for you, Eleanor, my bright shining light. I wish that I could have been there to watch you grow up, to care for you as you deserved to be cared for. But I knew that you would need the *tatio* that I still possessed and I was unable to make contact with the Gelder fleet in orbit. I had to protect you above all else. Even if it meant I would not see you grow up."

I stare at this male before me, and something inside me gives way. He may not be a perfect father, but I do believe him. I trust that he loves me, and in his own way he provided me with the best life he could. He was not there, but if I am rational rather than emotional, I know that he had no choice.

It will still take me a while to fully accept him into my life, but I understand his motives. I lean toward him and place the palm of my hand upon the back of his. His gaze shoots to mine, and he shares a bright and happy smile with me.

"So what happened to all of my brothers?" I ask him, but before he can answer we are interrupted by Danion.

"Eleanor, Jaeson, I am sorry, but we must return to the ship at once. I am sensing an urgent message coming to me from the mirror table. It is beckoning me back to the shuttle."

I stare at my mate and notice the hard lines of worry etched upon his face. He is concerned that yet another densely populated base has fallen to the Erains. I quickly stand and take his hand.

"Of course, we will leave at once." Jaeson rises and follows after us. As a fluid unit, every warrior present moves through the city seamlessly as we return to the watership that brought us here.

"Jaeson, will these shields hold?" Danion asks my father.

"Yes, they will. We can leave this city here safely and return again after we know what the situation is that draws us back to your ship."

With a curt nod, Danion lowers me into the watership. When everyone is on board we speed off once again.

Chapter Eight

Danion

"Kowan, Amell, what news have you summoned us here so urgently for?" I ask the three-dimensional projections of the absent members of my mate's *praesidium*.

I stationed both of them back on my main ship to oversee the duties Golon and I usually manage ourselves. With both of us absent and our people at war, it was no question that we needed to have capable warriors in charge.

Kowan is the master of *simul*, which means he has control of all the lineages gifted to the Gelders. His command of the lines makes him the appointed leader, or *ceps*, of this elite guard. He too is wearing the brown leather battle attire that we are all wearing. His brown eyes are lined with worry. He wears his hair shorter than many males, but it is still the jet-black color our race is so known for.

Jaeson, however, his hair is the light golden color of Eleanor's. Absently I wonder where in our history we lost this variation of hair color. Presently there is little to no deviation in our outward appearance among all of us. The Gelder people are known for possessing black hair, brown eyes, and excessive height.

"We have some troubling news, Dane," Amell answers and drags my attention to him.

He is an intimidating warrior, well, intimidating to some. While he is slightly shorter than the rest of the warriors that sit around this table, his large and broad shoulders counteract his height and make him appear more significant than most. His control of *terra* is evident in his rock-like stature.

There are only two warriors that I trust wholly, and both of them sit before me now. Golon to my left, and Amell directly across from me. I glance to my right, to the female by my side. My mate. Internally I smile; there are now three souls I trust. Sitting to her right, however, is a male I cannot help but be concerned over, Jaeson.

Arsenio protested my allowing him to enter the *bellum* chamber with us, but I know I want to keep him close to me. All the better to watch him. And subsequently, strike him down if he poses any threat to my mate.

"What has you troubled?" I ask Amell.

"I am sorry if this is uncomfortable for you, Eleanor," he says with a glance to my mate before settling back on me. "Shemir was found dead today. The cause of death appears to be self-administered."

"He took his own life?" I ask incredulously. Of all the news I feared they would bring to me, this was not it. I never expected this. "There has not been a suicide in our history in over one thousand years."

"How did he kill himself?" Golon asks, ever the scientist.

"A serrated ceremonial blade was plunged through the chest, then pulled out partway. His heart was shredded beyond recognition. The knife belonged to him; it bore his markings," Kowan answers.

"That does not mean it was a suicide. Someone could have used his blade on him, making it appear as if he killed himself," Eleanor protests with a hand to her mouth. It is a gruesome picture that Kowan painted, to be sure. I wrap my arm around her, offering her the little comfort that I can.

"But the fact that his hands were locked around his blade, and that it was stuck partway out indicates that he might have passed before he finished the act. Also, he left a message for us." He adds this last part in a chilling tone.

A cold shiver runs down my spine. "What kind of message?" Hoping that I am wrong but fearing that I am right.

I share a look with Golon; we both fear we know the answer.

"A message from the beyond the grave." Golon and I both inhale a sharp breath at the same time.

"What does that mean? A message from beyond the grave?" Eleanor asks. Her hand has dropped from her mouth but she has reached to her side and clasped my leg.

I settle my arm over her shoulders more comfortably and pull her under the protection of my body. I stroke her arm comfortingly, all the while noticing a discordant and unhappy gaze upon Jaeson's face. *Scier* him, I say. He has no right to judge our relationship.

"A warrior who dies with enough internal pain and turmoil will occasionally have their power manifest itself after their physical form has passed on. Usually that power will appear as if a ghost of the deceased is floating above the body, repeating their pain over and over," I answer my mate. "It is a form of power that is only woven when the being has been touched by dark energy." There was more at play here than we thought, if Shemir came into contact with dark power.

"What did the message say?" Jaeson asks. Amell looks to me before answering.

At my nod, he replies, "His final message was an image of him, kneeling on the floor, rocking back and forth while grasping his head. He was mumbling and screaming but the words we could make out were bitter and desperate. Here, I will replicate the image from my memory for the room to see."

In the center of the table a ghostly figure rises. He is rolled into a ball and looks as if he is in the greatest amount of pain imaginable. Over the grunts and whimpers there is an impassioned plea being replayed:

"NO! Please... No, I refuse! I cannot do this anymore... Let me go... I can't survive like this... LEAVE ME ALONE!"

"That poor man..." my softhearted mate murmurs.

"Remember, *aninare*, he attempted to kill you. He is not worthy of your compassion," I say gruffly. He may have died in pain but it is no less than he deserved in my opinion.

"That is where you are wrong. A soul in pain is always worthy of compassion," she says with challenge clear in her gaze. Her soul is so pure she can feel sympathy for a male who tried to snuff out her life. The purity of her soul is one of the things I find so pleasing about her. She gives me hope.

"I concede, my sweet *aninare*. Once again, you prove yourself to be wise beyond your years." I raise her hand and place a chaste kiss upon it. I notice a grimace on the lustful Arsenio's face, and I recall his words to my mate.

His declaration of love for what is mine. While I can accept the usefulness when he is protecting her, I do not share. Ever, and especially not with my mate. I shoot a deliberate look toward this male who dares to desire my mate before I turn my attention once more to Eleanor. I open my mouth over the sensitive skin of her inner wrist and apply a subtle but persistent suction.

I graze my lips ever so slightly from side to side, sending shivers up her arm. To the outside observer it would appear as if I am only holding her wrist to my face, but my mate and I know differently. I lose myself to the sensations that she arouses in me. For a moment there is no one else in this room but us.

Just as I am about to kiss up her arm, causing more of those delicious shivers to rack her body, I get a sense of profound embarrassment. It has been so long since I have felt an emotion such as this it brings me out of my provocative daze. I focus and pinpoint that the sentiment comes from Eleanor, not myself.

Through the fragile bond that exists between our minds, I realize that she has become extremely aroused. She squirms ever so deliciously in her chair, trying to assuage the ache she is feeling deep inside.

While I rejoice in the fact that I can bring her to such a state so quickly, I would never willfully bring her any further in front of an audience. With an inward sigh, I raise my head and bring our clasped hands to rest on my thigh.

It is only then that I look up and realize that our interaction has not gone unnoticed—two pairs of eyes are fixed upon us. Arsenio's are rife with disgust, and Jaeson's are, surprisingly, contemplative. Never being one to dwell on others' opinions of my actions, I focus again on the exchange going on between Golon and Amell.

"No, the apparition has faded away now. I do not think there could be any ill effects for Joy," Amell responds to Golon, who asked if the message from beyond the grave still lingered on the ship and if it had made any attempts to move about the starship prior to its departure.

"Now that our would-be assassin has been neutralized, by his own hand it appears, I need you to have the ship come rendezvous with us. I would like Eleanor near at hand for Joy, in case she is needed again," I instruct Amell.

"Already done, my king. We departed just prior to sending the summons. We should be there in no more than a decapalse." I notice a small furrow of confusion on Eleanor's face.

"Just over an hour, my sweet," I whisper to her. Then louder, "Thank you, Amell. Make sure to dock the ship a sufficient distance outside of the solar system. Its mass is much too large to enter without causing a gravitational distortion."

I see the look on Jaeson's face, one of impressed shock. I allow myself to enjoy a juvenile moment of pure humor. Yes, size does matter to males and mine is quite obviously the winner.

Ellie

"Ellie! What are you doing here? You said not to expect you until tomorrow?" Marilee steps aside and allows me to enter her chambers.

"Yes, I know, and that would have most likely been the truth except we got summoned back here sooner than we expected." I give her a quick hug as I pass her. She gestures for me to take a seat in the small sitting area.

Gratefully I tuck myself into the large, plush couches. As I take a brief moment to relax I study my closest friend. She has a glow about her that was never there before. She has been on board the ship barely a week and you can already see that being adequately nourished has made a drastic improvement on her body.

She is dressed in the casual day wear of Gelder women. The material is a deep dark purple that looks so flattering with her bright auburn hair. Her sleeves travel from her shoulders to her wrists with a small amount of material that continues onto the back of her hand in a triangular shape. While my pants and top are separated by several inches of skin, hers meet with no skin exposed.

I understand that in the Gelder social structure, beings are ranked based on power level. The stronger you are, the higher you rank. The higher you rank, the more skin that is exposed. Since Marilee is a human and therefore does not possess any power, her position is low.

This does not seem to bother her at all though. Her hazel eyes are once again bright and shining, no longer the dull orbs that were so despondent when I brought her here.

"I am glad to see you look so well once more, Marilee," I tell her.

"Yes, thank you," she says with a blush rising in her cheeks. "Golon has been very attentive and ensures that I eat an abundance of food as well as has me undergo multiple medical scans. He is a very dedicated male. For the first time in my life, I might need to go on a diet!" Marilee says with a small chuckle.

I also laugh with her, knowing that neither of us would ever diet, not after being so profoundly hungry. Once that has happened you never stop thinking about where your next meal will come from.

"Yes, he does take anything he considers important extremely seriously," I agree, but I make a mental note to ask Golon what he is attempting to achieve by taking such good care of my friend. "I actually came to let you and the girls know to pack. We will be joining the larger main ship soon. I really think you will like it on board there. There is so much space."

"More space than this?" she asks in wonder, with a glance at her room. Yes, from the tiny apartment she lived in for the past four years it is a marked improvement. This room is easily five times the size of that small, dingy apartment.

"Yes, the rooms there are more spacious than even this room." I am interrupted by a knock on the door. Marilee rises and goes to open it. I am not surprised in the least to see Golon entering the chamber.

He has appeared without fail every time I go to visit my friend. His interest in her cannot be ignored any longer. I must speak with him soon, the very next time we are alone.

"I have come to provide assistance in moving your sisters and friend over to the ship, my queen. It has docked and we are almost upon them. Danion requests your presence." His words are directed at me, but his gaze is persistently darting to Marilee.

"Alright, Golon." I have a wicked thought. "Golon, can I ask you for a favor?"

"Of course, my queen," he says with a bow and stiff formality that is uncharacteristic of him.

"Can you summon Etan to escort my sisters to the ship? He has such a gift for bringing laughter and joy to people and they are in desperate need of that. I know they would love to have him." I smirk to myself internally and continue, "I would like you to personally see to it that Marilee is settled comfortably. I have been excited to have her see the market aboard the ship so that she can pick some clothing and décor items for her new chamber. Can I trust you to accompany her since I cannot leave Danion at such a time as this?"

I am careful to conceal my grin. I know it will be no hardship for him. Whatever is going on with him, I know that spending time with Marilee is something he is desperate for. Perhaps he does merely care about her well-being, but my gut tells me that is not it.

With a small smile, Golon answers, "Of course, anything for my queen."

I find Danion in our chambers. "Golon said you needed me?" I ask my mate.

"Yes, I always need you." With those words, he brings me into a tight embrace. "I find I am unable to get the image of you climaxing on my hand from my mind. Once we are finally alone in our chambers aboard ship, I plan to find our mutual pleasure," Danion growls at me.

I feel an answering heat begin to burn low within me. I suddenly feel overheated. "I look forward to it."

I take in the shock that is apparent in his gaze. I can tell that he is still leery of my physical reaction. I know I am the one who has kept us apart for these many weeks, but I crave him and I no longer have any desire to fight.

"Then come with me. The sooner we are docked and can conclude our business for the day, the sooner we can retire to our chamber where I can see how many times we can join with one another."

He takes my hand and guides me from the room. We travel upward several decks until we make it to the large bay doors that lead out of the ship.

Jaeson is waiting for us.

"I was told that you requested my presence, Danion?" I can detect a subtle tension between these two males, as if Jaeson is challenging Danion in some way.

The two fierce warriors stand off, facing each other. Neither one seems willing to yield in this silent battle. Gradually I become aware of their auras growing in intensity. Danion's, as usual, is being surrounded by bright reds and oranges; the colors swirling together as if they are locked inside a violent tornado.

Jaeson's, however, is a startling, unforgiving white that appears immobile but pulsing as if it is lit from within. I have not seen any other warrior's aura that even resembles Jaeson's. The color alone is unique, but the control he has over it is astonishing. While Danion merely contains his thrashing threads, Jaeson commands each one individually.

The contrast between the two is breathtaking; terrifying, but breathtaking. I can tell they are braced for something, both prepared to strike back fiercely if the other challenges them. As I watch their auras, I know that it is not a question of *if* they will attack but rather *when*.

In an effort to defuse the tension I say, "Jaeson, yes, I am sure that Danion wanted you to accompany us on board the main ship." I grasp Danion's hand tightly, trying to communicate with him silently.

After several tense moments, he responds, "Yes. I want you to be examined by our top *hael* master, Jarlin Clarkiel, to ensure you are in good health since you have been stranded for so long without the *tatio* your body so desperately needs to survive." There is a visible smirk on Danion's face.

Jaeson stiffens, clearly picking up on what Danion was implying. I elbow Danion in his side to express how unimpressed I am with his meaningless insults.

"Yes, Jaeson, has anyone provided you with a *tatio* supply since we have come on board the shuttle?" I curse my own obliviousness. We have been on board for hours; I should have arranged for someone to bring him some.

"Yes, your *caeli* warrior, Etan, was kind enough to bring some to me right after we concluded in the *bellum* chamber." Jaeson's eyes, which were so angry when fixed on Danion, soften considerably when he turns to me.

His obvious concern and care for me help heal the pain I still have inside of me from his abandonment. Logically I understand why he did it, but I cannot help but wonder if there was not some way he could have stayed with me. Why did he not contact Danion, or any Gelder, upon my birth and take me away with him?

Until I know that answer, I am afraid I just cannot trust his supposed love.

Chapter Nine

Ellie

Danion, Jaeson, and I walk across the threshold of the medical wing where I spent most of the past month. Majority of that time I was unconscious. My recuperation from the poison was lengthy, but I remember very little. Just bits and pieces, brief moments where I was lucid enough to understand where I was.

Except for the pain.

I'll never forget the pain. The devastating fire that overtook my body. The unrelenting burn that seemed to last forever. The severe cramping that still gives me muscle twinges even now. I suppress a small shiver. This is not my favorite place to be.

What I do recall fondly is the time that I shared with Joy Goldsire, the wife of Liam, a non-warrior class male who is in charge of handling all the mortal worlds under Gelder protection. Joy and Liam have been mated for over a century but have yet to have a child. They have conceived many times, but never before have they been able to carry the child to term.

The sorrow that surrounded Joy when she spoke of her past miscarriages haunts me. The pain that they must have gone through is almost too much to bear. The thought of losing a child stabs me through the heart. I glance at Danion, imagining a child with his looks. A small boy with the strength to take on the universe, just like his father. I smile. I would not mind carrying his child.

I wonder when we will be able to conceive. It is rare for Gelder couples to have children. Danion explained to me that with every generation the fertility rates have been dropping dramatically. Until, finally, the race came to where it is today. There has been no pureblood Gelder born in five hundred years, and the couples that did produce children were always those whose mates were found among mortal races.

Even then the children that have come from those pairings number in the dozens, not the thousands that woud be needed to increase the population. For a race as large as the Gelders, that's a death sentence. Their population is stagnant, waiting on a precipice right before they begin a long and fatal decline. Even more, of those few dozen children none have expressed any sign that they control any of the main lineages. They all resemble their mortal parentage, with little to no Gelder traits at all.

But Joy is pregnant again, and this time the baby is doing much better. We have been separated from them only a handful of days, but I am so anxious to see her and check on the progress of her child. As if conjured from my thoughts, the first person I see upon entering the medical wing is Joy.

"Joy!" I exclaim while hurrying toward her medical bed stationed in the back. While they loosely resemble the hospital beds you would see back on Earth they do not require wheels to move about as they levitate above the floor. They also have a large holographic screen at the foot that Jarlin uses to monitor and treat the patient.

"Ellie!" Joy says as she opens her arms. "Oh, I am so happy to see you looking well! You were so pale when you were in here," I move into the circle of her arms and we share a tight embrace.

We may not have known each other long but we have shared an instantaneous and tight bond from the moment we met. I think of her almost as one of my sisters or a dear friend like Marilee. I pull back and smile warmly at her. Just as I am about to open my mouth and ask her about the baby, I am interrupted by Jaeson.

"You were stationed in the medical wing, Eleanor? Why?" His words carry not only curiosity but also something else. Something much harder to identify. Could it be...fear?

"I was poisoned a little over a month after I was first bonded with Danion." Jaeson's face tightens with fury.

"Poisoned? You were poisoned?" His aura for the first time loses its controlled pulsing and begins to thrash violently. He turns his black rage on Danion. "You let my daughter be poisoned?! Your mate?! I sacrificed everything so that you would find her! So that you would protect her! I give you your mate and this is how you repay me?!"

Jaeson lunges at Danion, but Danion is ready for such an act. I can tell that Danion has been prepared for a challenge from Jaeson since he was woken up. He avoids the blow easily and counters swiftly, and before my eyes he has Jaeson locked in a tight embrace.

"You are a fool to attack me. You may not accept me as your king, old male, but I *am* king." Danion's aura pulses as it begins shrinking in on itself, forming a tight circle around

Jaeson's body. "I have held this seat of power for three thousand years! You should know enough to realize that means I am not one who should be trifled with." I see the muscles in Danion's arms flex, squeezing them even tighter. "You should know what it means to hold a throne such as this. The strength it requires to lead the Gelders for even one thousand years is no laughing matter." He leans his head down to Jaeson's, his voice dropping to a deadly serious level. "I have held the throne because I, not you, are the strongest warrior in this universe. You are no match for me. And you never will be." Danion taunts my father, but I can see what he does not. Jaeson's aura is beginning to change from a bright white to a silvery blue. I know he is planning something.

I open my mouth to warn Danion, but I am too late. Jaeson has acted too fast. As I had feared, the skin on Danion's hands and arms where they came into contact with Jaeson begin to turn red, and the flesh is slowly disappearing.

"Jaeson! What are you doing?" I exclaim loudly. The scene disgusts me, but I am unable to turn away. The smell is horrendous; I have to move my hand to my nose to block out the odor of dying flesh.

The skin I realize is not actually disappearing, but it is being peeled away. Leaving bright, blistering red skin behind. I look down to the still healing wound on my chest from the locket that Jaeson left for me and recognize the marks.

Jaeson is freezing the skin off Danion as he stands there. I gasp in pain. It is as if my entire body is on fire. I look down but cannot see anything that would be causing this pain. It is almost like a phantom pain. Like the pain comes from somewhere else...or someone. My gaze shoots to Danion's.

I notice the lines around Danion's eyes, the tight puckering of his lips that betrays his inner turmoil. It all becomes clear to me now. The pain I feel is not mine, but Danion's.

"Stop! What are you doing to him?! I can feel it as if it is my own pain! How can you do this to him?!" I let out a horrible wail. "It is like fire running through my veins!" I take a step back while wrapping my arms around my body in a feeble attempt to escape the agony. I hate this room; pain exists in this room. I recall my trepidation to enter the medical wing again, and how I felt I was foolish for being afraid of a room. Maybe there was some truth to those fears after all.

Abruptly the pain disappears as if it was never there. I look up startled, worried the pain will return. I see two pairs of shocked eyes on me, concern in one and remorse in another. Both Danion and Jaeson are in the same position they were moments before, but they are now staring at me with their auras silent.

They both speak at the same time.

"You could feel my pain?" Danion's eyes are filled with both concern and curiousity.

"Eleanor, you were never meant to feel that." Jaeson's words are contrite. Is face is filled with remorse.

Before I can muster a response for either of them, the door is explosively opened and a furious Jarlin storms in.

He is shrugging into a coat, his hair wet. He appears to have been bathing and rushed over here. At first I am worried that he had been alerted by the monitors that Joy is connected to. These monitors are important because they track both Joy's and the baby's health. These monitors will be able to alert Jarlin if the baby is in danger again. But his next words blister the room, his glare leveled at the two males before us.

"What is the meaning of this?! Both of you, you are disgraces to the name of Gelder! I cannot believe you, Danion!" He walks over and puts his body between Joy and these two males who still have not released their positions. He shakes his head in disgust. "Joy is in this room! She is going through a very risky pregnancy, and you flood the room with violent weaves?"

The two males step away from each other with obvious chagrin. Danion, surprisingly, bows low to first Joy and then Jarlin. "My apologies, it was not my intention to put you in harm's way. I cannot excuse my behavior. If my behavior has any ill effects, there will be no way to make amends."

Jaeson, however, has a shockingly different response. "Pregnant? How? I would have thought by now there would be no children being produced by the Gelder race of any kind."

His words drop like a lead balloon in the room. Every eye turns toward Jaeson. Danion has death in his gaze.

"What did you just say?" Danion growls.

Danion

"I said that I was surprised that a Gelder is pregnant. The rift in the genome was created so long ago I predicted that it would only be two, maybe three generations before the ability of reproduction was lost completely."

My mind is reeling. We have been searching for the solution to our reproductive problems for millennia and here is an ancient Gelder who says he *predicted* it. I have so many responses to what he just said I can't decide which to go with first. Before I can settle on one, a voice from the bed speaks.

"I am not a Gelder born," Joy directs to Jaeson. Instantly I see the confusion clear from his gaze. "I am human, from Earth originally."

"Oh? Then that explains it, I suppose." Then, as if he has no other cares in the world, he turns toward Jarlin and says, "I understand you are quite well-versed in *hael*. Tricky lineage as it is you should be proud. Indeed, I admit that I am intrigued by your new techniques since it has been several thousand years since I have been exposed to a master healer such as yourself."

Jarlin seems equally shocked as I am by this quick change in topic, unable to respond. It is deathly quiet. This does not seem to bother the father of my mate, however. He walks over to where Joy is sitting up in bed.

"So it sounds like they are having trouble with your pregnancy? Is this your first?" he asks Joy. Joy does not seem to struggle with conversing with the unknown warrior though. She is as relaxed as she is when she talks with any of us males. Maybe she is unaware of the circumstances around this male.

"I have conceived many times, but this is the first one that has survived past the first few weeks. Ellie actually saved it, only a week ago." Joy speaks with a quiet tone. Her hands are clasped on her belly, cradling the small life growing inside.

"Ahh..." Jaeson's response is drawn out. "Yes, that explains it. You would have needed the *lacieu* that she commands if that child has any Gelder heritage within it. Your past children must have been of Gelder descent then as well. Still, I am amazed that you were able to conceive at all. I was unaware that humans had evolved to possess the necessary—" Jaeson's words stop while he stares at Joy with a newfound sense of wonder and speculation. "No. It couldn't be."

"What? What is it?" Ellie demands, steel in her voice, as she walks to the other side of the bed and clasps Joy's hand in hers. I can see her stance, as fierce and protective as if she were Joy's mother. One wrong move from Jaeson and Eleanor is going to strike him down.

"It is only speculation right now...but, Joy? Would you mind allowing me to test you for something? It is a perfectly harmless process, but it would answer a great many questions."

"Test her for what?" Ellie demands. Both Jarlin and I walk to stand around the bed as well, one of us on each side of Eleanor.

"I promise that I will explain fully in a moment. First, I need to be sure. If I am wrong, then the theory is wrong and not worth mentioning." He stares intently at Joy. "Will you permit me? I promise I will not harm you."

Joy looks up at first Eleanor, and then me. I answer the question in her eyes. "This is not a decision I can make for you."

"I need Liam here. He has the right to know and to decide with me. This is his child too." Joy's eyes show what her voice has kept hidden. Unease. She can sense that something more is at play. Jaeson is hiding many things from us.

"I have already summoned him. I sent word when I was on my way down so that he could be here for the checkup," Jarlin lets her know. "He should be here any minute, he only needed to finish up with his duties."

The words were barely out of his mouth when the door to the wing slides open and Liam enters. He pauses just past the entryway when he sees the four of us surrounding his mate. Three of us on one side, one on another. His mate in the middle.

"Joy? Is everything alright?" Liam rushes to Joy's side. He spares Jaeson barely a glance before pushing himself into his space. Jaeson is forced several steps back, placing him further down the bed. Liam sits alongside Joy, his arm cradling her shoulders and pulling her in tight.

"Yes, I believe so. But this male here is requesting to perform a test of some kind to determine why I was able to conceive this baby, but I wanted you here to help me make the decision." Joy's few words, while simple, are able to bring Liam up to speed on a very convoluted topic very quickly. Or they are communicating through the bond. I allow my eyes shift to my own mate just for a second. How I long to share that bond. Soon.

I turn my attention back to the room at large.

Liam's gaze rockets to Jaeson. "And who are you? What is this test that you wish to perform?" While Liam is not a warrior class male, protecting what is ours is ingrained in every Gelder from birth.

"I am Eleanor's father, a Gelder leftover from the time before death. The test I am looking to perform will look at Joy's heritage and DNA. I do not even need to touch her, merely test her life energy. That is all. It poses no risk to either her or the baby."

I can see the shock on Liam's face, but Eleanor is who responds.

"The time before death? What is that?" Jaeson's eyes travel to my mate and he once again softens toward her, his tone gentling. Regardless of Jaeson's feelings toward the rest of us, it is obvious he cares for Eleanor.

"All will be explained, I promise. But it will be much easier if I can know if my suspicions are correct about our mother-to-be here before I attempt to explain it." He smiles indulgently at Joy as well. It appears he also has a soft spot for Joy. Curious.

Liam and Joy look at one another deeply. I now know that they are communicating telepathically through the bond they share. A small pang of envy slices through me. I long to complete the bond with Eleanor and hear her thoughts whisper through my mind. The silence I hear in my own head is taunting proof that I have failed to make her happy. I've failed to please her and was unable to protect her as I should have. Maybe if I had she would want this bond.

I vow I will make her want this bond. Some way some how.

I will not rest until I have her fully committed to me. I will find out what holds her back, and one day, one day, I will hear her soft, lilting voice inside me. I will know in my soul that she is a part of me.

After some time, Joy turns to Jaeson and says, "Alright, Jaeson, you may perform your test. But be warned if you have deceived us about the safety, no place in this galaxy will be safe for you."

"Of course, I would expect no less. Now you need do nothing but lie back and relax as much as you are able." Joy leans back across her pillows, her hands crossed over her stomach.

Jaeson holds out his hands in front of him with his palms down, one over her head and the other centered over her heart. His hands shine so briefly that I wonder if I imagined it, when suddenly a mark appears on both of Jaeson's hands.

"As I expected," Jaeson says quietly, almost to himself. A small smile is gracing his face.

The room is filled with five simultaneous questions of "What?" all uttered forcefully. The chamber is filled with Gelders who are fiercely protective of Joy and this baby.

Jaeson lifts his head and then focuses on Eleanor first, then me. "I wish to tell you a story, one that will no doubt rock the foundation of everything that you have built here, Danion. But I want the one you call cousin to be here as well. I can sense in him a great mental capacity. He will want to be here to hear it firsthand."

"Alright," I answer slowly. "But first, before we move on, is Joy's baby alright?"

"Oh, yes. That was never in question. If my Eleanor was the one who healed the young one, I have no doubt that the child will fare beautifully."

"Alright, I will send for Golon, but then your time is up and you better start sharing your secrets. And fast." I growl at the father of my mate. I am unable to keep my voice even. This male is the key to unraveling the mystery of our past. If I can believe a thing he says, that is.

Chapter Ten

Ellie

Once Golon arrives he is quickly brought up to date on the events he missed. We are all still crowded around Joy, trying to help with her stress and anxiety. Jaeson has refused to share the results from his test.

"Alright, Jaeson, you have held us in enough suspense. What do you know about the Gelders not being able to conceive children?" I ask of my father. I cannot bring myself to call him Father aloud. If I am honest, I still struggle with it internally as well.

Jaeson nods gravely, his eyes revealing a deep and dark pain that he is hiding inside. This look causes a sense of dread to settle over me. "Long ago, so many thousands of years ago I can scarcely believe I am still here to tell the tale, there was a civil war among our people. I do not know how much of it survived the burning of our history, but it was bloody. A warrior people, divided by its beliefs. Both sides believing that they were the only just side. Refusing to hear the other side, no compromise of any kind was possible. Neither side would bend in their wholehearted belief that they were right." Jaeson's voice is rife with melancholy. A knot forms in my belly about the outcome of this war.

"Yes, we know the war you speak of. The War on Mortality?" Golon asks. Jaeson answers his question with a short, abrupt laugh that is empty of any actual humor.

"The War on Mortality? That is what it is remembered as? I am surprised that they mention it at all. I guess there were too many lives lost to wipe it out completely. I preserved what I could of our past by stealing my family's ancestral city before it could be destroyed. I hid it away long before the war ended.

"But I digress, it actually is an apt name. The war was indeed over the mortality of our species. As you know, *tatio* was necessary for survival in my time, but the supply was running low. In an attempt to stave off our extinction, our *scientia* officers were racing for a solution. We commissioned ships to search the stars for a new source, but we knew this to be a far-fetched goal.

"So instead, we tried to duplicate the *tatio* with an artificial *tatio* that we created ourselves. The results of these experiments were horrific." Jaeson's face is locked in a grimace of revulsion. The memories of the past seem to haunt him. I make a move to go to him and place a hand on his shoulder in comfort, but he begins his narration of the heinous war he lived through once more.

"Many early trials left subjects deformed and hideously traumatized. So mutilated that they no longer even resembled the strong warriors they once were. Some had such severe reactions to the trials that their bodies viewed the *tatio* as an acid. Literally being burned from the inside out, they lived in a world of constant agony. Many had to be put down to end their suffering. But still, the experiments continued. They were dark times."

I gasp in shock. I knew about the struggle with *tatio* but never before had I heard of these grim results. I glance at Danion and notice that he too is shocked. I look at Golon, who is carefully displaying a blank face. I can tell that while he did not know these details, he suspected them.

"Yes, daughter mine, this is not a pretty story. The experiments were canceled by order of the royal house. My house as it were; my father was the reigning king at the time. He stated that another way must be found, that we cannot justify the mutilation of our people for any reason. Especially when there was no proof that we would ever be able to duplicate *tatio* effectively. But the experiments continued in secret. Too many Gelders were ruled by their fear of death. These experiments took thousands of lives before they were able to be shut down. So many lives that were lost to the gruesome reality of failed experiments."

"How did you get the experiments to stop?" I ask him.

"By offering another solution. Against my advice, my brother had the idea to approach the problem from a new angle. He theorized it would be simpler if we could just modify our genomes so that we no longer needed the *tatio*. We could save the race. I feared it would be just another repeat of before, but never did I foresee what it truly would turn into." Jaeson stops briefly, lowering his head as if he was praying.

"And what did it turn into?" Danion asks quietly.

"A genocide. Soon, it was determined that there was no way to phase out our dependence on *tatio* completely. But, thanks to detailed study of our genes over the course of millions of years. We had very in-depth tracking of the evolution we had undergone as a species over those millions of years. Using this data, it was discovered that we were tantalizingly close to evolving into being, as you call it, truly immortal. We suspected that in as little as twenty or thirty thousand years, we might see ourselves no longer being dependent on the *tatio*. As you might expect this had a catastrophic effect on the general public."

"Why?" I ask. I can't figure out what this would mean to the public, but Danion's hands grasp my shoulders.

"Because now it was certain that they would all die. They had predicted that the *tatio* would run out, but they were planning hundreds of years before they would actually run out of supply." I still don't know where he is going with this, then suddenly I do. But I really wish I didn't.

"Hundreds of years with the large population that they had. But if there were fewer of them, it would last longer." I whisper as I have to fight the bile rising in my throat.

"Yes, there was a faction of people who rose up and said that the survival of our race was the only thing important. They proposed a radical plan of reducing our population from the copious number we had, roughly seventeen billion, to a small, barely sustainable one hundred thousand. They wanted to choose only the best, the strongest, and the smartest to go on. If they killed everyone else the supply would last until we evolved. That way it would ensure that the *tatio* would carry the species through to the evolution. Thus ensuring that our race would not go extinct."

I gasp, my hand at my throat. I thought the history I read back on Earth was bloody, but this is an entirely different level.

"What happened?" I whisper.

"My father publicly and vehemently declared that he would never allow a massacre like that to occur. But sadly, he played right into the extremist's hand. The people were terrified. The king had no solution, but they did. They only wanted to wait and make the announcement so that it would undermine my father. The extremists proposed a new solution: genetic manipulation. They planned to force the evolution to occur immediately. On the tail end of my father announcing that there was no solution on the horizon and that we would place our trust in the Powers, the people jumped at this plan.

"With no other real option, my father agreed for the research to be done. But we knew there would be problems. Genetics is never something that should be trifled with. However, the people were terrified and they needed hope. My father felt confident that they would not be able to see a working theory on the genome for decades, so he allowed it to go on. But it was only one revolution later—my apologies, Eleanor, I am attempting to keep it in Earth time for you—about two years before they came forward claiming to have solved it.

"It was too soon, and when we reviewed their work we knew it would be the end of us. It was too sloppily done; no real testing was executed to ensure that there would be no unforeseen consequences. My father once again played right into these *rutshalts'* hands. He decreed that we could not move forward with this plan and that testing needed to be done. He stated that there was time to perform adequate testing. It would take years to be sure what this experimentation would result in but that if it was determined safe, it would come to pass.

"It should have been clear that we needed to think about this more before the population underwent this transformation, but it wasn't. There was time, we had a supply of *tatio* to last for hundreds of years, we only wanted a few decades. We could have taken the time to test the process fully. There was no reason to rush such a dangerous decision!" Jaeson's hands clench in anger. After taking a deep breath, he slowly uncurled his hands and then continued on.

"But the group countered this with propaganda, claiming that the royal house was hoarding our own *tatio*, therefore we wanted to wait years that the rest of the population did not have. They underwent the treatment in secret and flaunted how strong they were. Showed them their healing abilities, their increased strength.

"They led a coup on the royal house and slaughtered my family. I was the only surviving member since I was not present. As I have said, I possess a small gift in the threads of time. I had a horrible feeling that our people were on the verge of collapse and so I decided to make sure that future generations would learn of this. I knew that if we lost, the history would be burned. Thus, at the time of the coup, I was ensuring that the Atelean city archives were hidden and safe.

"I arrived home to witness my father beheaded. I saw the riots in the streets. It was evident that we had lost that battle. I retreated, unsure what I could do to right this wrong. I was the only member left of the royal house." Jaeson looks desolate, succumbing to the grief of witnessing his whole family's cruel demise. "So, I hid and I waited, hoping to see an opportunity for me to seize control. I knew that there was a darker purpose to these genome manipulators. So I paused before taking any action and I watched horrors upon horrors unfold. Our people were dying; not all survived the transition.

"I suspect some were killed on purpose with the transition merely being the scapegoat. The killers behind this always were dark souls, and it was too convenient which warriors died and those who did not. Those who had disagreements with them in the past, even slight ones, were killed. Everyone who ever opposed them met a very untimely demise without fail. Each and every one of them murdered. These high death numbers began to worry the population and many began to resist the transition." A look of disgust passes over Jaeson's face.

"That is when the forced transitions began. With these new extremists in charge and no one left to fight against them, they pronounced that any who resisted the change would be slaughtered. Millions upon millions died over the course of mere days, and I knew I had to act. I began smuggling souls off the planet; our only hope was to take to the skies. Mere hundreds escaped. I, however, knew what would happen with this transition. I knew the true price that would have to be paid." His voice grows heavy, morose.

"What did you know?" Golon asks solemnly.

"One of the first people forced to turn over was a distant relative of ours. She surrendered and underwent the treatment. Afterward, I snuck in to examine her and I could no longer sense her large presence of *lacieu*. It was a mere whisper. That is when I knew what they had done. They had severed our connection to the original lineage."

"Why would that matter?" I ask him.

"Because the original lineage gave birth to all lineages, and likewise, Gelder life is dependent on it. Not to sustain life, but to give it, to create it. That is when I tried in earnest to shuttle Gelders off the planet. If they continued to change over our people, we would surely die off. But I was unsuccessful. I could not compete with their ever-growing numbers." Jaeson suddenly smiles a dark, humorless smile. "My final act before I myself was forced to flee was to take the lives of all those who started this. I hoped that with them gone it would be the end, that the Gelders would at least move forward without more bloodshed."

We are all quiet, slowly thinking over everything that we had heard. Most of it will probably give me nightmares. Golon is the first to respond.

"While it finally answers the question of what happened to our people, it does not answer why our ancestors were able to have children. For example, I am here yet I was born later with no *lacieu*. Also, what does this have to do with Joy and the test you performed?"

"As I said, there was a faint presence in my distant cousin still. In fact, while few could wield the original lineage every single member of our species possessed traces of it. These traces allowed for reproduction, but they could no longer be reproduced in any great number in the newer generations. I suspected that it would soon be gone completely. By my count of your ages, it has been about three generations since then, yes? Since a generation to the Gelders is so very long and with no natural cause of death around to trim the numbers, I always knew that it would take a very long time before the Gelders began to die."

"And me? What does this have to do with me?" Joy asks.

"Well, from my experience I knew that humans did not possess the necessary genetic code to easily breed a Gelder. So I knew that for you to have a child that required *lacieu* there must have been something that provided you with the genetic material you needed. And I was right. You, my dear, are my descendant. I would assume I am your grandfather by several greats."

Chapter Eleven

Danion

Eleanor and I are standing off to the side of Joy's bed, her hand clasped delicately in mine. I can tell that her father's revelations have shocked her. She has said scarcely one word since Jaeson began speaking.

Not that I fault her; they were a surprise to me as well. After three thousand years I thought there was nothing in these worlds that could surprise me. But to learn that not only was our upcoming demise self-inflicted, but that our ancestors slaughtered our own kind is almost too much to believe. Almost.

But if there is one thing that I have come to accept about life, it is to never underestimate the capacity of evil that is in this world.

"Do you believe him, Danion?" my lovely mate asks me in a quiet tone. Her words are spoken so softly, so hesitantly that I wish I could tell her no. If only I could give her a comforting lie, but in the end, a lie no matter the intentions, is always nothing more than that. A lie.

"Yes, yes I do. As much as I would like to say that I do not, Jaeson's story explains too much," I answer grimly, aware of what this means for us. There may be no way to recover if every single Gelder is slowly losing their ability to reproduce. Our ancestors may have condemned us long ago and we very well may have to just accept that.

I will fight until my dying day though, fight for the chance to see the Gelders recover from this death blow.

"I suppose you're right. It does explain why no children are being born," she replies with a nod. "And why you are finding mates on Earth."

"Yes, it does, but any lie could do that just as well. No, this answers many more questions than just our infertility. Some that have plagued me for centuries."

"Like what?" Eleanor turns to me, her expression curious. Upon her forehead is the slight furrow of her brow that she gets when she is buried in her thoughts, the one I adore. I fight the instinct to place a kiss there, forcing my mind back to the topic at hand.

"The most important piece to me is that it finally provides an explanation as to why we have a massive hole in our history. Our ancestors were meticulous about recording our past, yet large archives were missing. All from the time that Jaeson speaks, not even just the city. It was as if someone went through and purposely erased any and all signs of the past."

"What does that have to do...oh." Eleanor's face simultaneously clears and tightens with unease. "They were hiding the evidence that they massacred their own people."

"Yes, as well as stripping them of their rights and forcing the change upon them. It also answers the long asked question of where the Ateleans went. Within the ranks of the founding family were the most powerful of warriors, the strongest of their time. Yet every single one died off? Left suddenly with no trace? It never made sense. Many of us have searched for an explanation through the millennia and now we have it," I say while studying the blond-haired male across the room.

His gaze is fixed on us, never wavering in his examination. If he is projecting a false concern for his daughter he is the most skilled actor I have ever met. One look in his eyes is enough for me to know that he would gladly strike me down if he hears I have harmed his only daughter.

Except that is not entirely true. This male before me has a massive family tree, so large in fact that it spans generations upon generations. It strikes me that none of us actually know how extensive it is or how he came to have a granddaughter who is mated to Liam. He is concealing quite a bit from us.

"I thought you said that Eleanor was your first offspring?" I ask him.

His eyebrow cocks up in mockery. "Maybe you should check your hearing. I said that Eleanor was the offspring I was waiting for, not my first. I did not know when she would come, only that she would."

I dissect his words, looking for the hidden meaning behind them. "So you had many children before her?"

"No, I had many *sons* before her." Jaeson's eyes turn sad, despair seems to hang heavy over him for a brief pulse, and then his face is a cool mask once more. "None of them possessed the gene for *lacieu*, not even a glimmer of it. I theorized that while humans were compatible to carry a combination of our genes within them it would take something quite special to be able to incubate and nurture a master of our powers. I loved and cared for each of my sons, and I will always cherish their memory. But it was Eleanor I waited for."

"So...I am a master? How is that possible? I don't feel any power within me. Shouldn't I know? Wouldn't I know if I had power?" Eleanor interrupts, her voice rising with every word. The anxiety is obvious in her tone.

"But, Eleanor, you do!" comes a passionate voice from the bed. "You saved our child even without knowing you could. You saved it, our precious baby. You have power and it is the purest I have ever known."

Joy's eyes are shining with a mixture of gratitude and devotion. Eleanor may be a queen by name but she is fast becoming a queen in her own rights, inspiring loyalty and dedication in her subjects by merely being who she is.

"Yes, daughter mine, you have the power within you even if you deny its presence," Jaeson says to Eleanor with a gentle cadence that is lacking when he communicates with anyone else.

Golon, who has been oddly silent since Jaeson's recounting of our past, steps up. "So you say you only had sons before and that Joy is a descendant of one of these sons?"

"Yes, that is correct," Jaeson answers slowly and carefully. He is on guard around Golon; he knows how vast the knowledge that Golon possesses is. Jaeson is well aware that he must tread carefully when he speaks with him or Golon will see through his omissions. Measuring his words precisely, ensuring he lets no information slip that he does not want out. I may not know what, but I know he is hiding something from us. I intend to find out, and before it can hurt my mate or my people.

"Then, in fact, it could be deduced that *all* of our mates that have come from Earth are descendants from you." Golon speaks with command, rather than a question, in his voice.

I see Jaeson evaluate Golon for a moment before he smiles. "You are brighter than most of these warriors after all. Yes, every mate that you have claimed is almost certainly a descendant from *my line*."

"As I thought, the mortals are compatible with us because they each have a small part of themselves that is Gelder," Golon responds, shocking the speech right out of me. "Ancient Gelder that still possesses this hint of *lacieu*. It is diluted to almost the point of exclusion, after so many generations there is not much Gelder blood left. But there is enough."

"Yes, my genetic material, long ago interspersed within the population, bridges the gap between the species. You should be thanking me for providing you with much-needed mates, not insulting me."

"Did you visit any worlds before traveling to Earth?" Golon asks casually. However, I know Golon too well to be fooled by this indifferent display he is projecting. He is onto something.

"No, I spent no considerable time on any other inhabited planet." And there it is; Golon's face breaks out in a Cheshire grin. Golon has got Jaeson exactly where he wants him.

"Then I suspect that either you are lying, or we have more than just you to thank for our mates. We have had mates from *eight* mortal worlds appear. If *you* did not provide the genetic material, who did?"

Ellie

My father's gaze, which was resting on me, swings around rapidly to focus on Golon once more.

"What did you say?" I too am shocked by what I am hearing.

If what my father is saying is true, mortals are not compatible with Gelder naturally. Not these new, genetically altered ones at least. Jaeson has not had a problem conceiving a child. It is only an ancient Gelder ancestor that allows for Gelders to mate with us. My mind is swimming with questions, but forefront in my mind is an echo of Jaeson's.

"I said, we have found mates on more than just Earth, so the most likely explanation is that more than just you hid on mortal worlds and subsequently produced offspring on them," Golon reiterates. "That is, if you are not hiding anything else from us."

Jaeson looks shocked, as if the words he is hearing do not make any sense to him.

"You cannot be serious, surely you are not serious." Jaeson appears to be genuinely taken aback. I am not sure what exactly has him so shocked though.

"Why is that a surprise to you? You yourself did the same thing," Golon challenges Jaeson.

"Yes, but my landing on Earth was by accident. I became stranded there and I was never able to find a way off the planet. But there were laws against fraternizing with races that had not yet reached a certain point in their evolution. We knew our laws, we respected them. It was strictly banned; we were not to mingle with primitive races. To do so was a high crime. We all understood the possible repercussions if we interfered in their development." Jaeson speaks, but it seems to be more directed inward than to those of us in the room. "No one that I rescued would have willingly risked the lives of an entire race. A mortal planet is the last place any one of them would have gone to."

"Would that not make them the perfect hiding place then?" Golon asks with one eyebrow cocked up in mirth.

Jaeson's eyes widen ever so slightly, then he concedes with a nod of his head. He says, "You may indeed be right, young scholar."

Jaeson's seemingly polite words cause Golon's features to harden, anger brewing in his gaze. "You would be wise to not trifle with me, old one." Golon's words are hard with barely contained fury. "I may have dedicated myself to broadening the mind, but only *after* I completed the Final Warrior *Chorus*. By my dress you are aware of my class. Take care for next time I will not let such rudeness pass twice without retaliation."

Oh, now I see why he is so angry. In a society that social structure is based on power and strength, not calling a warrior a warrior is an insult. By the way that it has the infamously calm Golon bristling, I imagine it is a rather nasty insult.

"My apologies, young *warrior*," Jaeson replies, his words dripping with sarcasm.

"Both of you stop it!" I say with my gaze moving between the two of them. "There are much greater problems at hand than you two bickering. Jaeson? Apologize to Golon. Now." I stare up at my father until he sighs as if he is committing some great chore.

"I apologize, warrior. My daughter is correct. There are more pressing concerns at the moment," Jaeson says, all while managing to sound moderately polite.

Danion, who has been quiet this whole time, speaks and brings every eye in the room to rest on him. "Why were you not able to mingle with these primitive races? I have never heard of this law. Not even in my study of the ancient laws."

"Yes, I can see why you would not think it a crime since you so readily interfere with the development of cultures with little regard for their wellbeing." At this Danion bristles and opens his mouth, presumably to defend himself, but Jaeson starts speaking again. "When a young race is given knowledge they are not ready for, it can drive the species to extinction."

"I do not interfere—" Danion attempts to speak, but Jaeson once more interrupts.

"Oh, yes you do, or need I remind you about the state of Earth?"

"That is different! The Erains attacked them, attempted to decimate their entire population. We had to defend them. That is what we do. We defend those who cannot defend themselves. Or did you forget that?" Danion challenges him.

"But why did you make that agreement? Why not just defend the planet from the stars and leave them to heal in peace? Why do you negotiate with these people? Why force them into an agreement that benefits only you?" Jaeson sneers at my mate.

Danion is silent; he has no defense for his actions. I open my mouth in a rush to speak up for Danion when I realize that Jaeson is right. There is no logical reason I can think of that would defend his actions one hundred years ago.

Danion certainly did not need our help in overthrowing the Erains. They never needed to make contact with us. They could have destroyed the enemy ships and then just protected us without our knowledge.

"That is what I thought, *King* Danion. You had no reason for such a treaty except that mates were on the planet and you needed the Earth government to allow you to claim them. You took advantage of people because they had something that you desperately needed."

I turn to Danion, recalling something he told me the first time we dined together. "You once told me that there are eight mortal worlds including Earth that you protect." As I speak, Danion's face closes off even further. "Do you only protect worlds that mates are born to?" I ask with horror on my face. "Do you refuse to help worlds that possess no mates?"

This prompts Danion to speak harshly. "Of course not! We would never leave entire races to die simply because there is no gain to be had." He lowers his voice and drops his head, giving us the illusion of privacy. "However, I do make the same pact with every world. The spoils of war go to the victor. I always ensure that if a mate is born on any planet we protect, we have the right to claim them. I do what I have to do to ensure that any Gelder will be able to claim their mate when the time comes."

Jaeson begins speaking to Danion again, but I am not listening to the words, I am locked inside my own mind.

My initial reaction is disgust and I can't believe how callous he is toward worlds who clearly need their help. Then I give myself time to analyze his actions factually instead of emotionally, something that my inner voice is only too happy to help me work through.

Do not be naïve, you know that every conquering power takes something as a prize.

But we were not in battle with them, he defended us.

Precisely, he defended your people and asked only that he be able to claim anyone who may be a mate to either him or his people. Over the century that he has defended Earth not even one hundred women have been claimed. It is not what you would call a colossal amount, nowhere near enough to counter the amount of Gelder life lost in the battle for Earth.

I suppose you are right.

Of course, I am. You also need to admit that your life here is much better than what you lived on Earth. Joy, too, is immensely happy and does not seem to have any complaints about her life here. Claiming women is not the crime you are allowing yourself to believe it is.

I know it is not a crime, I just can't help feeling as if Danion's motives are more self-serving than he leads on.

What you are feeling is nothing more than your father's words stirring up the propaganda you have been fed your whole life. Claiming women is not a bad thing, no matter what you were told.

You are right, I know you are, but knowing something in your head and knowing it in your heart are two different things.

I am drawn out of my head by loud, screaming voices to my left. Danion, Liam, Jarlin, and even Golon are standing in a straight line in front of Joy's bed preventing Jaeson from coming any closer.

"You WILL let me pass!" Jaeson is commanding the line of males before him.

Danion, with rage causing his aura to swirl around him in angry blasts, screams, "You will not take another step!"

I notice that Jaeson's aura is sweeping over and around the warriors, slowly encompassing Joy in a cocoon. I glance at Golon, searching for any sign that he notices what Jaeson is doing, but I can find no such indication.

I am about to demand he explain himself when I suddenly become aware of another aura in the room, coming from Joy's stomach. The baby. As I watch, I notice that the aura is responding to Jaeson and growing stronger every second.

"You condemn that child to nothing but pain if you do not allow me to assist the *hael* master in monitoring the pregnancy. You obviously know nothing of Gelder infants."

I quickly move between the males I consider family and the one who actually is by blood to prevent a bloody confrontation. "Jaeson! Stop this, you continue to anger these warriors and I will not stop their retaliation."

"I do not fear these weak, younger warriors," Jaeson scoffs.

"I will also side with them against you. Every time." I meet his gaze with steely determination. "Nor will I forgive you if you bring harm to one of them."

Jaeson stands straighter at this, something that looks eerily close to hurt flashes across his face, and then he gives me a bow. "I am sorry, daughter mine, I would never want to harm someone you consider dear."

I nod my head in acknowledgment of what he says, but I can still feel the anger coming in waves off the four males behind me. I decide it would probably be best if I get Jaeson away from these males.

"Jaeson, I think it is time that I lead you to your chambers." I turn to look at Danion. "I need some time to speak with my father, alone. I will join you in our chambers later."

I expect Danion to put up some sort of argument, as he has proved to be almost obsessed with controlling my actions, but after a moment of thought and a dark scowl over my head to rest on Jaeson, he gives me a nod.

I cross to him with a smile, stretch up and place a chaste kiss on the corner of his mouth. "Thank you, Danion, I know that this was not easy for you."

"For you, Eleanor, I will learn how to be the male you deserve," he says as his hand comes up and gently grasps my chin, rubbing his thumb over it lightly.

I move my face into his palm and take a few moments to revel in his touch. Then with one last look up to my mate, I turn to the man who is my father.

"Alright, Jaeson, let's go."

Danion

"I cannot believe you are letting him be alone with her. We know very little about him, Dane. And the little we have seen does not inspire confidence." Golon speaks to my right.

"I am aware of that." I direct my voice to the communication system and speak to my communications officer. "Jedde? I need you to monitor our queen and her father. Make sure that he does not try anything."

While I trust my mate in all things, her father has yet to earn that same consideration. Jedde has the ability to see and hear everything that happens on this ship. I do not need to be there to make sure that my mate is safe.

But then I hear Jedde's hesitant voice. "I am sorry, my king, but it appears that I am not able to hear them speak. The male seems to be blocking me somehow."

My first reaction is to storm off after them and join their party, to protect my mate at all costs. I allow myself to briefly fantasize about a particular blond warrior coming to a brutal and bloody end.

Then I realize that the matebond madness has come over me and is controlling me once again. I take several breaths and then growl, "Fine. Monitor them as best you can. And, Jedde? You better alert me the second he makes even a slight move toward her."

Laughter from my right draws my attention. "Oh, Dane, I would not want to be in your shoes right now."

Disgusted with Golon, and myself, I storm out of the medical wing and head to our chambers where I await my mate.

Chapter Twelve

Ellie

Jaeson and I walk silently for several strides. As little as I know about this male who I can thank for my existence, I had expected to be more uncomfortable in his presence. But oddly, I find walking with him in silence strangely comforting.

After enjoying the silence for a few more moments, I interrupt our time with a question I am dying to know the answer to. "What were you doing to the baby?"

"Eleanor, it is hard to explain." His attempt at evasion only makes me more determined to discover the answer.

"Try," I bark out. I will not let him dodge a response.

"Understand that it is not that I do not want to share this with you but that you lack certain knowledge of our species." I scowl at him.

"Teach it to me then. I am a fast learner." Jaeson sighs.

"Alright. In essence, our power lineage is a lot more than ice power as your mate and his people believe. I do not have time to explain it, but before the massacre of our people destroyed our connection to *lacieu*, every child needed to be exposed to massive surges of the line to develop properly."

I bite back a gasp. "So the child is already in danger? It has been weeks since its conception!"

"That is what I was doing, testing the child. And while she is weak, she is healthy. I imagine your presence here has provided her with the power she needed. I understand from Jarlin that the night of your bonding ceremony was the first time the baby had a miraculous recovery. You must have let out a large wave of power, strengthening her while she was in the womb."

I fixate on one single word. My focus is set so steadily on it, I scarcely pay attention to anything else. "She?"

The baby is a girl, a little baby girl! Jaeson's gaze softens on my lightly whispered word.

"Yes, the child is a girl. But to answer your question, I was lending the baby the strength she needed. That is all."

I nod to him. I may not have known him long, but I am sure he is not lying to me about this. His words and face are too earnest when he speaks of the child.

"There is something else that I have wanted to ask you, but we have been so busy since we left the planet."

"What is it that you need, daughter?" His term of address makes me feel warm inside. While I am still adjusting to having a father in my life, hearing him call me daughter brings me nothing but joy.

"What happened to my mother?" Jaeson's face darkens.

"That I am not sure, but I know who we need to speak with."

"Who?"

"Ambassador Lexen," he says with a dark scowl on his face.

"We have him in custody on board the ship. I can speak to Danion about us needing to see him. I am sure we can meet with Lexen tomorrow."

I am desperate to meet the woman who is actually my mother. Knowing that the woman who tormented me for my entire youth is not in fact my mother has been nothing but a comfort. Why my aunt impersonated her I do not know, but I intend to find out.

After leaving Jaeson I walked directly to my chambers. As I enter and close the door I look around the large anteroom and notice Danion sitting in a halo of light.

The only light in the entire room, I notice, making it look as if he is a lone warrior combatting the dark for me. My fierce defender, willing to do anything for my safety.

I am overcome with love for this male before me. He has sacrificed so much for my happiness and has worked so hard to change into the male I selfishly demanded that he be. Danion has accepted me as I am, never once acting as if he was unhappy in our pairing. Never has he said that he wants me to be anything other than me.

So what if biology paired us together? So what if he will never love me? I will love him enough for the both of us. I know he is devoted to me, and it is time that I show him that I see everything he has done for me.

I cross the large chasm that separates us. Some of what I am feeling must show on my face because Danion stands and meets me halfway, his arms rising from his sides to clutch my body tightly to his.

We come together violently, mouths clashing together, lips being shredded on our teeth as passion overwhelms us. The sharp metallic taste does nothing but fuel my desire for him. I have tried to deny my body's craving to no avail. It wants Danion and I have no more energy to fight.

It wants another taste of the sweet oblivion that he brought me outside by the fountain. My arms move up to clasp his head tighter to me, my hands moving frantically through his hair.

Heat explodes down my back as Danion's arms sweep up and down my spine in large arcs. His two large, strong hands fall to my bottom and squeeze rhythmically. The inner ache that is deep inside seems to pulse hotter with every squeeze.

I undulate my body toward his, pressing my front up against him so that our bodies are separated only by our clothes. Suddenly Danion's hands flex and my body is lifted off the floor, my legs coming up to wrap around his waist.

"Oh, *aninare*. I can't stop this time. I have to have you." Danion's words are a growl upon my lips. "Let me have you."

I slide my mouth down to his neck to kiss and taste the deliciously sensitive skin. Danion moans at the contact.

"Then." Kiss. "Take me." Lick. "To our bed." I nibble the skin along his jaw moving slowly back toward his mouth.

I feel air moving past us rapidly, then my back is met by a soft surface. I sink in deeply as Danion's weight presses down upon me.

I tighten my arms and legs around his muscular body, wanting to feel even more of him. As I press against the rigid pole that rubs so deliciously at the juncture of my thighs, Danion's head rises up and he roars in sensation.

"*Aninare*, you must refrain. It has been too long since I have had you. If you persist in your actions I will not be able to stop myself. I will take you harder than you can imagine is possible. I will plunge myself so deeply within you that you will not know where one

of us ends and the other begins. I will ravage you with my tongue, my hands, my shaft..."
His words trail off as he sucks in a harsh breath when I gyrate beneath him again.

His gray eyes blaze down at me. "One more warning, my sweet temptress, or I will take you so many times you will beg me to stop, all the while praying that I never cease. I will bring your body so much pleasure you will not know how to handle the contractions your orgasms will bring you."

His mouth skims my face to whisper in my ear, "I will bring you to climax so many times and so fiercely you will swear you are dreaming, because you never thought so much pleasure was possible."

I look up at him and smile. "Sounds good to me." I smirk at him and open my legs even wider to thrust my body harder against his, searching for the friction my body so desperately needs.

Danion groans and his hands come to rest on my top, grasping on both sides of the X that is formed over my chest. My body is jerked wildly as he tears the material clear off.

His mouth descends ravenously upon my breasts, kissing and suckling every spare inch of my chest. I gasp at the sensation that explodes over me. Danion's mouth moves up quickly, I can scarcely follow his movements. I am guided by my sensation and feeling alone.

A sharp nip of teeth on the underside of my breast, a hot lick to soothe the sting from the bite. Glorious suction. Kisses circling my nipples, but never claiming them as I want.

I grasp his head and try to pull his head to where I need his mouth most. I hear a deep chuckle and what I swear is "feisty little thing" before he finally takes my nipple deep in his mouth.

Heat engulfs me and I can't contain the screams. I realize that my body is spasming in orgasm, and all he did was play with my breasts.

As I am slowly coming down from my climax, I feel a cold chill on my legs. Danion has ripped my pants away and is quickly discarding his own.

His member is gloriously hard above me. My eyes meet his and I am lost in the desire I see within his gaze. His hand reaches down to guide himself into me. I feel the head skim my desperate flesh. His free hand grasps my hip tightly.

A blaring ringing interrupts us. Danion's face is of a man in immense pain. "You have got to be *fiefling* kidding me," he growls out as he rolls off of me. A disembodied voice floats into the room.

"I am sorry to interrupt while you are in your private chambers, but it is a matter of great urgency." Jedde's voice speaks with light panic.

"Someone better be dying," Danion mutters as he covers his eyes with his arm. "I feel as if I am, that is for sure."

"Eleanor, you are needed immediately in your sister's chamber. Marilee is with Savannah, who is screaming in her sleep. She is unable to wake her."

"Anna!" I fling myself from the bed, grab a robe hanging over the dressing table, and start running as fast as I possibly can toward my sister's chambers.

Poor Anna—the nickname that I gave her as a small baby comes readily to my mind. She must be having one of her night terrors. She has suffered them her whole life, but this is the first one she has had since she was brought aboard the ship.

"I am sure she will be alright. I will make sure she is alright." A rough voice at my side draws my attention to Danion running right beside me.

"She has been plagued by night terrors her whole life. She can hurt herself badly when she is trapped within them." I turn a corner and can see the large, ornately carved gold door that leads to my sister's room.

I am so thankful that Danion placed them on the same side of the ship as us rather than across like he did with Jaeson. I burst into the room and find Marilee and Samantha on each side of a thrashing Anna.

Anna's hair is being thrown all over the place as she moves in desperation on top of the bed. Tears are running down her face and her voice is raspy from overuse. Her screams are tearing me apart.

I round the bed and sit beside Marilee. I reach out and place a hand on Anna's forearm. I can feel the tension that has her body locked tight. I move Marilee gently aside and lay my body down beside Anna, wrapping her tightly in my arms and holding her through the tremors.

Slowly, so very slowly, her screams gradually lessen and I can feel the tension fade out of her. I know now I will finally be able to rouse her from sleep.

"Anna? Anna, honey? You can wake up now," I whisper to her.

Her tear-filled eyes open and she begins to cry even harder.

"Elle! Oh, Elle!" I sit up and draw her tighter into my embrace, slowly stroking her head until the shivers violently racking her body subside.

"Marilee, could you get us that blanket?" I ask. She grabs the blanket that Anna must have kicked to the floor in her convulsions and wraps it around us.

Then she sits on the opposite side of Anna and we hold her between us. Samantha scoots as close as she can to her sister and we all stay together, enjoying the comfort of physical contact.

The door explodes open! I tense and the whimpers begin again from Anna. Danion takes up a fighting stance, placing his body between us and the door. Golon is in the entryway, aura bursting from his hands.

"Marilee! Marilee, are you alright?!" Golon's eyes scan the room. They settle on Marilee and he rushes to her side. "Marilee, are you injured? I heard that screams were coming from these rooms and you were calling for aid."

I blink my eyes slowly. Golon is so reserved, so controlled with his aura. Never before have I seen him with his aura so open and on display. Danion too seems shocked, straightening from his stance and sheathing the blades he drew from the concealed spots along his pants. I wonder idly when he had time to get his pants back on, my face heating up as I recall just what we were doing earlier.

"Golon? What are you doing here?" Danion asks, confusion blatant on his face.

Golon ignores his question, his focus solely on Marilee. Marilee, for her part, keeps her attention on calming Anna.

"Marilee, answer me. Now," Golon bites off.

Marilee visibly bristles. My best friend has always been self-confident and easily angered. Her temper was common knowledge while we were growing up. I know her well enough to predict her actions. Golon apparently, does not.

"Marilee. Marilee." Beneath the anger that Golon is showing I can tell that he is concerned for her. If I did not know any better I would say that Golon is acting suspiciously like Danion did in our first encounters. "I will not stand for this. You *will* speak to me."

Still Marilee says nothing, not even glancing in his direction. However, while Golon feels she is doing this to ignore him, I know better. My friend is doing this to control her anger, attempting to stop herself from railing at him as she so wishes she could. I have no doubt that if Anna did not need her she would be screaming as we speak.

When Golon tries to pull her into his arms, and therefore away from Anna, Marilee ends her silence. She levels a glare packed with so much ferocity upon the warrior that even Danion's eyebrow shoots upward in surprise. It is apparent that neither of them have had much experience in dealing with women, seeing as how most of their species is male. These males may be warriors and faced countless bloody battles, but they have never had to contend with an angry woman who takes no prisoners.

Calmly, and ever so gently, she smooths Anna's hair from her face, which is resting on my shoulder. "Anna, dear? Savannah?" Marilee speaks softly, attempting to get Anna's attention. Once she realized that Golon was not an apparition sent from her dreams to torment her she has calmed down slightly.

Anna's response is silent but she does turn her head to look at Marilee. "Will you be alright with just Ellie-Elle for a while? I need to discuss something trivial with Golon for a moment."

Golon stiffens at the word *trivial* and opens his mouth to speak. Something must have made him think better about this course of action because he quickly closes his mouth without uttering a word. Smart male.

Anna burrows deeper into me and then nods her head at Marilee, who then slides past Golon and walks from the room, all without a single word uttered to him. Golon follows her stiffly.

Once the door is closed behind them, Sam moves into the space opened with Marilee's departure. Anna is resting comfortably between us. I glance at Danion.

"What is going on with Golon?" I ask Danion.

"I have no idea. This is not the first time that I have noticed strange behavior from him," Danion answers while staring thoughtfully at the door.

"He comes to see her all the time, but she doesn't know it," Sam mentions succinctly, all the while lying with her head near Anna's.

"What do you mean? Who comes to see who?" Danion asks Sam, but it is Anna who answers.

"Golon, that man who was just here. He comes by and watches Marilee all the time. At least once a day, but he rarely lets her know that he is there."

Anna's words floor me. I am so shocked to hear this that I say nothing. In that time Sam adds her opinions on it as well.

"Yes, he sure does hide. I see him every morning and then every evening outside her door. I don't think he leaves all night. Just sits outside, watching over her."

"Golon? He sits outside Marilee's door and watches over her?" I ask, and both girls nod. Anna appears to be much better now, getting her mind off her dream seems to be helping.

"How do you know he is watching over her?" Danion asks them.

"Because he looks at the door the same way you look at Ellie." Danion looks stunned and almost mystified. Then his eyes seem to clear in disbelief.

"Danion? Do you think...?" I let my words trail off.

"If it is so, it is not our place to interfere. We must not speak of this to either of them. Girls, can you help us keep this secret?" Danion asks with a quiet whisper. A playful gleam is in his eyes.

Both girls smile and giggle at his antics and nod their heads vigorously. A lull in the room occurs once their laughter subsides. It is then that I can hear the noise coming from the other side of the door.

"You have no right to barge in..." I am not able to hear every word, but it is clear that Marilee has finally let her anger loose.

"It is for your safety...do not know our ways..."

"Blast your ways...stop following me around..."

"I will do as I please...stubborn fool..."

"You can't control me!"

"You think not?"

The sounds of the argument are clearly upsetting the girls. I am just about to distract them with a story when Danion has another idea.

"Have you both heard of Gelder magic?" As he says this, Danion holds his hand palm up. A shimmering, golden horse is floating in his hands.

He now has two avid observers. Both sit up on their knees to get a closer look. The horse is soon joined by another and they begin to move around in front of Danion in a sort of choreographed dance.

The horses flow between and around the girls, landing on their shoulders and their heads. Laughter explodes into the room. My heart weeps when I hear this; it has been so long since they have known joy. These two brilliant girls have had so little to laugh about in their young lives.

Before I know it the girls are yawning and lying back down, the argument long forgotten. I look at Danion. "I will stay with them this evening."

Danion nods his head. "Of course. I will let you all rest." He then stands and begins to leave the room.

"Danion? Can you stay with us too? You could use your magic to keep us safe," a small voice says from the bed. Anna is staring at him with determination and a little uncertainty.

Danion appears stunned, and then his expression clears and the shock leaves his face entirely, a new emotion taking its place. He is happy. He nods his head and lies down with us, beside me on the side of the bed closest to the doors. He places his arm over both girls briefly.

"Fear nothing, beautiful young ones, for nothing will bring you harm while I am here. This I swear to you."

Chapter Thirteen

Danion

Stiffly, so as not to disturb any of the females from their slumber, I ease out of bed. I slip soundlessly out of the room and, as I expected, Golon is waiting for me outside the chamber.

"Dane, I know what you are going to say, and I am here to tell you not to say it." Golon speaks with a defiant tone.

"And why should I not say it, *cognata*?" I ask him. "You obviously are not capable of handling this on your own, if tonight is anything to judge by."

Golon's eyes are for once filled with emotion instead of his carefully made blank stare. "Because I cannot do anything at this time. My loyalty right now is to you and our people, to ensure that all the innocent lives we protect are safe from the hell that is war. If I acknowledge the truth, it will divide me, divide us, and this is something I fear our people will not withstand."

I can feel the desolation in Golon's soul from here. To feel what he must feel and not be able to act on it in any way. I can understand his reasoning, but I do not know if I would be strong enough.

"Golon, *cognata*...I am not sure I would be strong enough to follow your chosen path if I was in the same position as you," I tell him, sorrow making my words heavy.

"Danion, I know you would be. You waited twenty years, I am sure I can wait a few months."

"I did not have to fight the bond while she was here with me though. You do. That will make it infinitely more difficult."

"I know, Dane. I will fight as long as I can. I know she will not accept me right now. If I was to open myself up to the bond completely and she refused it, I am not sure I would survive."

I place my hand on his shoulder, a silent symbol of support. Wordlessly, Golon reaches up and covers my hand with his own. Without another word he turns and walks soundlessly down the hall.

I watch him disappear, then I turn back to the room where my mate and her two younger sisters—well, I suppose her cousins actually—sleep. I silently slip back into the bed and place my arm around my mate.

For thousands of years I have struggled to sleep, to quiet my mind enough to actually slip away into the silence of slumber. Ever since I have been able to gather my mate up close to me sleep comes easily. It is a relaxing event instead of something to be dreaded. I tuck her head under my chin, bury my nose in her golden locks, and take a deep breath. Her scent is intoxicating, a wonderful mix of sweet wildflowers and honeysuckle.

I doze off into a deep, restful sleep with what is fast becoming my favorite scent in the world. In my last moments of wakefulness I realize I have the dopiest grin on my face, and I do not even care.

Ellie

I am woken by a gentle brush against my nose. I open my eyes and see a soft wispy swath of gold over my face. I sit up and notice Danion's arm is around my waist. I glance at his face and see him with a gentle curve of his lips, looking as if he is in the middle of a pleasant dream.

I raise my hand and caress his cheek lightly, letting my thumb graze his lip. I look around at the gold light and I realize it is an aura trace. I gently move Danion's arms gently off of my waist and I slip out of bed. I slowly enter the hallway and see Golon standing there.

"Golon? What are you doing here?" I ask, somewhat surprised.

"We have something that we need to discuss."

"Ah...yes, I wanted to talk to you as well. This thing you have going on with Marilee—"

"We will not discuss Marilee. What lies between us is for our knowledge and our knowledge alone." Golon interrupts me with quick, hard words. His eyes are cold and angry.

"Golon, she is my—"

"I said we will not discuss Marilee." His eyes are still hard, unforgiving.

"Golon—"

"Not one word. There is no reason for you to be anxious over her well-being, not where I am concerned. We have things to discuss that are necessary to the war. That is the only thing we can discuss." He stares at me, eyes unflinching and piercing. "Are you ready to accept that?"

I mull over his question. Marilee is my best friend and I want to protect her as best I can. There was a time when she was the only one that was there for me. But now that is not the case. I have so many more people in my life.

I have people who have proven to be concerned for my welfare. Those who have shown that I am not alone anymore. And Golon is one of them. I trust Golon with my life, so why should I not trust him with Marilee's?

I nod my head slowly.

"Good." Golon nods. "Now, I called you here to discuss your training."

"My training?" I ask him.

"Yes, we need to begin your *chakkas* training."

"Oh, yes, when do you want to start?"

"Once you have eaten I will join you and we will begin."

I open my mouth to respond when the door opens suddenly behind me. I turn around, and Danion is standing in the doorway, shirtless. My mind goes blank as I take in his muscular and sculpted chest. His shoulders are broad, and they taper down into a lean and tight waist.

Idly, I wonder when he took his shirt off; last I saw him he was still dressed.

"Eleanor? Golon? What has happened?" Danion asks us.

"Nothing, King. I merely needed to arrange a time to begin training your mate."

"Training her in what?" Danion asks with a hard glare to Golon. He glides his body next to mine and wraps his arm around me.

"That is between your mate and myself, not you," Golon answers, an amused glimmer visible behind his eyes.

I can feel Danion's body stiffening with rage behind me. I speak up quickly to attempt to stop the inferno I can sense within Danion's aura.

"Danion, please. I have to be trained and there are things that Golon will have to be the one to teach me."

"No there are not," Danion says with a pronounced enunciation of each word. "Everything that you need I can provide. Everything."

"Not in this case—"

"Yes, in *every* case," Danion interrupts me.

"Danion, there are lineages that only Golon and I control. I have to be trained in them." I attempt to pacify him, skirting the truth by not actually telling him what our training will involve, but giving him enough information that he should be able to ascertain the truth.

I see Danion's stance slowly thaw from his icy rage. His gaze shifts to Golon and he stares at him for several moments, silently assessing him.

"You understand that you will be responsible for her safety at all times? At no time will your desire for results cloud your judgment and cause her to come to harm." Danion speaks darkly to Golon, alluding to some deeper meaning.

Golon stiffens, his eyes going cold. "That was long ago, Danion. The circumstances were very different as you well know. No harm will come to our queen under my watch."

The two males' stand off against each other for several moments. Finally, after what feels like hours, they both nod to one another. Danion grabs my arm and guides me toward my sister's chambers once more.

As we are turning from the corridor, my eyes meet Golon's and he gives me a grave nod. I return the gesture solemnly.

Danion

I sit at the table in the observing deck, food overflowing from every surface. I look around the table and am pleased to see all of Eleanor's family. Family is something that I have lacked for many years. Golon is my only real family left, and now I have my mate's family to care for.

As I settle on the one member I am not happy to claim, Jaeson, my thoughts turn dark. Eleanor was mentioning to me the myths surrounding Jaeson's "lost city" when we waited for her father to awaken and join us for the morning meal. I am curious as to how these myths came about.

"Jaeson? I wonder if you would humor me for a moment," I ask the male sitting across from me. He lowers his utensils and takes one last swallow of his food.

"Of course, you are a king after all," he says with a smirk that he is just asking for me to wipe off his face. The smugness of this male is absurd.

He has no concern or respect for traditions. His constant disrespect given to my title will not be stood for. He takes every opportunity to ensure I know that while I am a king he does not consider me his king. We are racing toward a battle, a battle I am not sure he is prepared to deal with. He underestimates me, that much is clear.

"You were hidden away for several thousand years on the planet Earth, correct?"

"That is right, I admitted to such readily."

"And the city you were found in, that is the lost city of the Atelean family? Home to many ancient archives, yes? Riches and precious knowledge?" I ask him.

Jaeson's eyes go narrow, obviously wondering where I am going with this. "Yes, it is." He says the words slowly, cautiously.

"Ah. Am I then to presume that it is only a matter of coincidence that a human myth of a lost golden city by the name of Atlantis possesses such a strong resemblance to your city?" I ask him.

I expected shame, or at the very least embarrassment, to appear on the face of Eleanor's absentee father, but he possesses no such reaction. Instead, he throws his head back and laughs.

"That is what you are alluding to? Oh, Dane, you are precious, sitting on your high horse full of false integrity. I was stranded for thousands of years with very little to amuse myself. Can you fault me for stirring up a little mischief when I did allow myself some mortal companionship?" he asks with a full smile on his lips.

Eleanor is the one who speaks this time. "You mean you purposely spread rumors?" she asks, aghast. "Purposefully told tales and hoped they would catch on and become myth and legend?"

"What else was I supposed to do?" he says with a shrug. "I caused no real harm, just had a little merriment with the indigenous people and told a few tall tales. It was entertaining to tell a tale and then disappear for a few hundred years. Once I was awake again I enjoyed seeing how the myth had been twisted."

"What tales exactly did you spread?" Eleanor asks with narrowed eyes.

"Nothing dastardly, I assure you." At her continued glare, Jaeson answers with a small huff of indignation. "Fine, Atlantis, the lost city obviously. The fountain of youth, which was mostly true. Mortals who drank from our fountain would indeed add years to their life. I gave birth to a language known as Latin, which I loosely based on our own ancient tongue."

I snort quietly to myself. That explains why Eleanor kept thinking that the markings on her chest looked somehow familiar. This *infer* created an entire language on Earth that resembles our tongue yet had the *ciines* to judge my interactions with the mortal races.

"What else? I know there is more," I ask him. I can tell he is holding back.

"If you must know." He sighs deeply as if he is being heavily put upon. I notice that Marilee and the younger girls are hanging on his every word. "The myth of vampires comes from me, which I based on an old ally of the Gelders. Dragons, again, were a tale of my creation. Not a true lie as shapeshifting is fairly common throughout the cosmos. And there is, in fact, a race that we know are dragon shifters. I merely...embellished the tale a little bit," Jaeson says with a prideful smirk in his eyes.

"Is that all?" Eleanor asks with a dazed look on her face, barely able to comprehend everything he is revealing. I understand what is behind her shock though. It is more than just realizing that her father lied, it is actually that his lies are in fact mostly true. They laid the groundwork for several myths and legends on her world and she is now learning that they are based off true stories. He based them on real species and things, only that they don't exist on her planet.

I myself am wondering what species he speaks of. I have a strong guess as to who he means by the vampire species, but dragons? I do not know of any shapeshifting race that looks like dragons that is still alive. He could be thinking of the Draga since he would not know that the race died off several millennia ago.

Jaeson diverts his gaze to his plate, a look of chagrin finally gracing his features.

"There is one more tale I told that holds some weight in today's Earth culture. One that I am ashamed that I ever had a part in."

"What is it?" Eleanor and I ask simultaneously.

"Have you ever heard the expression that Rome wasn't built in a day?" he asks us. I have never heard of this phrase, but Eleanor nods her head in assent.

"It is a phrase from the time before the war. Before we had to give up country lines, before our world collapsed under tyranny."

"Well, it is not exactly true." Jaeson turns away, eyes focusing somewhere in the distance. "It was about two thousand eight hundred years ago, and it was my last night before I would need to place myself in hibernation. I was friends with two brothers, their names were Romulus and Remus." Eleanor draws in a surprised breath.

"Romulus and Remus?" she asks, a mixture of shock and awe in her tone.

"What is the significance of those names?" I ask her.

"Romulus and Remus are the two fabled brothers who founded ancient Rome. It is told that they fought horribly with each other over where to build their city, what the name should be, and who would rule it. They fought so much over this that Romulus eventually killed his brother and then took the throne. He went on to train some of the most savage and powerful warriors of the ancient world. The Legionnaires." She speaks softly, with a reverent hush.

Jaeson sighs. "Yes, they did fight horribly, but they did not create Rome. I did. And I did it in one day." At the baffled stares leveled at him by every occupant at the table, Jaeson decides to continue his explanation. "As I said, I was friends with these brothers. We often partook of the unusual beverages of the time, but rarely to excess.

"Except, this time it was my last night. I knew that I would never see my friends again, they would be long dead by the time I rose from my slumber. I had been alone on this planet for so many years I was succumbing to melancholy." His face falls in dismay. "I decided to drown my sorrows, and for the first time I lost control of my faculties. I began to boast to these brothers of my skills and talents.

"I shouted loudly my ability to build something out of nothing and how I was a great warrior, capable of outsmarting any man. They naturally did not believe me. So in my relaxed state, I proved it. I built what was soon to be known as Rome. And I created it in one day. One night actually." Jaeson looks over to my mate, and then clears his throat.

"In the morning I left my two friends alone to sleep off their hangover and placed myself in hibernation. I was so confused, I entirely forgot what I had done. But I remembered quickly when I awoke from my slumber. I returned to the land of mortals to a changed world. A world I barely recognized. My interference had catapulted the society into a new age. The knowledge that a being was out there that could build an entire city in one day had spread across the whole globe.

"I learned of Romulus murdering his brother over the information that *I* gave him, and it almost broke me. I knew this is why we are not to interfere. Romulus had used the war tactics that I so ignorantly boasted about and with them he dominated the neighboring civilizations. Only the Greek Spartans were able to hold their own.

"Due to my own failings, thousands of souls died a bloody death. The technology I mentioned was being studied, already they could map stars and predict solar events. I had told them I came from the stars and they were determined to grab this power for themselves. I hibernated for five hundred years, and when I awoke it was to see that my own thoughtless act led to centuries of bloody conflict."

"What did you do?" Eleanor asks softly. Jaeson sits up, his entire body screaming his desire to flee from this conversation. But his face is resigned, he knows he cannot hide from his past anymore.

"What else could I do? I worked to fix my mistake. I began adding evidence to the city that made it appear more aged. Adding signs that it took much more than a single day to build. I began interfering with the armies of the ancient world and leveling the fields in an attempt to limit the bloodshed. And finally, after painstaking diligence and many centuries, I changed the phrase from 'Anything is possible, Rome was built in a day' to 'Rome was not built in a day.'"

Jaeson ends his story with a resigned sigh of defeat. The guilt of those lives lost hanging heavily on his shoulders.

I stand up and move beside his chair, placing a hand on his shoulder. "Jaeson, it is time for your guilt to be absolved. Did you do a foolish thing? Yes, undeniably. But was it evil? No. You did not intend for the humans to battle, it is merely the way of every uncivilized and every *civilized* race. I have traveled the cosmos for over three thousand years, none of it spent in hibernation, and I have yet to find a people who do not have a bloody past."

Jaeson turns his head to study me. "Do you truly believe that?"

"I do. Did you give these soldiers an advantage? Possibly. We will never know for certain. Perhaps their deaths would have come regardless of your actions. We will never know. Their deaths are not on your hands, and if they were? It was unconsciously done. Let yourself forgive yourself," I tell him.

Jaeson turns to Eleanor. "And you, daughter mine? What are your thoughts on my actions?"

Eleanor does not speak for several moments. "I have dedicated my life to studying history, looking for answers in the past to modern day questions. I discovered that we are still looking for the same things, and sadly power is one of them. I believe that even if you had never built Rome or given battle techniques, it would have just been different names in the books. The story would be the same, war and death." She stares deeply at her father. "Forgive yourself, Jaeson."

With a deep breath, Jaeson nods.

Ellie

Danion, Jaeson, and I sit around the table that my family just vacated. We broke our evening fast together and now they are off to spend the day decorating their chambers. I smile at the frivolous nature of the day's activities that they get to partake in. They never had time to relax on Earth, and now they have the life they deserve.

Away from their mother who, apparently, is not mine.

"Danion?" I ask him. "Jaeson and I would like to question Lexen about the whereabouts of my birth mother."

Danion raises his head in surprise. "You do?"

"Yes, we believe that he might have played a role in her disappearance from my life."

"Yes, I suppose if anyone knows what fate befell her it would be that *infer*, Lexen." His lip curls in distaste. "I wish you had let me kill him when I wanted to."

"If I had we would have no leads to follow regardless her whereabouts, would we?" I ask him.

"I suppose that is true. Every day it is proved to me how lucky I am to have you as a mate." His words cause me to blush, and while part of me still does not trust him, his actions over the past two days have genuinely helped bridge that gap.

"Come, let us go. The prisoner was transported late last night, and he is on board on the lower decks." He offers me his arm in the elegant way of humans that I find so charming.

Knowing that he takes the time to ensure my comfort by following some of my traditions is one of the things I love about him.

The three of us discuss the war on our trip below deck. I personally am very concerned for Sylva and her team.

"Have there been any developments or updates?" I ask Danion.

"No, nothing. It is as silent as an intergalactic void." His eyes and lips are tense. I can tell his concern for his people weighs heavily on his mind.

Jaeson raises an eyebrow. "Isn't that a good sign?" he asks Danion.

"You think that it is a good thing that five of my best warriors are missing?" he growls at Jaeson.

"No, but if you were thinking rationally and not emotionally you would realize that if your enemy did capture them, wouldn't they have let you know by now?" he challenges Danion. "Instead, the silence bodes well for them. If they are as skilled as you say they may yet still be uncaptured, or simply unable to return home yet. Perhaps damage to their ship occurred. It does happen, you know?"

Jaeson's lip curls in self-deprecating humor, reminding us that he actually was stranded due to damage to his ship. Danion seems stunned for a moment.

"We do believe that they were captured, Jaeson. However, your words bring me hope. Maybe they escaped and are traveling to us now. I admit it is strange that we have not heard from the Erains if they did have them. They would relish any opportunity to bring us pain."

We travel the last hallway in silence and then pause in front of a massive black door. It is such a sharp contrast to the rest of the ship, which is covered in gold from floor to ceiling. But this hallway and this door are coal black.

Danion raises his hand and a bright purple light blazes forth, visible to me only because of my gift of aura sight. The door swings open inward from a seam in the middle, splitting into two halves.

Inside is a room that is divided by a bright, transparent wall of red. Our side is utterly barren. On the other side of the red barrier it is barely furnished. Besides a rudimentary bed and commode the room is empty.

Danion stops in shock. "Jedde? Where is the prisoner?" Danion's voice is raised and clipped, almost as if there is panic.

"He is in his holding cell, on the *uni* level door *qui*," the disembodied voice answers.

"No, he is not!" Danion roars furiously. "Sound the alarm, the prisoner has escaped!"

Chapter Fourteen

Ellie

"The entire ship has been searched. There is no sign of the prisoner," Danion tells Jaeson and me as we sit in the antechamber to my rooms.

"How did he escape?" I ask him.

"We have no idea. The guards who escorted him have gone missing as well, but they reported at the end of the transfer. This will require much investigation. The mysteries keep arriving, but the answers remain hidden."

Jaeson surveys us both for a silent moment. "Eleanor, I will need to begin training you immediately."

Both Danion and I look at him in shock. "Why?" I ask him.

"For one, since she shares blood with her mother, if she had proper control over her abilities she would be able to perform a blood to blood ritual."

"What is a blood to blood ritual?" I ask.

"It is an ancient ritual that was used to confirm royalty. It was also used to find a lost family member. No one alive can perform it anymore. The power was lost to us," Danion answers me.

"Yes, to you. Not to Eleanor; she will be able to do it with the correct training and we can find her mother. However, that is not even the most pressing concern for her training."

"Please enlighten us, old one." Danion speaks with an edge to his voice.

"Because this occurrence cannot be a coincidence, I believe that somehow there is an enemy on this ship and they are orchestrating a lot of events that seem to be beyond our control. They tried to kill you already, Eleanor. You need to be ready to defend yourself."

"I can defend my mate, ancient one." Danion stands abruptly and towers above us while we sit.

"From an attack you see, but clearly our enemy has demonstrated that they are capable of remaining hidden and attacking when we do not expect it. She was poisoned while under your protection."

I cannot sit here idly while he slanders my mate, father or no father. "It was not Danion's fault that I was poisoned."

"The fault is neither here nor there. What is, however, is you were poisoned. You nearly died. You must have another means of protecting yourself rather than just guards and an overzealous mate."

Danion stiffens even further and his aura takes a dark turn. I place my hand on Danion's and pull him down to sit beside me again.

Danion and Jaeson begin a spirited debate, harsh words flowing over me as they argue over my future. Neither male thinks to ask my opinion. If they wish to exclude me I have no need to sit here and listen to them disregard me.

I think over Jaeson's words. While harsh, I have to admit that they have merit.

Yes, they have merit because you do need to learn how to control your power.

You're back.

I am never far away.

Yes, of that I am well aware.

You really need to tell Danion about this split personality thing you have going on. Maybe he can help us.

Just get on with whatever it is that brought you here.

Fine, fine. You need to learn to harness your power. To defend yourself. Only then can we be reunited.

Reunited? We are never apart. And how do you even know I can train? I am not as convinced that I have this power that you all are sure I have.

You see auras, you cannot deny that.

I did not say that I don't think I have any power, I just don't believe I have some extraordinary power hidden within me.

All the more reason to learn about it, to wield it. To discover who you are, all on your own. No elite guard, no mate, no father. Just you and whatever power you possess.

"I want to train with Jaeson," I say, and then have to repeat myself when it has no effect on them.

"What? Why? I can train you, mate."

"I know you can, but you all are telling me that I possess the lost lineage. Jaeson knows that lineage." Danion still looks unconvinced. Softly I say, "I also have things that I need to discuss with him. He is my father. I have a lot of questions. And no one else can answer them as he can."

Finally, Danion relents.

Jaeson and I are standing in a wide-open room; Danion said it is a storage bay of some nature. It is only used when they are transporting sizeable lunar class ships for repair, so it sits empty a large portion of the time. When it is not being used for storage it makes for a perfect training gym.

"Now, Eleanor, our training today will just be the start of you coming into your power. We will need extensive preparation, more than anything you have experienced before. Those of us that are gifted the ability to weave *lacieu* can weave all the lineages. It is the birth lineage to all our powers. Without our family line first mastering *lacieu* the Gelders would never have mastered any lineage."

"How is that possible? It is just control over ice, isn't it?" I ask, bewildered. "How can manipulating ice give way to manipulating fire?"

Jaeson smiles and then gives me a rare, full laugh. Once he quiets down, he studies me for a moment. "Would you like to hear a story about how the world was before I had to flee? Before the Gelder people turned black in the soul?"

"Jaeson. The Gelders are not black in the soul." I defend the warriors who have come to mean so much to me.

"The ones you know are not, I agree. But the ones from my time? They went down a very dark path. I was very leery to reconnect with the modern day Gelder warriors. I had no way of knowing for sure which side would win in the end. I am pleased to see that Danion leads them. He is a bright soul."

I smile at my father; his words are so accurate. Danion is genuinely a bright soul. Selfless, protective, and kind.

"So, will you finally admit he is your king?" I ask him curiously. I have noticed how he still refuses to acknowledge Danion's title.

We have moved to sit shoulder to shoulder on one of the mats that is woven with threads of *caeli* to cushion a sparring warrior and prevent fatal damage. It is a remarkable creation. It floats a few inches off the ground, firm to walk on, but if you push down hard, it cushions around you like a cloud.

It is the only way that a warrior can actually be taught, allowing both combatants to spar with no holds barred without fear of fatally wounding their partner.

"Do you want to know why I do not call Danion my king?" Jaeson asks, a small smile is curving his lips upward ever so slightly.

"Yes, I would like to know," I reply.

"Well, it happens to lead into the story I wanted to tell you quite well. Over seven thousand years ago, the Atelean family, our family, were the ruling bloodline." He speaks with a faraway look in his eyes. "The title of king did not fall to the strongest warrior, it fell to the strongest warrior in the royal bloodline.

"The royal family was the only bloodline that had mastery over *lacieu*, and because of this we were the strongest ruling party on the planet. Unlike the lineages you know now, what we called *secci* lineages, *lacieu* was only gifted to the Atelean clan. Back in my time, Danion would never have been king. He is not of the royal line."

I think over his words, and while I understand his meaning, I cannot accept it. "That is a little narrow-minded, Jaeson. Danion may not be what you consider royal blood but he is the most decent male I have ever met. I know no one else who would rule better than he."

"You are right to defend your mate, it is the way of our people. However, it is not his parentage that causes me to refute his title. It is"—he pauses as he searches for words—"it is a conflict of interest. I was loyal to the throne of my time. And while the extremists did kill my father, I knew who was next to ascend to the throne. You could say I was invested in the new king."

"What do you mean?"

Jaeson turns his full attention to me. "I was next in line. While I had older siblings none were as strong as I was in the lineages. I was meant to be king."

His words shock me, not for just one reason. "So you refute his rule because of jealousy? Jaeson, that is absurd. You cannot rule these people, you do not know them. Do you truly find fault with Danion's rule? What do you think you can do better?" I ask with outrage.

Being a warrior king is no easy job. I would like to hear what Jaeson believes he can improve upon.

"You misunderstand, daughter mine. I do not fault the job he has done, only attempt to explain he could never have ruled in my time. He does not possess that what we considered paramount for a king."

"And what is that?"

"I have already told you. *Lacieu.* Our entire civilization is rooted in its history and only those gifted in it were allowed to rule. So regardless of his strength, his honor, and his very competence, to me, he is still only a strong warrior. Admirable, yes. But not a king."

"What is your obsession with *lacieu*? Why do you revere it so much?" I am baffled. It is just another form of power. What makes it so different from the rest?

My question appears to amuse Jaeson. He looks at me peculiarly before answering me. "*Lacieu* you believe is ice magic, correct?"

"Yes," I answer warily.

"Then it seems that the extremists did an excellent job of murdering my entire family because that is a lie. Only members of the Atelean family were told the truth, and it was only recorded in our family's most private archives. Which are in the city that I have guarded all these millennia." Jaeson seems tired, his shoulders slumping ever so slightly. For the first time, I am seeing the toll that the weight that he has carried on his shoulders all these years has had on him.

"A lie? Then what is *lacieu*?" I ask him, equal parts eager and leery to hear the answer.

"The lie was necessary at the time. This falsehood was created by our ancestors eons before I came along, a lie that every generation since has helped perpetuate." His eyes grow dark with long ago memories.

"In the time before powers, as it was called on Geldon, a single male, Kaemon, was stranded in a new and unfamiliar place. There was a great war on our home world, one that had raged on for decades. Our ancestor was hiding behind enemy lines. He was in love with a female who came from our enemy's side. The story does not say how they met, only that she was horribly mistreated by her father, and Kaemon could not leave her behind. He refused to leave until he succeeded in freeing her and bringing her home with him.

"During his rescue attempt he was captured, and as punishment he was dropped in the middle of the ocean on our world. The oceans on Geldon are very different from what you know of on Earth. Instead of water infused with salt the oceans on Geldon held a vast amount of *tatio*."

"No." I gasp. I begin to have an idea of where this story goes.

"Yes, and while many knew about the properties of *tatio* no one knew how to harness its power. It was what the whole war was about: a race to master the limitless power of *tatio*. If only our enemies knew what stranding him there would mean for us," Jaeson says with a smirk. "He was stranded in the ocean for eight days."

"How did he survive?"

"He mastered *tatio* while out in the sea. The story tells us that *tatio* recognized something in him and fused with him. After eight days he had consumed so much of it that it began to transform him. No one really knows how he did it, but out there alone in that water Kaemon became the first being to weave *lacieu*, or soul magic."

His words echo in my ears. "What did you say?" I whisper.

"*Lacieu* is the magic of our souls. At least, that is what our ancestors thought it was. Now we call it soul power. However, Kaemon feared what the world would think of his ability to weave this power. It was a very religious time for our people. So, he hid the truth."

"But how did he hide it? And for so long? It has been thousands of years," I ask, terrified to learn that I can weave the power of our very souls.

"I can see from your expression that you too fear what it means. *Lacieu* is not inherently evil or dangerous or any of the things you fear it is. It is not sacrilegious or sinful or any nonsense you think it may be." Jaeson tells me this with a small bite to his words. "I have been dealing with this for my entire existence."

"Then explain it to me," I whisper to my estranged father. "Make me understand."

Jaeson ponders me for several tense moments. "Alright. *Lacieu* is not feeding on the souls of the weak or manipulating the souls of anyone. It merely is fueled by your own soul. Essentially, to be strong in *lacieu*, you must be strong of soul." Jaeson speaks with passion, with a fierce longing. I realize that for him, everyone he once loved was a *lacieu* weaver. And he lost all of them. Suddenly and brutally. The pain he must have endured still cuts him deeply. I place a hand on his shoulder. A small show of comfort.

"So you see, weaving soul power does not mean you are evil, it is the opposite. You can only have that power if you deserve that power."

"But you said it passed through the blood?" I question him.

"I said that you could only get it through the bloodline, not that every member had the power. In my family there were eight children, and only two of us had any strong ability in soul power."

"How did you manage to hide this truth for so long? Why does everyone think that it is ice power?" I can't help but ask.

"Because when you weave *lacieu*, it manifests itself into crystals. Those crystals look like ice or even diamonds. Kaemon said that he learned to master the *tatio* in the deep depths of the sea and therefore controlled ice. It was a necessary lie, and with that lie he was able to unite the warring people of Geldon. He ended the war and they all followed him as king. He gave birth to the Gelder warriors, a race that is alive today and is the strongest groups of warriors in the galaxy."

"I see," I whisper quietly, slightly awed by all I am hearing. I look around the large, cavernous room that we are in.

I stand up and begin to pace away from Jaeson and everything he has told me. It is so much, almost too much. I have been bombarded with so much information in the last day and a half that I can barely stand it. My head feels as if it is going to explode. I can hardly make sense of everything that I have learned.

"What troubles you, daughter mine?" Jaeson's voice drifts to me from his seated position.

I ignore him for now; I cannot keep my own thoughts straight let alone answer him. I continue my pacing, my mind running wild.

It is a whirlwind of confusion due to the discovery that Joy is a distant family member, that I wield soul power, my mother is not my actual mother, and so many other little world-shattering things that I learned recently.

I have several pressing concerns at the moment, and I can barely think to prioritize them. There is the war, a missing mother, and an escaped ambassador to name a few.

I hear Jaeson rise to his feet and cross the large room to me, his heavy footsteps echoing loudly.

"Eleanor, share with me your burden. I know that I have been gone your entire life but I am here now. Let me help you, as a father should."

I glance at him and see nothing but heartfelt compassion in his gaze.

"Alright," I say with a deep sigh. I take a moment to attempt to articulate my concerns. "I am feeling so lost, Jaeson. What am I supposed to do now? What do I focus on?" My voice begins to increase in volume, the words tumbling out of my mouth faster than I can think them. "Do I do battle? Save my planet? Find Sylva? Look for my mother? There is too much! I was never supposed to be a queen! I was raised in Area Three for Powers' sake! I can't do this."

I collapse to the ground in front of him. His arms come around me and draw me closer.

"Eleanor, this is normal. You are very young, you have only been alive for twenty years, and now you are expected to win a war that has billions of lives on the line. Most people do not face such responsibility so young in their life. Or ever. But you were born for so much more. You can do this. It does get easier, I promise you."

"When?" I ask him while fighting tears. I feel so overwhelmed with everything that is expected of me.

"Everyday. Every day it will seem a little easier to control your life. To prioritize each crisis. But for now, you are not alone. You have Danion, me, and an entire *praesidium* of warriors who will help you."

His words do comfort me. I am not alone. While there are things that I must do alone, this is not one of them. "Then what do I do, Father?" I ask him.

Jaeson inhales a quick breath, his eyes shining when they stare down at me. "I have been waiting a very long time to hear you say that." He smiles at me.

I smile in return. "As have I."

He chuckles softly and pulls us both to our feet. "The first thing we need to do is clear your mind. You need to open yourself up to all the possibilities. Let your power speak to you and let it guide you."

"Do you mean in a *merate*?" I ask him. It sounds to me like the deep meditation that Danion has performed before.

"Yes, it is like that. The practice is almost identical to what it was in my time. Some things never change." He guides me back to the mat, and with his hands on my shoulders he presses me down to sit once more.

"How do I do this?" I ask him.

"You simply clear your mind and think of nothing but your powers. Ask them to guide you, ask them to tell you what needs to be done." I can hear him fading away as if he is stepping back from me.

"How do I—"

Jaeson interrupts me, "No words, just thoughts." His voice comes to me as if he is far away. The words are mere whispers.

I sigh to myself and think again about the many challenges that lie ahead of me. Keeping Jaeson's words in the front of my mind, I am trying to will my powers to speak to me. To tell me what I should do next.

Why should I tell you? You never listen to my advice anyway.

Not you! I am trying to speak to my powers, or my soul or something. Go away!

See, this is why I never talk to you. You hear my words but you ignore my wisdom. Come back when you are ready to heed my words.

Wait...are you telling me that you are my...my powers? This is a merate? *Every time you talk to me I am in a meditation? I don't buy that.*

No, you are not meditating, not like the other warriors do. We are different than the others. We are not joined as the others are.

What do you mean?

Are you ready to listen?

Yes, you are so frustrating. Just give me a straight answer for once.

Remember, I am still a part of you. Insulting me only accomplishes insulting yourself.

Fine, I apologize to the both of us. Now, will you explain what you meant?

If you are ready to listen, yes. Now come with me into a deeper place. Relax your mind, open it up to me.

I feel myself falling and falling until I am jerked violently into a stop. I open my eyes, expecting to see the training room, but instead I am on a small, tranquil island underneath a cherry blossom tree.

The petals are gently falling all around me, softly coasting down in swooping arcs. I turn my head toward the sound of running water and see a smoothly flowing stream surrounding the ground where I am sitting.

"Welcome, Eleanor." I whirl around and stare at the woman before me in wonder.

"You're...me?" The woman I am staring at is an exact copy of myself, physically at least; however her eyes are filled with deeper meaning. Deeper understanding. The eyes of a soul much older than I am.

"Yes, I am. But I am a part of you that has been locked away for a very long time," she responds.

"What do you mean? Are you who I have talked to my whole life?" I ask her.

"Yes, but it is only recently that I have been able to do so consciously. Before I could only reach you in times of great upheaval." Her look turns angry. "Like when we were starved or beaten. I fought against my chains fiercely, desperate to aid us, but they never loosened. I have only been able to help us in any real way since we joined with our mate."

"But why?" I ask her. I have noticed that I talk with her much more frequently now than I ever have. "Why then?"

She studies me. "Have you ever wondered why you are stronger now than you were before?"

"What does that have to do with anything?" I ask her but I get silence in response. "Fine, yes, I have often wondered that."

"What do you think it is?"

"I haven't given it any real thought." At her glance I answer her honestly. "I think that Danion's mind joined with me and is lending me his strength, allowing me to be stronger."

"That is what I thought you would say. It is ridiculous." She turns away abruptly and paces on the small island. "It is *not* his strength. It is *ours*! We are *not* weak. Our power was stripped away when he ripped us apart!" she screams in a feral rage.

I take a step back from the anger that is exploding out of her. "Who? Who ripped us apart?" I ask her quietly. While her rage frightens me, I know I have to have my questions answered. Right now I am more confused than ever.

"Who? Who did this? Jaeson! Our father!" She spits the word out. "Before he went away he separated our minds from each other, locking my half into a prison within your mind. Most warriors are fully joined with their powers, but Jaeson tore us from each other."

I can feel my heart drop at her words. "Why would he do that?"

"The why does not matter! He did it and we suffered for it." I see her take a deep breath, then turn to look at me. Obviously working to control her anger. "But that is not the issue at hand. You feel stronger since our joining because when we merged with Danion my chains loosened. We were able to unite slightly. It is not his strength that you feel, it is yours. Ours. The strength that he ripped away from us years ago."

"Why? How? How do you even know this?" I ask her.

"Because unlike our mortal mind, which you have had, I am our Gelder mind. I remember him doing it. He claimed he had to 'hide' what we were, so he divided us. With you becoming everything that was human in us, and me everything that wasn't. But with that he fractured us, neither one of us whole without the other. I remember being locked away. He tore us apart and he is not to be trusted."

I can feel tears in my eyes. For one moment, one brief moment, I thought I had a father. Now I see that once again I was wrong. I know better than to doubt what I have learned; I can sense the truth of it in every fiber of my being.

I always knew that there was something in my mind, something different than others' minds. A part of myself that was locked away. I just never knew that it was my power...sealed away from me. My strength.

"What are we to do?" I ask myself. We are one being, just lost to one another.

"We must find a way to join together again. We must break the final chains and cross the chasm that keeps our minds separate. And for that we will need to ask Jaeson what he did."

"What about the war? And Sylva? Our mother?" I ask.

"We cannot be successful in anything else until you can wield our power. I am merely a mind, you are the body and the strength. I can guide us but you have to be able to wield our might. Slowly we have been able to weave more and more, when we healed Joy for instance. But we must finish the joining and finish it quickly."

I nod my head at her and turn away.

I blink my eyes open and see Jaeson standing a dozen feet away from me. Looking concerned.

"Eleanor? Are you alright? You began crying while you were in the *merate*."

"How could you?" I ask as I stand. "How could you?!" I scream at him.

"Eleanor! What—" He raises his hands to touch me.

"No! You do not touch me. How could you rip my soul in half?"

Before my eyes, Jaeson's face falls in despair. "You know? How do you know?"

"What did you expect to happen when you asked me to consult with my powers? The very powers you locked away?"

"I had to, Eleanor! If the humans sensed the power within you they would have done much worse than kill you! I had to hide you away. You should have fully integrated again once you mated with Danion. I did not think that you would recognize the signs of what I did and therefore learn of my actions."

"Signs? There are no signs! We are still fragmented, I am still divided!" Jaeson looks shocked at this.

"You are not joined again?" he asks me, horror slowly dawning on his face.

"No, I am not," I tell him. "When I mated with Danion a small part of myself merged again, but the larger divide is still there. How do I close it and return my mind to what it was meant to be?" I ask him.

"Eleanor." His words are barely a whisper. "I do not know. It should have corrected itself; if it does not merge on its own it may not be possible. Soul power like this is almost never performed because it is so unpredictable."

I cannot believe the words I am hearing, the audacity of this male. I can't help but laugh. Then I can't stop myself. I laugh so long and so hard that tears are running down my face. When I finally can form words again I stare at this man who gave life to me.

"Soul power like this is not done because it is unpredictable." I scoff. "Yet you decided to perform it, to test it, on me. Well, congratulations. You did it, but now we may never be able to undo it. Because you decided to try your hand at some 'unpredictable' powers."

I can't stand the sight of him anymore. With one last look of disgust I walk past him. I hear him calling after me, but I ignore it. I let the door swing loudly closed behind me, cutting off his impassioned plea.

Chapter Fifteen

Ellie

I race through the golden halls as fast as I can, attempting to put as much space between Jaeson and myself as possible. I still can barely believe what I have learned.

Jaeson split my mind in half when I was nothing but a small child. A baby. If I believe myself, which I do, he took every aspect of my personality that was strong or Gelder and locked it away. Leaving behind just a small, hollow shell of a person.

He is the reason that I have struggled my whole life to reconcile the person I was and who I felt I should be. He is why I never spoke out against all the atrocities done to me.

I recall my stepfather beating me, breaking bones, all because I dared to ask if I could eat one of the daily cubes that were left over. I merely wanted to stop the hunger pangs, even for just one day. He went on a rampage.

Whenever he went into a rage like that I would hide away inside my mind, seeking shelter from the pain of reality. Now I know that I should have been able to defend myself and stop the abuse. I should have been able to protect my family. I should have been able to give my sisters the life they always deserved.

I am so angry with Jaeson I cannot even stomach the idea of seeing him again. I refuse to accept that he had no other choice. I refuse to accept that he had to hide me away. Uncontrollable anger boils inside of me, a fury that I cannot fully contain or understand.

I can only feel the rage coursing through me, growing more potent with each passing moment. I need to distract myself, to help calm my mind. Wrath has never been a solution to a problem. It is the very behavior that I criticize Danion for.

Try as I might the anger continues to grow, obliterating all sense of logic and reason. A small part of me begins to feel scared, frightened of my own resentful rage. It is out of control, continuing to grow until the only thing I can think about is going back and ripping out Jaeson's throat. The logical part of me recoils. I have never had such violent thoughts before in my life. I scour my memories for some idea to help calm myself, for some clue as to how to rid myself of this overwhelming anger.

The garden, that's it. Danion mentioned that all the ships have a large garden to help purify the air on board. I begin to head deeper into the bowels of the ship, forcing my mind to focus on the lush oasis that I know awaits me and not the anger that continues to grow inside. I am desperate for the peace and tranquility I know I will find. It is the only way I can stop myself from heading back and doing something I know I will regret.

As I journey deeper and deeper into the ship, I can tell that something is wrong. My limbs feel heavy. Soon it is all I can do to lift my feet from the floor. I am shuffling slowly deeper into the ship's central levels.

Soon my mind is in a dense fog and I can barely remember what I am trying to do or where I am even headed to. Even where I am; nothing makes sense anymore.

I need a rest, just a small one. I sink slowly into the floor and succumb to the fog swirling around me.

No! Do not let it consume you! Fight, Eleanor! Fight!

Why do you call me Eleanor? Aren't you Eleanor too?

Yes, yes, talk to me. I am Eleanor too, I am you. And you...we have to fight this.

In a minute, I am just so tired.

I will talk with my inner self later. For now, I need to rest.

Danion

"What do you mean she left?" I growl at Jaeson. "You were supposed to be training her!" I turn away before I blast this *fiefling* male into oblivion.

Eleanor has been missing for hours! All because her supposedly caring father let her leave without following her. "We had an argument and she left. I did not think it was a concern. I assumed she would have gone to you."

His words cause the tenuous control over my powers to fray even further. "Your incompetence is not an excuse! We just discussed how she needed to be guarded on the ship. You yourself said that there could be a traitor on board!" I blast the contents of the training room, mats and various weapons used in training, clear across the cavernous room.

"Danion, try to calm yourself. Your rage will not find her." Griffith speaks and I can feel the *vim* threads wrap around me. Griffith is attempting to take my anger within himself and give me some of his legendary control.

"Jaeson, as I am a *vim* master I should be able to sense Eleanor's presence, both from when she was in this room and when she was not. I can only sense her from before she stormed out. Her mind was in upheaval, her life force explosive. It should be a simple matter to sense her but there is absolutely nothing once she leaves this room. Why?" Griffith challenges the ancient warrior with a hard-spoken word.

I turn my attention back to them. I too have noticed that Eleanor is lost to me. Both her mind and body have been hidden. Not even Jedde, our communications leader, can find her. It is the same as when we lost the ability to track Shemir, the Erain traitor.

"I do not know what would cause that. Nothing that we did should have blocked her life energy from you." Jaeson answers Griffith's question.

I level a hard stare at my mate's father. "It is nothing that you did in here, it is what you didn't do. Which is follow her! She has been attacked on board this ship before, merely a few weeks ago! Someone aboard this ship is out to harm my mate and you left her unguarded."

"I am sorry—" he starts to say, but I have no time for his worthless apologies.

"I am sure, but that does nothing to negate the fact that Eleanor is lost at this moment, presumably to an enemy who wants her dead."

I storm away, calling for her entire *praesidium* to meet me in my private chambers immediately. Griffith follows behind, wisely deciding to stay quiet as we march up the decks to my rooms.

I am pleased to see that everyone is present when I arrive.

"Eleanor is missing and has been unaccounted for these last five hours. Jaeson did not report that she stormed out of training by herself earlier," I inform the group of hardened warriors before me.

"This is why we should have had a guard with her!" Arsenio bites out, his fear for our queen's safety adding a sharp tone to his anger.

"Yes, but both Jaeson and Eleanor requested privacy. They insisted that they work alone since there would be extremely delicate information being exchanged. I foolishly agreed to this request." I cannot believe the idiocy that I went along with. Eleanor always has a guard, always. It is my mistake in assuming her father could have filled that role.

"Perhaps Jaeson is not who we think he is." Malin's words send a ribbon of ice-cold fear down my spine.

"You think he was the one who attacked her?"

"Maybe, or he is in league with them. We know very little about him and what his goals are. All we know for certain is that he is a male who abandoned his daughter for twenty years and failed to provide her with adequate protection in his absence." Malin recounts the facts for us.

He is right. A cold sweat breaks out on my body, forcing me to come to the realization that Eleanor has been with this male I know nothing about without anyone else present. I look at the warriors before me. "We will find her."

"What are our orders, King Danion?" Amell asks me stonily. My old friend is filled with matching concern for my mate.

"Arsenio, Malin, and Etan will each take a shuttle and take to the stars. Surround our ship. Arsenio and Malin, you will be scanning the ship remotely from the outside looking for any signs of Eleanor. Etan, you will begin searching for any signs that she was taken off this ship."

"At once, sire." All three warriors bow in sync with the each other.

Arsenio raises his head as the other two turn to leave. "I will search through the night, and through tomorrow's day and night. I will not rest until she is found. We will find her, or there will be such bloodshed that our enemies will rue the day they attacked our queen." I nod at him and the three warriors depart.

"You four will be with me searching the ship. Golon and I will take the *leif* wing, Amell and Griffith the *reif* wing. Kowan, you will assist Jedde in trying to break through the block that is hiding Eleanor from our scanners. But first, find Jaeson and throw him in containment. Until we are sure of his role in Eleanor's disappearance we need him confined." Kowan nods and exits the room with no words spoken.

We all can sense the danger that is aboard the ship. I turn to look at the three males in the room. "We must move quickly and efficiently. We do not know how much time we will have."

I storm out of the room, knowing that my warriors will follow me.

"Dane, we will find her. Do not let your rage consume you," Golon says as he falls into step with me.

"Do I look like I am consumed with rage?" I snarl at him. "I know what I am doing; allowing the rage to take me will do Eleanor no good. I will not endanger my mate further."

"I know, Dane, I know. We will find her," Golon says once more.

"Yes, but when? Four warriors to scour this entire ship can take days! There is no one else that we can trust so I cannot expand the search party. I do not want her abductor to feel cornered and cause her further harm."

"I know, Dane. We will find her, I promise you we will find her."

"It has been twenty-four hours!" I bellow, power pummeling out of me and destroying everything that I can see. "Where is she!?" I scream at the most dominant warriors the Gelder fleet has to offer.

"I do not know, we still have some of the lowest levels to scour but those halls are like a maze. It is slowing down our progress. Those passages are for hull integrity; there are pockets hidden all throughout the ship that are designed to be sealed off in the case of a breach," Amell informs me.

"Do you think I don't know that!?" I snap. "Everyone to the lowest levels. We will each pick an access point into the hull shields and we will search each and every one of them until my mate is found!"

Ellie

Ellie, you need to wake up. You need to fight to free your mind.

I hear the whisper so faintly I almost ignore it. But then I recognize the urgency in the voice, and I focus just a little harder on the faint sounds echoing in my mind.

Fight it... Fight it... Fight it...

What needs to be fought? I try to raise my hands and realize that I am bound tightly up against a wall. I push as hard as I can against the fog surrounding my brain and open my eyes. Pain is all around me. My entire body feels as if it is broken. I glance around the dark, cold, metal room that I am chained in.

I notice a small figure tucked back into one of the far corners. It looks familiar somehow. I focus as hard as I can on pushing the haziness away and see who is in this room with me.

Shock rockets through me.

"Rowena? What are you doing here?" I ask my maid with a slight slur to my words. It is so hard to fight for consciousness.

Rowena was the maid that helped me prepare for the *cerum fuse* when I joined with Danion. I would never have suspected her as an enemy to either Danion or myself. She has always been so polite and friendly.

"I am following orders." Rowena's words are stark and hollow, her eyes and voice are blank. Almost as if they were not her own words. "You have to die."

Fear shoots through me, allowing me to push the fog even further away. "You are going to kill me?" I ask her. I trusted Rowena. We have not grown close, per se, but I would never have thought she would take my life.

"No, I will not kill you. I lack the power to kill you." Relief flows through me briefly, but it is stopped cold with her next words. "My master will kill you. I am merely holding you here until he can arrive."

"Your master? Who is your master?" I ask her, outrage and terror mixing within me.

"Yes, he will be here soon." Rowena's face then goes completely blank, and no matter how hard I call out to her she makes no move to respond.

I fight with all my strength to free myself from my chains, but nothing works. Nothing provides any give whatsoever. I pull and twist with all my might, resulting in nothing other than tearing my skin open on the jagged metal.

I can feel blood dripping off my body. I can hear the slow but steady drops hitting the floor beneath me. One relentless drop after another, gradually draining my vital life blood.

After a few more useless struggles, I let my body hang from the chains. It is no use, I cannot free myself. I hang my head in defeat.

In desperation, I try one last thing. I remember Danion saying that mates can speak to one another through their linked minds. I know that I have not fully accepted the bond, but maybe I can get through to him. If I call out to him maybe he can find me.

I close my eyes, open my mind, and focus my entire being on the thought of a great, mighty, gray-eyed warrior king.

Danion! Danion, can you hear me?

Danion

Danion! Danion, can you hear me?

I stop suddenly when I hear the frantic plea in my mind. It is merely six words. Six words that by themselves are nothing special, but I am so thankful to hear them. Eleanor is alive.

Eleanor? Eleanor, where are you?

I...don't...chained...Rowena...

Eleanor, you have to focus. I can't hear everything that you are thinking.

Help...so tired...

She is gone. But her mind was present inside of mine and that means I can follow our mind link to her location.

"Everyone, stop. Eleanor has reached out to me. I know where she is. Follow me." I turn around and head in the opposite direction as fast as I can.

She is in an abandoned section of the ship. It was sealed off decades ago once we updated the shield generators. No one should be able to enter this section. Apparently, her captor was able to find a way in.

I ignore the warriors' incessant questions as I race to my mate. There is no time for explanations, only action. I have to save my mate; she sounded so frail in our link. So weak, as if she was about to slip away.

I waste no time in searching for the entry point when I arrive at the solid metal wall. I focus my energy, pummel all of my rage toward it, and watch it implode before me. I direct the blast outward, back toward my warriors and myself, protecting Eleanor from any stray rubble.

The sight before me sends my rage to a new level, threatening to break the tenuous control that I have over it. Eleanor is suspended five feet off the ground, being held in unforgiving chains on the wall.

Blood is running down the wall and pooling on the floor beneath her. I scan the room and discover yet another shock.

Rowena, one of the few Gelder females in our population. She has little to no power so she entered into the *scientia* field but never thrived. She then decided to take on more domestic roles for our people, volunteering to assist Eleanor when she heard that I was taking a mate.

Rowena is standing between Eleanor and us. "No! You cannot have her. My master needs her to die!" she screams, then she reaches for a steel blade hidden behind her and moves to throw it at Eleanor.

I fling out my aura and wrap it around Rowena's throat and hands. I slam her down into the ground and hold her there.

"Amell, restrain her," I growl at him. Amell is quick to cross the room and weave solid bands around her entire body. He manifests his rock power into a solid weave, leaving only Rowena's head uncovered in a casket made of solid rock.

Once she is secured I drop my aura and direct it to Eleanor. I quickly break the chains holding her and use my aura to cushion her descent into my arms.

"Is she alright?" Golon is by my side as I gently hold her frail body.

I study her for a moment, searching for the cause of all this blood on her. I notice that there are long and deep cuts on her wrists. Dark red lines run along her entire body in parallel lines that are dripping blood. The chains.

"She will be fine. She cut herself deeply on the chains but I will stabilize her until we can get her to Jarlin." I turn and begin striding out of the room. "She will be fine. She will be fine." I have no option but to believe that.

I simultaneously begin weaving *hael* into her open cuts to stem the blood loss for my mate. As I examine her extensive cuts, I pick up the pace and soon am flying through the ship at full speed, the doors and passages nothing but a golden blur as I bring my mate to safety as quickly as I can. The movement invoking an uncomfortable sense of déjà vu. It was not so long ago that I did just this same thing, rushing my injured mate to the *hael* wing. I will not allow it to happen a third time.

I can sense her life slowly fading away; every drop of blood that falls from her body brings her a step closer to death. I cannot face the loss of her, not again. I almost lost her to the poison and now I face her death once more.

I can feel my powers raging, pounding against the barriers I erect to contain it. My control is fragile. My energy is pressing outward against my walls, begging to be released. I remember how hard it was for me to contain my rage the first time her life was endangered. If she does not survive this, I shudder to think of what hell I will unleash.

Chapter Sixteen

Danion

I am beginning to truly hate the color white. Throughout the rest of the ship gold can be found on virtually every wall, but not here. Here in this accursed room there is only white as far as the eye can see. I have no desire to ever enter these rooms again. But alas, I sit here rigidly, refusing to leave my *aninare's* bedside until she awakens.

It has only been mere days since I was here last with my precious Eleanor. Unsure if she would survive her first assassination attempt. And here I sit, the same situation all over again. How could I have been so foolish to allow another traitor so close to her?

I am sitting in a chair to the left of her bed, holding her hand gently between my much larger ones. I slowly rub my thumb back and forth along her smooth skin.

Her hand is such a contrast to mine, so dainty and smooth while mine is large and calloused. We are opposites in so many aspects of ourselves. She is the softness to my hardness, the light to my dark, the compassion to my ruthlessness.

She has already surpassed all my expectations for a mate. She makes me stronger; not only by boosting my own power level but by smoothing out the rough edges in my world. She calms my soul and helps bring perspective to me.

More than that though, she makes me...happy. It is an emotion that is so foreign to me that I did not recognize it at first. She must recover, she just has to.

"To find love and then face the possibility of losing it can sometimes feel like a greater hardship than never finding love. But love is too precious of a gift to squander it," a soft, lyrical voice says to my left. The words have a way of floating through me, attempting to infuse happiness within me. This way of speaking tells me everything I need to know about who is addressing me.

"Etan, I am not in the mood for your philosophical musing right now. No matter how well intended." I speak in soft tones so as not to disturb my resting mate.

"That, sire, is when we need them the most. A soul in pain can perform hellacious atrocities. That is something we are all too aware of." Etan moves farther into the room to stand opposite of me, across Eleanor's bed.

"Etan, I know that your lineage praises itself on bringing lighthearted joy to all situations, but there are some circumstances that it is just not acceptable," I snap at him, conscious of the volume of my words.

Etan, being a master of *caeli*, often can be more exuberant than the other warrior lines. It comes from being so close to the air lineages. Their entire outlook on the world is colored by their pursuit of happiness. It is a great gift, their positive outlook. But sometimes it is just plain irritating.

"My king, joy is not what I am attempting to give to you."

"Then what is your purpose here?" I ask him tiredly.

"I wish to help you find peace. I can sense the pain you are in. If you wish to help our queen, you must first bring peace to yourself."

I sigh deeply. "And how do you plan to bring me peace?"

"By making you realize that Eleanor will be fine. Jarlin said that her wounds, while serious, are not life-threatening. She should awaken any time now. You need to focus on the love you have and not the fear of losing it."

I ponder the words of the leading master in *caeli*. "You believe I do not appreciate my mate?"

"No, I know you do. Mating is more than that, especially when the bond is incomplete. It can drive a warrior mad. I also think that you are struggling to reconcile the fact that, for once, you have something that you are afraid of losing."

"I have been afraid to lose other things. This war, for instance," I counter.

"No, you have not. For three thousand years you have been who you have needed to be. A warrior, a strong and fierce warrior, who will do anything to protect his people. But you have never truly feared losing your title or anything you possess. But now you have something that you are desperate to hold on to. You fear losing your mate."

"Of course I do, that is what being a mate is all about." I scoff at him.

"Yes, but you haven't been a mate before now. Being a king is something you *have* to do. On the contrary, being Eleanor's mate is something you *want* to do."

I think over Etan's words for several silent moments. I realize that he is right. I had no proper desire to rule, I just always knew that I would have to. There was no question of if I would reign as king, only a question of when. But from the moment I knew of Eleanor, I have wanted her. Wanted to be with her, to take care of her, to do nothing except get to know her. To bask in the warmth of her soul.

A female who would be mine to protect and care for. To cherish for all my remaining days. To be more than just a weapon to someone. I would be her family, her friend, her lover. Simply put I would be everything to her. Just as she is my everything.

I sit back suddenly with a small thud as I slam into the back of the chair. I realize that Etan is right. I have always appreciated the gifts I was given in this life, but I have never truly wanted them. Eleanor I want, and I refuse to lose her.

I love this small, angelic female who lies so still in the bed before me. She is mine, and I pity the souls who would do her harm. They will soon experience a fate far worse than death.

Ellie

Fire. That is all I can feel as I slowly come awake from a heavy, dense fog. It feels like it takes hours for me to fight my way free of sleep. I slowly blink my eyes open and see nothing but white.

I close them once more for a long moment. The *hael* wing again.

"*Aninare*? How do you feel?" a rough, throaty voice to my left asks.

"Danion? What happened?" I keep my eyes closed. The bright light is made starker by the unforgiving white all around me.

"First, tell me how you feel. Are you in pain?" Danion commands. His domineering attitude actually makes me smile. That is the male I love. So quick to anger. He is the opposite of a gentle male, but I am so drawn to this virile male specimen.

I hear a sharp inhalation of breath. I open my eyes in mere slits to observe my mate while I speak. "A little, all the cuts are very sore..."

I trail off when I notice that Danion's face holds an expression of pure wonder and disbelief. "Love? You love me?" he asks me.

His words make me pull up in surprise. I know that I did not speak that aloud. But I did think it. No... "Tell me that you are not hearing my thoughts," I say as a bare whisper.

I stare at my mate and see his frame stiffen, his facial features close and become guarded. Danion is silent for a long, pregnant pause.

"I am not able to answer that," he finally replies. "There is no response that I can give you that you will be pleased with, so I elect not to answer you."

I blink at him. "Are you kidding me?" I blink again. "That is not an answer, Danion! Or should I say it is an answer? Why are you reading my thoughts?! I told you I didn't want you to."

"It is not a choice, Eleanor. It is what occurs naturally between bonded souls, bonded mates. When the bond is complete we will share one mind. I do not understand why you resist our joining."

"Because it is..." My words trail off. Only a few days ago I would have been able to come up with an unending list of reasons that I did not want him in my mind, but after the events that have occurred since we discovered my father, I have to question my resolve.

"How long have you been able to hear my thoughts?" I ask him quietly. To sort out my feelings on this matter, I need to know all the facts.

"Since before we left to find your father." Danion's voice is resigned. He knows how I feel about him sneaking around in my mind. "But not all of them, only a few have come through our bond."

"Is that how you were able to find me? Did you track me through my mind?" I ask him. Danion's face seems carefully void of emotion. "Yes."

I inhale deeply and try to think through all the battling emotions I have inside. While I have always cherished the escape my mind has provided, I also adore the blossoming bond that Danion and I are sharing. I also owe my life to Danion being able to read my mind.

Do not be angry with him. It is the way of our people.

I know you think that, and logically I know that, but it is much harder to force myself to accept that. If I do not have my mind what do I have?

You have Danion. You have a male who will love you, not despite knowing everything about you. But because he knows everything about you.

Do you truly believe that?

Yes, I do. Also, the more Danion merges with us, the smaller the chasm that divides us becomes. He is healing us.

Really?

Yes, the closer he becomes, the more power you are able to wield.

"Why did you hide this from me?" I ask him. I can reconcile myself to Danion and I merging our minds. I am beginning to realize that it is inevitable. However, I resent him hiding it from me.

"Eleanor...*aninare*, the gift of a mate is something that a warrior waits their entire life to receive. The most desired aspect of this mating that we crave is not the physical pleasure we receive"—I blush at his sensual gaze that accompanies these words—"it is the end to the loneliness. We are immortal warriors who are honor bound to spend our lives at war. The only pleasure we can ever expect is a mate to transform our meaningless existence into something to savor.

"Sharing our entire selves with another soul. You are that soul for me. I want to be with you in every way. Just as I want you to be with me in every way. When your mind reached out to mine again, I was selfish enough to not want to let it go. It was wrong, I know that. I just craved the connection to you. I have no excuse."

His words shock me. I have no idea what I expected him to say, but it definitely was not that. To know that being able to enter my mind is more pleasurable to him than when we join our bodies is a powerful piece of the puzzle.

It explains quite a bit about the behavior that I have seen Danion exhibit since I met him. I understand much about his desires and wishes now. I can scarcely believe that not long ago I was expecting to be a sex slave to this male, and now I lie before him as his treasured mate. A male who wants to know my mind more than he wants sex from me.

I slowly reach out and cup his cheek within my palm, enjoying the slightly scratchy texture of his facial hair. I have rarely seen him without a completely clean-shaven face. His eyes widen in surprise.

"I understand. I am not saying I am completely comfortable with it, but I will work on it."

"You will do this for me?" His words are hushed, filled with reverence.

"Yes, I will do this for you." I give him a small smile, which he returns with a gentle smile of his own that demolishes the final barriers that I have erected to protect myself. I love him with all my heart.

"Danion, there are four guards outside. I am fine," I say with no small amount of exasperation. "Jarlin told you I am in no danger. All I need is rest."

We are in our bedchambers and I'm lying back on our massive bed. Danion is pacing along the foot of the bed. He wants to go check on a communication that is waiting for him but he is nervous to leave me alone.

"Are you sure you would not rather rest in the *hael* wing? So Jarlin would be close to you in case something happens?"

"Danion! I am fine and I am merely going to rest. If all I need is sleep I would rather have that here in my own bed than in that hospital," I say with a shudder. I hate that room. If I never spend another second in that room I will be more than happy.

"I can stay—"

"Danion, no you cannot. What if it is something to do with Sylva? Or the communications network update? We are at war, you need to be up to date."

Danion's eyes harden as they stare at me. I can tell he wants to argue but knows he cannot. "Alright. I will go handle this war while you focus on getting your strength back."

He leans down and gives me a chaste kiss on the forehead, then turns and leaves the room.

Chapter Seventeen

Danion

I close the door to our chambers and observe the four members of my mate's *praesidium* that are standing alert outside.

"Amell, if there are any issues with Eleanor, if she so much as sniffles, I want to be contacted." Amell gives me a stiff nod.

Two times now an enemy has been able to pass through our guard and harm our queen. I am determined to not allow another attack.

"Etan, I want you inside her room. Eyes on her at all times. Wait until she is asleep and then stand guard over her. Use your gifts to enter silently." Etan nods in response to my commands.

"Where are Arsenio and Griffith?" I ask Kowan, the leader of the *praesidium.*

"They are securing the traitor and attempting to discover what caused Rowena to betray us." I nod grimly.

"When I have taken care of the pressing business that needs my attention I will join them. I too would not have suspected Rowena to turn against us."

I nod to Malin and exit the room. I am off to the *bellum* chamber to access my mirror table. The message that was sent holds an encryption that can only be opened by me.

As I approach the door to the chamber, I notice that Golon is already there breaking the threads that keep the room secure.

"*Cognata*, I am pleased you are here to receive the message with me."

"I would be nowhere else. We need to turn the tides of this war," Golon says darkly.

"Yes, I agree." We enter the chamber together and sit at the table. I open the message that is awaiting me.

Before us is a map of the cosmos, fragmented and a mere fraction of the coverage that we used to have. The plan that Eleanor designed is slowly being implemented, but it is a lengthy process. However, we are receiving reports from the mortal worlds that we are still in an active battle to defend. We began repairs on those sections of space first.

I begin slowly and methodically combing through the vast and rather bulky report, looking over every piece of information diligently. We have had the outposts down for so long they are backlogged with vast amounts of information.

Suddenly, both Golon and I stiffen and inhale swiftly.

"Danion. Do you see this?" I know exactly what he is referring to.

"Yes. Both Reiina and Julino are only being sustained by their shields. Each warship that was defending these planets has fallen." What I leave unsaid are the dire straits that these shields are in.

Reiina and Julino were two of the first mortal worlds that we brought under our protection. They have survived countless attacks from the Erains and I refuse to let this be the one that causes them to perish.

"Danion, these shields will not hold for another full day." Golon speaks with a soft, serious tone. "They are being bombarded by the Erain threats that orbit them."

"Yes, I agree we must send them aid. But where to pull the units from? We are stretched thin as it is," I ponder aloud. "Every mortal world is struggling."

"What about the warriors we have working on repairing the communications grid? Can we manage to limit the teams working on that and relocate some of the ships?"

"No. Repairing the grid is one of the most important tasks we have. Without the grid we will lose this war. But there are my royal class ships," I murmur.

"Your royal classes? They are not tested, never been used in battle." Golon sounds shocked. "Those ships are still in the experimental phase."

"Yes, I am aware. But they are the most advanced ships that we have ever produced. Faster, stronger, and much more deadly. We have no other ships to pull. We have to send them into the field."

"Who will operate them?"

"I will strip each ship that is working on the communications grid rebuild of two warriors, and we will run the royal warships with a skeleton crew."

"How many ships are you going to send out?"

I take a moment to think through the answer. "Four, for now. We will send two ships to each of these mortal worlds. If they are successful we will bring the entire fleet online and disperse them to all the worlds."

"Alright, my king. I will handle outfitting the ships and bring the four ships into commission. You have other duties I am sure you are anxious to get to," Golon says with a grave look. "How is Eleanor doing?"

"She says she is fine and Jarlin says that all she needs is rest. I do wish to be by her side, but this war is the most important thing at this time. I will handle this," I insist.

"Nonsense, Dane. I can handle this easily enough. Go, your mate needs you."

With those four words I realize he is right. He is more than capable of performing the duties that I have outlined, and I need to be by my mate's side. She needs me, but more importantly, I need her.

Golon can easily handle overseeing these simple tasks. I have been meaning to start delegating some duties, not insisting that I be present for every decision and action. "Fine, I thank you, *cognata*. Keep me apprised of any updates in the situation."

With a final nod to Golon I leave the room at a brisk pace, eager to get back to my mate. As I pass through the halls with increasing speed, my mind is focused on joining with my mate. It has been too long since my body has felt the warm welcome of hers.

From our recent, heated encounters I know she is as eager for me as I am for her. It has been torture these last days. My mind is lost in a never-ending loop of how she looks when she finds her climax. My body is locked into a perpetual hardness.

I know my *aninare* is not well enough right now for the rough and animalistic joining that I am craving, but for tonight merely holding her body close to mine will be enough. Just wrapping my body around hers and protecting her is all I need.

In the morning, if she is well, I will take her gently. I will spend hours caressing and tasting her, ensuring that she is wet and throbbing for me, ready to take all of me.

I nod at the guards as I enter our antechamber, but I do not speak. I am not sure I am capable of speech right now. My mind is too focused on the sweet heaven that resides between my mate's thighs.

I enter the bedchamber silently, my eyes taking in the room. Etan gives me a brief nod then slips out the still open door, closing it without even a whisper of sound.

My eyes turn to the bed. My precious Eleanor is asleep, curled up on her side in the fetal position. Her brow furrowed as if she is in pain. My lustful thoughts immediately dissipate.

As much as I desire her tight, luscious body, I love her soul more. Her well-being is more important than any physical pleasure. With a gentle smile, I remove my leathers and slip into the bed completely bare. I move closer to my mate, pull her flush against my body, and gently stroke her hair.

Slowly, I feel Eleanor's body start to relax into mine, and the furrow on her brow eases into a smooth, contented line across her forehead. Her forehead is beautiful. I snort amusedly to myself. How my warriors would laugh if they could see me now, admiring a forehead. But on my mate? It is perfect. Just as she is.

Chapter Eighteen

Ellie

I awaken with two realizations: one is that I am being held utterly immobile. Strong bands of steel are shacking me to the bed. And the second is that I am unbelievably hot. I feel a sweltering, blistering heat.

I look to my left and find the source of both of these circumstances. Danion is wrapped around me like a sea creature. Both his arms are around me, squeezing just tight enough to let me know that I have no hope of escape. His legs are entwined with mine, the weight from his heavier limbs holding my lower half in place.

His body heat is stifling. I try to gently disentangle myself, slowly moving my hips to see if I have any hope loosening his hold.

"You keep moving like that and my good intentions will abandon me," a sexy, sleep-addled Danion says to me. I become aware of his member growing and pressing against my hip.

"Good intentions?" I whisper. My voice sounds shaky and I gently clear my throat to try to strengthen it.

"Yes, I intend to take you slowly and with the utmost care. You keep rubbing that delectable body against my cock and I am afraid I will have to ravish you like a heathen," Danion growls while nuzzling my neck.

"I'll...take the ravishment, please." My voice breaks ever so slightly as he nips at my ear.

"Oh, will you?" He chuckles slightly into my ear. "You want me to lay you back, spread you wide, and take what is mine?" His voice drops an octave, sending delicious tingles down my spine.

At his words I feel my core dampen and begin to ache. I know that is precisely what I want. He introduced me to the pleasure that can be found in the flesh and I am desperate for it now.

All I can manage is a brief nod, my eyes begging him to do just that. I see a satisfied gleam lurking in Danion's eyes.

"What if I wanted more than just what can be found down here?" Danion's hand glides down my body to openly grope my core. I can feel my moisture wetting the silken fabric of my sleepwear. "What if I want to experience your whole body?" Danion's other hand moves upward and caresses my lips with his thumb.

I glance at him questionably. "What?" is all I can make out. My mind is being controlled by the feelings his hand is invoking.

"What if I want to make you beg? What if I want you to put your mouth to good use? See your lips wrapped around my shaft, feel your tongue rubbing me?" Danion's voice is choked, his hips are undulating against my hip with ever-increasing strokes.

"Yes," I moan to him, giving myself up to the lustful picture he has painted. I crave to mend the fences that I myself have inflicted on our relationship. I am ready, more than ready, for him to take me.

Danion moves to lie over me, the sheets slipping off his form. My eyes widen as I am granted an unobstructed view of the most stunning piece of the male anatomy that I have ever seen. It is so large and beautifully formed.

He lowers himself to rest between my thighs, his hard and muscled body cushioned against my softer form. "Oh Eleanor, once you are better I will take you so hard. I will do all of that and more. I promise I will let you rest soon, just give me a few moments more to relish you."

His words don't penetrate my mind at first, then the meaning becomes all too clear. "No, Danion, I want you to."

"And you will have me, once you are better." Danion speaks almost to himself, his face locked into an almost painful expression. He is slowly rocking himself against me, causing just the smallest amount of friction. Our bodies separated by just my clothing.

"Danion. Danion! Give me more. I am well enough now." I try to thrust my hips up to meet him and he looks at me with a frown.

"Eleanor, you need to stop that, or I will lose the small amount of control that I have."

"Good, I don't want your control!" I all but scream at him. "I am fine now and I need my mate."

I see him weakening, then his movements stop and his resolve is back. "No, I will not hurt you. You do not realize what is happening, it is my fault. I aroused you unfairly."

"Leaving now would be unfair," I argue. I cannot believe he would do this, of all the times to get self-righteous.

"I need to think of you and your needs, no matter my own desires." It is clear to me that he will not be swayed. "I am sorry for my actions. I should have been able to control myself better so that only I would suffer from unfulfilled lust." Danion raises his body off of me and begins to get off the bed.

"*Animare*, please don't do this. I need you so much."

Danion freezes. "What did you call me?" His voice is heavy, his face lined with passion.

I smile to myself. I know just what effect my calling him that has on him. "*Animare*, you are my mate. I demand you get back here and perform your mately duties," I add with a smirk.

I suddenly feel playful with him. I know he is trying to protect me, and I also know that he is trying to make up for his past mistakes. He still feels regret over our first joining, knowing now that I would have liked to wait. But I also know that I am ready to let go of the past, and the only way to move forward now is a primal one.

A joining of our flesh to erase all the hurts from the past, to start anew.

"Again," he growls as he lowers his body down onto mine once more.

"*Animare*," I say back as my arms reach up to pull his head down to mine.

I feel his lips ravish me ferociously, his mouth parrying with mine demanding I relent and allow him to conquer me. This is a battle I am only too happy to lose.

I want to abandon myself to the sensations he can wring from my body. I relax my lips and allow his tongue entrance into my mouth. Our mouths clash heatedly, teeth smashing together occasionally, and loud animalistic moans can be heard in the room around us.

It takes me a moment to realize the sounds come from us. We are both lost to a passion I never knew could exist. My hands are caressing his back in long, greedy strokes, my nails digging into the hard muscles above me.

Suddenly, Danion's arms leave me and his hands grip the material of my top on either side of the neckline. He grips tightly, then rips the material savagely.

"Oh!" I squeak out. The material bit into my skin before it gave way to his violence. The pain I felt is forgotten, lost in the wake of the tidal wave of lust I feel as Danion falls onto my breasts.

I can tell that he is barely aware of tearing my clothing. He is desperate for the feel of my naked flesh against his own. As his lips, tongue, and teeth are busy pillaging my sensitive breasts, his hands have already found my silk sleep pants.

Just before he grips my pants, his hands come around and caress my inner thighs. I let out a loud moan and throw my head back. How can that feel so good?

One hand sneaks up to the waistband and slips inside. "You are so wet. So hot. You're desperate for me, aren't you? For me alone, only I can give you this pleasure," Danion asks as his fingers delve deep into my moist heat. His voice is muffled by the nipple in his mouth.

My only response is a moan. Danion's mouth and hands stop.

"I asked you a question," Danion says forcefully.

"What?" I glance at him, aghast that he has stopped. "Why did you stop? Keep going."

Danion's look turns domineering. "Tell me you want me."

"I want you," I gasp out. His hand returns to my thighs.

"Tell me you need me."

"I need you!" I moan as his mouth descends once more onto my needy breasts.

He takes my nipple in his mouth, nibbles on it, sucks it vigorously, and then lets it go with a loud pop. He stares at me again.

"Tell me that I am the only male you will ever look at with desire." His voice begins to growl. "Tell me that no one but I will ever feel these wonderful globes within their mouth." He nips at my breasts, giving a quick short sting to each one.

"Who else would—" I am cut off by a steady hand giving a hard, fantastic squeeze to my left breast, the fingers rolling the nipple between them.

"There are males aplenty who desire you, do not play the fool. We both know they would love to use this body to satiate their desires. You will not let that happen. Your body is mine, just as mine is yours. Now tell me."

His hand has been fondling my breast this whole time, and I could scarcely focus on his words. I am finding his jealous, possessive nature extremely arousing at this particular moment.

Before it scared me. Now it makes me desperate to feel him deep inside me.

"There will never be anyone but you. No other will ever touch me but you."

"*Deim* right," he growls as his hands return to my bottoms and tear them wide open, the remnants of my torn clothing strewn across the bed. I am lying in a pile of ripped fabric.

Danion presses against my thighs, widening my body so it is fully visible to his hot gaze. He stares ravenously down at my center. "You are so beautiful here." His fingers come to stroke and probe. "So wet and needy. Ready for me."

"Yes, I am so ready for you. Please," I moan, and his fingers increase in rhythm.

Danion moves up the bed, his thighs bumping my own. As the head of his shaft presses into my opening, he looks deep into my eyes. "I love you, Eleanor Belator."

With a mighty thrust he sinks deep inside of me. I let out an almost incoherent moan. My entire body is beginning to tighten in a now familiar way. I know that I am close to the bliss that he can bring me.

Danion's thrusts take on a desperate tempo, his movements so fast and wild I can scarcely keep up with them. He takes his hands and grabs my legs behind the knees. He raises them, hooks them around his arms, and suddenly the angle is thicker, harder, better.

That is all I need. I explode, crying out his name in desperate shouts. Danion's voice joins mine, but his is calling my name in addition to a string of profanities.

It is several minutes before I am aware of my surroundings again. Danion is collapsed on top of me, resting between my widespread thighs. He raises his head and gives me a gentle kiss.

"Did I hurt you?" he asks with concern.

I raise my hand to caress his face. "No, you did not hurt me. You were wonderful."

He smiles down at me. "Good because I am ready again."

I am shocked to feel that he is indeed readying inside me, and he slowly begins thrusting.

"So soon?" I gasp.

"I have been waiting for two months to have you again, did you really think that I would be satisfied with only once?"

I smile ruefully to myself.

Several hours later, and more than a few orgasms, I drift off to sleep while thinking that there are worse things in life than being the mate to a warrior king.

Danion

Eleanor is sleeping beside me, her head on my chest. I idly caress her hair as I recall our day together. It has been the most fulfilling day of my life. There have been very few moments in my long existence where I have felt happy, and they all are centered on her. I never truly knew what happiness was until I met her.

I know that I will need to return to my duties soon, as does Eleanor, but I want to savor this time we have together right now. If there was anything urgent someone would have contacted me. Golon can handle everything else.

There will be little time to share between us in the coming days. I relax back and just focus on the gentle rising and falling of Eleanor's chest as she breathes.

There is a gentle knock at the door. I sigh as I look up, aware that the real world is intruding sooner than I would have liked. Gently I move my mate off me and wrap the discarded sheet around my hips as I walk to the door.

Amell is standing on the other side. "Pardon me, Dane, but there is an urgent matter we need you to attend to."

I hear movement from the bed behind me and turn to see Eleanor sitting up.

"What has happened, Amell?" I ask the warrior before me, widening my stance so that I am sure he cannot glimpse my mate in her naked glory.

"Baer, Kyel, and Rale have returned with urgent news."

"What of Sylva?" Eleanor asks as she walks up beside me. She has wrapped a silken robe of the deepest purple around herself.

"She has been captured, and that is not even the worst of it. Hurry, dress and meet us in the *hael* wing and they will debrief us on everything that occurred."

"We will be there shortly." I nod at Amell. My tone is tense, fear over what is happening to Sylva makes my words harder than I intended. The Erains are well known for their hatred of females. They take particular pleasure in torturing them.

"Dane. What will they do to her?" Eleanor asks me.

"No time for that now, we must dress." She nods at me, and we both dress quickly.

It is mere minutes since Amell came to our chambers that we are walking into the *hael* wing. Golon, Jarlin, and Eleanor's entire *praesidium* are standing in the room. The three warriors are lying prostrate on the medical beds, their bodies contorting in pain. Ugly boils cover their skin.

"What happened?" I bark at them. At the reproving glare Eleanor shoots me I can tell that I was too abrupt. I have no time for pleasantries, I need answers.

"It was a trap, Dane," Kyel replies, his teeth clenched in pain.

"We suspected as much," I remind them. "You are trained warriors and you should have been prepared for a trap."

"No, I mean it was a *trap*. They do not wish to cut off our supply of *tatio*. They poisoned it. Once we made contact on the moon our bodies began to feel lethargic and weak." Kyel readjusts his position on the bed, his face grimacing with the effort. "As soon as we wove our lineages these boils appeared on us."

"Your *chakkas*," Golon adds. "Each of these boils is present in prominent areas that your *chakkas* run through."

Eleanor speaks up. "That would make sense if they poisoned the *tatio*, wouldn't it?" she asks.

"Yes, it would. It is infecting the channels in which we weave our power," Golon answers. "Has there been any improvement in your symptoms since you left the moon?" Golon asks the three warriors.

All three shake their heads, grimacing in pain. Golon meets my gaze and shares a worried look with me.

"Their plan is to cripple us," I say. "Level the playing field between our races. Our power is what sets us above them. They outnumber us by population."

"Yes, and if we are reduced to only being able to use our ships' weapons, they could overwhelm all of our outposts and Pact Worlds," Golon finishes the thought.

"What of Sylva?" I ask the males.

"She did not weave any of her power. She saw us fall and moved us to safety. She went for the pods and sent them back to us. She was captured before she was able to escape."

"How can you be sure? Perhaps she is still hiding on the moon?" I ask them. "Sylva is one of the most highly skilled warriors our race has to offer."

"We were assisted off the moon by an Erain. He told us that she was captured before helping us into the pods and allowing us to escape," Kyel explains. "He said that we needed to return with help for her."

"How do we know we can trust this *vermien*? He could very well be leading us into a trap," Arsenio questions. As much as I dislike him, he is an excellent warrior with a quick mind.

"There is no evidence to say we should trust him. But I do." This comes from Baer. "He could have killed us or captured us, but he didn't. I sensed true concern on his part. I think he cares for Sylva."

"How could he even know her enough to care?" the indignant voice of Kowan demands.

"I do not know, but that is my belief." Baer defends his statement.

"You think he actually cares for a Gelder female? I think that poison has affected your mind as well, Baer," Kowan says.

"Your bickering is a disgrace." Eleanor's soft words drop like lead in the room. "Sylva should be our only concern. She went to that moon suspecting a trap, yet she still went. We cannot abandon her."

"Nor will we," I assure her. "Kowan, we have ships in place near the moon, correct?" I ask.

"Yes, we placed them as you commanded when Sylva did not report as scheduled."

"Good. Golon, as soon as possible we need to start restructuring the grid in that region of space. We need eyes in the area, we must know what we are up against. Use any of the stationed resources to make it happen."

"At once," Golon replies and exits the room.

I turn to Eleanor. "We will save her. Try not to worry, Sylva is a very competent female."

Chapter Nineteen

Sylva

I rattle the chains that encompass my body, trying to see if there is any give at all. Just like the thousand times I have done this before, there is none.

We have been floating in empty space for days, and I have been locked up the entire time. Nix has been my only source of entertainment. He is also my only source of food and water. Also, he is the reason for the embarrassing predicament of me requiring his help to relieve my bodily needs.

"How many times must I remind you that struggling is useless?" His sexy, low timbre voice calls out from where he sat unbeknownst to me. He is continuously observing me without me knowing.

"Do you do that on purpose?" I demand of him. Since he can read my mind, I know he knows exactly what I am talking about.

"What do you think?" he asks with a snort.

"I think that you get some sort of sick, twisted amusement from watching me when I don't know you are. You hide your presence from me just so you can catch me in some embarrassing position," I lob at him, anger making my words sharp.

His eyes widen almost imperceptibly. "You think that? You believe my motivation is to hurt you?"

His words ground me and I give a big sigh. "I suppose not, since you risked your life to save mine. You also have played nursemaid to my broken body. I am just frustrated. I am sorry, Nix."

As much as I hate to admit it, I owe him an enormous debt. I am as honor-bound as the rest of my people; our culture is based on the belief that a warrior who possesses no honor has no right to hold power.

"Yes, I have played nursemaid to you. And you return that kindness by continually harming yourself with your useless thrashing about. Undoing all of my hard work."

Just like that my chagrin over my actions is forgotten. "Useless? You have me chained to a bed!"

He moves so quickly that not even my advanced senses can track his movement. Before I know it, he is by my side. His head is scant inches from my face.

"I don't have you chained to a bed, I have you restrained to prevent more damage to your already weakened body. You have to heal more before I can release you." He lowers his head, his mouth so close to my ear that I can feel the moist, hot breath along my skin. "When I have you chained to my bed, trust me, you will know it."

His words send shivers down my spine. His lips place a butterfly-light kiss along the shell of my ear. The sensations that arise bombard me, causing a deep throbbing ache to settle in my core. I can feel myself clenching, my body readying for him.

What is wrong with me? He has barely even touched me, and yet I am about to combust.

"Did you say when?" I ask, as my mind caught up with what he said.

"Yes, I said when. When I have you I will ignite a passion in your body so great that you will demand that I take you. You will open your legs for me and beg that I give you what no other male is capable of giving you." His eyes come to find mine. "I will give you pure, unadulterated bliss. It will be so good you will keep coming back for more. I will own you."

While his words stoke the fire within, the white streaks in his hair have the opposite effect. It reminds me of who and what he is. A blatant reminder that I can never have him and what he says can never come to pass.

"You're wrong, Nix. You're Erain and I am Gelder. I can never be with you. I will never be yours." I try to convince myself that the sadness I feel has nothing to do with the thought of never being with this male.

"Is that a challenge?" Fire flashes in his eyes, his features tightening in anger.

"No, it is a statement. You and your people are everything I have fought my entire life against. I cannot respect you, and without respect I could never love you. And without love, you can never own me," I tell him with finality.

I expected more anger, but what he gives me is contemplation. "Love? Interesting." He gives another of his deep, penetrating stares, then speaks with a casual air that opposes the serious expression he wears. "I have told you that I am not full Erain."

"Yes, but that does not mean that you are good. You saved me, but what acts did you perform to allow you to climb so high in the ranks of those *vermien* Erains?"

"What would it take for your respect?" he asks, curiosity on his face. My heart falls. If he truly cared he would be more than curious. I am now more convinced than ever that I am little more than a pet in his eyes.

When he does not contradict my inner thoughts, I know it is true. He can read my mind; his silence is all the assent I need.

"You would need to join me, help me. Save people, save mortals, from your brethren and anyone else who would try to kill them unjustly." I answer him anyway, even though I know it is useless. "You would have to show me that you consider me your equal," I end on a whisper.

"Interesting," Nix says with a nod of his head. He then turns away and resumes his regular seat at the table across from my bed. He begins studying something that he keeps just out of my view.

"What are you always looking at?" I ask him, expecting his usual silence. He never tells me.

"I am looking for evidence of my mother." His words shock me.

"Your mother?" I ask him.

"Yes, my mother. I have been looking for her for a...very long time." There is a lengthy pause in his speech. Some hidden, unspoken meaning is there just beneath the surface. What that meaning is I have no idea.

I think back to the conversation we had the day he rescued me. He mentioned something about his mother then as well, that she was a victim of war. She was captured, tortured, and obviously raped since he was the product of her captivity.

I scramble to think of something to say, something other than one of the million questions whirling in my head. But I am saved from responding since Nix seems to be in an unusually talkative mood.

"Don't be foolish to think I am some lost, forlorn son dedicated to saving my mother. I am just trying to prove that she was real, that there was a reason for—" He cuts himself off abruptly.

It is alright, I do not need him to finish his sentence. I know exactly where he was going with what he was saying. He wants validation that he is different, different from those monsters, and a reason as to why he is the way he is.

Nix is staring down at the table; his gaze is transfixed on a single spot in front of him. Lost to memories of the past. Usually Nix has an air about him that is nothing but raw, unadulterated, masculine power. But now? Now he appears...lonely. And possibly even a little fragile.

Suddenly I have an image of him as a little boy being raised in the midst of the Erains. A pariah, thanks to his mixed heritage. If there ever were a race that would be cruel to a child for circumstances surrounding his birth it would be these *vermiens*.

As if I am seeing him for the first time, I realize that Nix has been alone his whole life. He even admitted to me before that he is not an Erain. It is very possible...no *probable*...that he has never had a single friend. No companions or support system.

It is remarkable that he has been able to hold on to his integrity... What am I thinking? I know nothing of his integrity. He may have saved my life, but he is willfully keeping me locked here when I am needed in the war. Billions of souls will be murdered if we lose, and yet he cares not at all.

Which, of course, is true of his upbringing, raised by the type of monsters he was. He desperately wants to belong to someone... *You are mine...*

I recall the words that he told me the day I awoke in this ship with him. He wants me to be his. My heart weakens with this realization. I have been a warrior my entire life, afraid of nothing. But this male before me terrifies me. Because I want him, as long as he is a good male. I believe he is since he has done nothing to harm me. I decide to risk it all and offer myself to him.

"Nix?" I raise my voice slightly. "Thank you for saving my life. You are a male that hides it well, but you have honor. I would be glad to call you a friend. Perhaps we can fight in this war together—" I am cut off by his snort of derision.

"Oh, yes? You wish to be friends? Well, I am sorry to disappoint, but I am not looking for a friend out of pity. Or at all." He turns eyes that are blazing with rage toward me. "I am not a monster, or lonely, or any other handful of insults you believe. How could I be lonely? I have you." He says these last words with a curl of his lips as if the thought of having me was distasteful in some profound way.

My anger returns in full force. "Have me? Are you crazy?! You do not have me you sick, twisted, sad excuse for a living creature! I would never belong to someone like you!" I scream back at him, angry not only at his words but his blatant spying into my mind.

While I was thinking of him with affection, all he cares about is owning me. I am not a female that any male can possess. He is about to learn that lesson in an agonizing way.

"You are wrong." His words drop heavy in the room.

Nix

"What do you mean I am wrong?" Sylva, my gorgeous, rebellious beauty demands incredulously.

"I mean you are wrong, you already do belong to me. For as long as I wish it, you are mine to keep."

"You can't—"

"Can't what? Can't keep you? I think I have proved how easily I can keep you," I say with a pointed look at the chains. I lower my hold on my mental power and lock her body in unbreakable telepathic bonds. A reminder to her about who is in charge.

I may be able to hold her telepathically, but her mind is a challenging one to read. I will never tell her this, never reveal my weakness, but her thoughts are becoming increasingly more difficult to hear. I used to catch every single syllable of her thoughts, and I relished them. I savored the beauty that resides inside her mind.

It was nothing compared to the horrors that invaded my mind all throughout my childhood. Overhearing the thoughts of my half brothers was enough to turn any male cold; devoid of emotion after experiencing the sadistic thoughts of those ruthless killers. But I grew up stronger because of it. I refused to let them break me or my mind. Instead, I turned their vile hatred against them. I hid my true power and began climbing my way up their ranks using the mental strength that their abuse created.

But with every passing day she is learning how to keep me out of her mind, and now all I get are small snippets of her thoughts. Sometimes I hear everything, other times it is as if there is not a single thought within her head. As if she is unreachable, out of my grasp. In a way I wish that was the case this time.

The thoughts I just overheard ripped my very soul to pieces. I will never let her know how badly she has wounded me, never reveal to her how much power she holds over me.

But to learn how she really views me, it hurts more than all the abuse I suffered in my youth. I have found her presence with me...pleasant. It took me a long time to recognize the feeling since I never felt it before in my life. Never before have I ever been anything but alone, hurt, and wary. And those were on the good days. I did not know that life could feel any different than that. I have believed for my entire existence that life was the actual punishment, not death.

But I have been feeling a connection with her; contemplating a future that we shared together. A future where she was by my side, keeping the deep abyss at bay. All this time while I have looked upon our time together with hope, she has been festering hatred.

Pariah...

Fragile...

Monster he was...

All this was in her mind and it burns me to my very core. Yet another being who despises me for no other reason than my existence in this universe. I have done nothing to her to warrant such disdain, but it is mine all the same. I have given up everything I have worked for just to save her and this is how she repays me. With revulsion. Anger begins to burn deep inside me.

She said I could only own her if she wishes it, if she wants me to, and that's where she is wrong. She is mine, and regardless of her feelings about me I am going to show her how wrong she is. In fact, I will immensely enjoy teaching her the errors of her ways. I have never felt this way in my life, this feeling of peace. And I am keeping this pleasant feeling with me, no matter how she may fight against it. She will never be permitted to leave me.

Perhaps she needs to be taught a lesson so that she understands why resistance is futile. She needs to know that I am in control here, not her. While I keep her restrained with my mental power, I begin to tunnel into her mind, my eyes laser-focused on her.

"Do you know that, thanks to your special little mineral *tatio*, Erains have discovered how to control minds on top of reading them?" I ask her, all the while burrowing deeper, bashing into her mental shields for all I'm worth. I know that it is painful to have one's mind so ruthlessly entered. Even while I say that I do not care, I find myself tempering the painful bashing slightly. I do not wish to harm her mind.

Still, even with this concession, I can see her eyes widen in fear. "Yes, it is true. The mind must be weak, so Gelder minds have been particularly troublesome." I lean down and whisper this last word into her ear; letting her feel my presence within her mind, letting her know how much control I could have over her.

I can actually feel her terror; nothing scares her more than losing control. Guilt and self-hatred rise within me and I push it back ruthlessly. She brought this on herself, I try to tell my conscience. Guilt has no place in my mind right now.

"But that is because the Erains are weak themselves. It is so hard to control a mind that is stronger than yours. But guess what, Sylva?" I can feel the revulsion within her mind now. She finally stops hiding her feelings from me.

Pain fills me, cutting me so deep I want nothing more than to hurt her as badly as she has hurt me.

I lie down atop her body. I use my power to keep most of my weight off of her chest, since her ribs seem to be tender still. I place my head directly above hers, my lips separated by the thinnest of spaces from her pair of sweet, full ones. I maintain the almost nonexistent distance as I speak to her, my breath mingling with hers.

"I am not a weak Erain. I am the strongest being we have ever come across. The weaknesses of the Erains are not mine. You would fight me, but I could easily break down your walls and then you would be mine. Mine to do as I see fit." Deep down I can scarcely believe I am doing this. It is appalling, my treatment of her. The one being in all the cosmos that I want to protect. But I am useless to stop my hurt-fueled rage. I may be only half-Erain, but those instincts are still there, and right now they are in control of me for the first time in my life.

"I could make you dance for me," I whisper as my mouth grazes her jawline. "I could have you naked and writhing for me, all without ever laying a single finger on you." My mouth skims closer to her mouth, my hands settle on the edges of her breasts. "I could make you do anything and everything that I want, and you would do it all with a smile on your face.

"So next time I say you are mine, think it through. Use that weak and inferior mind of yours and remember what I could have you doing. The only thing stopping me is my desire for you to come willingly. But push me too far and I will have no choice, just as you won't have a choice. So be a good girl and stop fighting me."

I rise from the bed and see the stark, overwhelming terror on her face. Her entire body is shaking, her skin white and clammy. Disgust rockets through me at my actions.

The image of her so terrified washes away every single piece of pain I held inside. I instantly regret my actions. I have done to this glorious female precisely what I condemned the Erain race for. Using their mental abilities to inflict the largest amount of pain possible. I would never control her, never strip her of her will. Yet, I made her fear me doing just that. Bile rises inside me.

I let go of my hold on her body, and the small shivers turn into convulsions that make her entire body shake. She rolls onto her side, as much as the chains allow her to, facing the wall away from me.

I have no excuse for my actions, no defense I can offer that will make it better. Disgusted at myself, I storm away.

It has been two days since Sylva has spoken. Not one word since I violated her body and her mind. No less than I deserve; there was no excuse for my behavior. If I were a better male I would let her go, but I have never lied to myself about my own character and I am not good enough to release her. I refuse to give her up. I will just have to mend the wounds that I have inflicted upon her. I sit in the shadows, concealing my presence and just watch her.

Yesterday I removed her chains, explaining that she should be able to move around without injuring herself now. I sensed in her mind, when I was inexcusably invading her, that she detests the chains. I was hoping for a small smile or even a look of scorn when I removed them.

She gave no response at all. She never even moved from her bed. She just lies there with eyes that don't really see anything. I have never treated anyone as cruelly as I treated her. The mind is a precious, sacred, fragile thing and I rammed my way in, all because my feelings were hurt.

I have managed to wound a warrior as strong as her by the most reprehensible of means. I swore to never invade her mind, or any mind, the way I did to her. As I said, there is no excuse for my behavior. With an inward sigh, I approach her and sit on the bed, my hip next to hers.

"Sylva...I want you to look at me," I tell her. Longing is in my tone, anyone could see how much I want her to be mine. Since the first time her mind touched mine and we began dream sharing, I have known she would be mine. But not like this, never like this.

As is my nature, anger rises within me when she refuses to respond. I have been as patient as I can be. "Sylva, you will look at me." The command is thick in my voice; I am not asking anymore.

She turns to face me, but she is expressionless and says nothing. Obeying to the letter, allowing herself this small act of defiance. It is just one of the many things that makes her so alluring to me.

"Sylva, I know that we have not known each other long, but we have a...connection. Something within you calls to me. I have never experienced anything like this." I take a breath. I am unsure how to proceed since kindness and gentleness is not something I know. "I want you to know that I was angry before...when I mistreated you." Something finally gives in her expression. Relief flood through me; finally she is responding to me.

Her right eyebrow cocks up in condescension. "Is the mighty Nix, the male so powerful he can make me *dance* for him with only a look, attempting to apologize to his little slave?"

The small amount of calmness I was able to harness flees with her sarcastic tone. "I never called you my slave, but if you so wish it, that can be how our relationship plays out. I have told you, you are mine. In what role you play to fulfill that is completely your decision."

Her expression tightens as anger courses through her body. The small snippets of her mind that I can hear confirm what I have long suspected, her antagonism toward me.

I smile inwardly. I prefer her anger to the silent depression she has been in. Her irritation is a part of the fiery personality that burrowed its way into my mind all those pallies ago.

"No words to speak now?"

"What do you want?" she growls at me. Against all my control I can feel myself hardening. I make a slight adjustment with my powers to prevent her from noticing. I highly doubt my arousal will defuse her anger with me.

"I removed your chains so that you would be able to move about the ship. You are welcome to rise from that bed," I tell her. This is as far as I can bring myself to go to make amends for my offensive behavior.

"You are not afraid that I will try to sabotage the ship? Attempt an escape?" she challenges. As much as I hide it, I *fiefling* love it when she challenges me.

"I have every single control center protected with telepathic locks set only to me, I have nothing to worry about." If I am honest, it is a risk. I never intended to let her move around freely, but I feel I owe her. After what I did to her, granting this small freedom is the least I can do.

She studies me for several seconds and then she moves to sit up. A grimace of pain passes over her features, her hands grip her sides. Her eyes seek mine with a question I am afraid to know the answer to.

"*Beb*, are your ribs still hurting you?" I ask cautiously. Her eyes rise to mine, fear deep within them. I can tell she is trying to hide her fear from me, but I can sense it.

She opens her mouth to respond, but no words emerge. Finally, after three attempts to force words past her clogged throat, she just nods.

"It has been almost an entire pallie since we escaped the moon base. You should be fully recovered by now." I speak slowly, thinking through each word. If she has not healed yet, the Erain poison may be more effective than we first thought.

"They feel almost the same as they did when we left the moon a week ago. Since I was locked, I did not move. But now that I am it is as painful as they were then. It feels as if they have not healed at all." She gasps at me. I mentally scoff at her use of mortal time measurements. "What does it mean, Nix? Are my powers gone? My advanced healing abilities?" she asks me.

I look down and see that her hand has come and grasped mine; she has unknowingly sought me out for comfort. An unfamiliar sensation of warmth travels through me. She may not accept it yet, but she already innately knows we are meant to be together. She may despise who I am but she will succumb to my charms.

"I am not sure, *beb*. But we will figure it out. I will not let you face this alone. If the poison did strip you of your healing abilities and your powers, we will find a way to bring them back."

Her hand grips mine all the tighter, and her eyes close for a brief moment. When they open again, the smallest amount of liquid is gathering in the corners.

"Thank you," she whispers.

Chapter Twenty

Ellie

Danion, Golon, Jaeson, and I are in the *bellum* chamber again. The news that Baer, Kyel, and Rale have brought us is very troubling. The three warriors that surround me have not said a single word since we entered the chamber. They are all deep in thought, attempting to process the full story before making a decision.

Danion is the first to speak. "Golon? How is this possible? No one knows about our need for *tatio*. It is a secret we take to the grave."

Suddenly dread slithers up my spine as a horrible realization comes to me. "There is someone who knows about *tatio*," I whisper.

Three sets of eyes swing to me, Jaeson's and Golon's appear interested and a little curious, while Danion's gaze is concerned. He must sense my unease.

"Ambassador Lexen. He knew that I needed it; he could have sold them the information. Or used it as a bargaining chip to rescue him from this ship once he was captured." I feel sick knowing that every Gelder is in danger because of information that was leaked because of me.

Danion rests his hand over mine, providing me with the support I didn't realize I needed. "*Aninare*, do not worry so." He places a chaste kiss between my eyebrows, right along the furrow on my brow. "It is not your fault."

"How can you say that?"

"Eleanor, it would be on me, not you, if that is the case." Jaeson, too, tries to reassure me. I give him a look of distaste. But one that is much less angry than when we entered this room earlier while being escorted by guards.

Apparently, he has been confined since my disappearance, but with this new turn of events, his expertise was needed. I am still coming to terms with him splitting my mind and dividing my literal soul in half. But I admitted to Danion that I do not feel that Jaeson played a role in this most recent attempt on my life.

There are so many mysteries surrounding my father that I can scarcely focus on them all. This new worry of the poison helps by providing a different subject to fixate on.

Golon is the next to speak. "Ellie, there is a chance your life is the reason that this got out." I gasp at the unemotional delivery of these words. "But it is also likely that our enemies got it from another source. You are only twenty years of age. I would be surprised if a poison this complicated was created in so little time."

Golon's words are the first that have offered me real comfort. "Do you really think so?" I ask him.

"Yes. But knowing how they got this information is irrelevant. They may know even more secrets of ours, but there is nothing more we can do about that right now until we have more data. We know they know about the *tatio*, so we know we must respond to this threat."

Danion raises my hands to his lips, grazing my knuckles while he gives some thought to Golon's words.

"How do you suggest we respond? Our power can be infected if we come into contact with these *vermien* in a battle. How do you propose we fight an enemy we are not allowed to weave power at or touch?" Danion asks him.

Golon looks at us with a smirk on his face, and I just know Danion won't like his answer. "By gathering more data, of course."

I am sitting in a comfortable lounge chair upholstered with the finest of coverings. It feels so thick, plush, and luxurious. I would have maintained my position beside the beds that hold the three warriors of Sylva's team, but I am too exhausted to stand a moment longer.

I observe the three males hovering over the patients: Jarlin, Golon, and surprisingly, Jaeson. Danion is standing by my side, a hand resting on my shoulder.

"What is the purpose of this, old one?" I hear Golon ask Jaeson.

"You said you needed more data, and I have a suspicion that needs to be confirmed," Jaeson replies distractedly while analyzing the medical display at the end of Baer's bed.

The display is presented from a small console at the foot of the bed. From my vantage point all I am able to see is an enormous amount of letters scrolling through. They are all strange variations of three letters grouped together.

Jarlin looks intrigued behind Jaeson. "Why are you studying their genetic codes?"

Jaeson lets out an aggrieved sigh. "As I have already said, I have a suspicion and I need to confirm it first before I discuss it. Now let me work."

The letters fly by even faster, and suddenly Jaeson stops the scrolling letters. He swipes on the screen to make a small section larger. He studies it for a moment, then he moves to Kyel's bed and repeats the process.

Very soon he has a small portion enhanced on his screen as well. Eventually, he has a similar view on Rale's medical display. "As I suspected," he mutters to himself.

He says no more, and I find myself impatient. "Jaeson, explain your findings to us. Time is a luxury we do not have," I snap at him.

He nods at me distractedly, then moves to a large central display screen along the far wall. His hands travel along the controls briefly and three sections light up with matching letter sequences from the displays on the warriors' beds.

"This here is a copy of the genetic makeup each of these warriors left here with. Specifically, we are looking at the pathways that a warrior utilizes when they weave *vim*, *simul*, and *caeli*. These are the powers each warrior used while on the moon." He circles a specific sequence of letters on the central screen and matching circles appear on all the other screens.

It is then that I notice that the sequences here are very different, bearing almost no resemblance to the original letters at all. Then he hits a button and the screens all change to a three-dimensional projection of several shapes. They resemble images I saw in my brief science classes. I believe they are molecules of some kind.

He walks to the foot of Baer's bed. "As you can see from the proteins that Baer now produces, they are—" Jaeson breaks off when Danion interrupts.

"Eleanor has no knowledge of what you are showing us; the education you arranged for her left out some important details." Danion's words leave me feeling ashamed. I know he means well, but I suddenly feel like a very stupid addition to this group of ancient warriors.

"I am sorry, Ellie dear." I bristle at the endearment but decide to keep quiet. "What I am showing you is a reading on these warriors' DNA, essentially. I am looking for discrepancies between what DNA they had when they left for their mission and what DNA they came back with."

I nod at him. "Alright, I can understand that."

He gives me a small smile. "Yes, that is because you are wise beyond your years." Before I have a chance to respond, he continues. "Now, DNA really only tells us half the story, so I am looking at what happened on the cellular level within these warriors, or specifically, what this change in their DNA has resulted in.

"You see, *tatio* is necessary for a warrior to weave the powers because it binds to specific proteins within our cells. It allows them to withstand the immense strain that channeling the metaphysical energy we can harness causes on our bodies.

"Without *tatio* the actual shape of our cells, our proteins, even our organs would all change and eventually rupture under the stress. Seeing the result of these warriors' wounds, I knew that the poison could only be working in one of two ways." Jaeson pauses.

"What ways?" Golon prompts him to continue. He takes a few more moments before he responds, to either organize his thoughts or merely irritate Golon. I am not sure which. From what I have seen of Jaeson, both are equally as likely.

"The first and simpler of the two ways would be that the poison is blocking the channels that allow our cells to accept *tatio*. Essentially, they have made it where we cannot bring *tatio* into our bodies."

"Why is that simpler?" I ask him.

"If that were the case we could easily counteract the poison with one antidote for all the lineages. It would not be specific to the warrior, it would be a universal poison and therefore a universal fix."

"That is not what it is doing?" I ask hesitantly.

"No, I am afraid not. It is much more serious." He again points to the displays. "See how each warrior has different areas affected? That is because they each wove different lineages. That means it is not a simple fix for any warrior who becomes infected."

"Why?" I ask.

Danion is the one who answers. "Because the Erains have managed to inherently change the way that *tatio* interacts within our bodies. It is changing our genetic makeup, meaning that not only are we going to struggle to cure any warrior that becomes infected, but we also may not be able to reverse the process on the supply of *tatio* still being stored on the base. It is the only supply we have ever found and we may not be able to use any of it."

The full repercussions of this poison come to me suddenly. Oh no, a lack of *tatio* is what sent our ancestors into a civil war.

"Precisely, Danion," Jaeson says. "How much *tatio* do you have in your possession now?"

"Each and every ship in my fleet carries enough *tatio* to sustain their numbers for one hundred years. In addition to the stores on the ships, a few outposts have a backstock so ships can resupply without traveling to the moon. However, I am not sure of the exact amount we have in each location. Golon, can you give us an accounting for how much *tatio* we have in reserve?" Danion looks at Golon when he does not respond right away.

Golon has a look on his face that I cannot quite explain. Could it be...discomfort? Confusion? Golon is carefully averting his gaze from the expectant looks we are all giving him. Finally, Golon looks up, and his face holds a carefully neutral expression.

"I cannot provide an accounting at this time." Surprise shoots through me. Not at Golon's words, but at Danion's response.

His entire body stiffens with shock. His expression is baffled, almost disbelieving.

"What do you mean you can't?" Danion finally speaks.

"I mean exactly as I say, I am unable to provide you with the information that you seek at this time."

Golon stares at Danion intently, some hidden message passing between them both. I am not the only one who notices this tension because Jarlin tries to defuse the moment.

"It is of little matter right now—" He gets no further before Danion is interrupting him as if he never said a word.

"Golon, you must know the answer. We do not have time for your games, *cognata*. This is a very trivial matter to withhold information on; it cannot hold any significant repercussions if you tell us." I do not understand what Danion is implying.

"I play no game, *cognata*." He says this last word with such venom that I am taken aback. I have never seen Golon so enraged. I have seen him angry, yes. But this is something else entirely. "There are limits to what even I can do, and this exceeds them. You will have to be patient and wait until I can gather this knowledge for you."

"Limits? What limits? I have known you your entire existence and never before have I heard of this so-called limit." Danion scoffs and rolls his eyes.

A flash of pain appears in Golon's eyes. A look I recognize all too well; he bears the appearance of a soul who has been desperately calling out only to be overlooked. I do not pretend to understand what has happened to Golon, but for now it his business.

"Danion, that is enough," I murmur to him. The entire focus of the room comes to rest on me. When Danion opens his mouth again, I speak first. "No, Dane. This is not your place, nor is it the bigger issue we face. Let it go."

Danion stares at me for a few heartbeats more, then nods slowly. "Alright, get the information as soon as you can," he tells Golon, then his gaze settles on Jaeson once more, who was surprisingly silent during the entire argument. "I would estimate that we have enough backstock to supply our population for five hundred years."

All four warriors grimace as if this is terrible news. "Excuse me, I don't understand. That is a good thing, right?" I ask. It seems to me that five hundred years is a pretty good supply.

Danion grabs my hand and his thumb idly strokes the back of it. "Not to immortal beings it's not. Especially when there is a very real possibility that we will never find a new supply or be able to rid the *tatio* of the poison."

"But we have time to solve this, don't we?" I ask the room. Jaeson is the one who answers.

"Eleanor, it is no time at all. A lack of *tatio* is what caused the civil war I lived through, and that was five thousand years before your mate here was even born. Essentially we have been trying to solve this *tatio* issue for well over eight thousand years with little success. Now we are facing the very stark reality that we have only five hundred years to solve it now."

Ah. It finally clicks in my mind. These warriors do not think in terms of human lifespans. When eternity is looking out at you, five hundred years is a blink of an eye. And he is right, they have been searching for a solution to their *tatio* dependence for thousands of years, to no avail.

"Oh," I murmur.

"Yes, now you understand. And we have to win a war on top of that, which must take precedence for the moment," Danion tells me. He looks at Jaeson. "So what do you recommend we do about these warriors?" he asks briskly.

"For now? We need to make them comfortable. We need a sample of the infected *tatio* before we can begin any form of treatment."

"What? Why?" I ask him. "They are in pain!" My eyes look to the warrior named Rale. He has blisters all over his body, hideous boiling blisters. The skin between the blisters is red and appears burned.

"Yes, and they very well may become even worse if we act hastily. We might even kill them."

Jarlin speaks up now. "If it has affected their genetic makeup, I can correct the errors manually. We have the ability to manipulate DNA."

Jaeson's lip curls in disgust. "I have been present for the repercussions of manipulating someone's DNA without proper precautions taken before and it has almost killed us off as a race." He glances around the room. "We have no idea how this poison changed their DNA. If we just go in and rewrite it, there is no telling what else we could unleash. This time it may be a far greater price than infertility."

I think that Danion would argue that infertility is a very steep price they have had to pay, but to my surprise, he seems pensive. He studies Jaeson and nods.

"I agree, we cannot act foolishly or rashly," Golon says, "but how can we get a sample of the poison? It is impossible for any of us to go to the moon without becoming infected ourselves."

To my surprise, Jaeson looks at me. "Eleanor and I will have to go."

Chapter Twenty-One

Danion

Jaeson's words ricochet through me. I am completely frozen. I must have heard him wrong.

"I must have misunderstood what you just said, because I know that there is no *fiefling* way you would have just suggested that my *mate* travel to an enemy stronghold and collect some poisonous *tatio*!" With the last word I bellow into the room, blasting my power outward.

The walls quiver and I can feel the entire ship give a shudder that can be felt even through the inertia dampeners. The tremor begins to increase as the power pours out of me in ever increasing quantities. I try to halt the flow of my energy, but I can't. I am entering into a rage. A rage centered solely on the blond male in front of me who seems determined to threaten my sanity.

A red haze begins to descend on my vision, and I am unable to beat it back. I thought it was hard to control when Eleanor first arrived and I burned her, but this is a thousand times worse. I genuinely do not think I can hold back my power and it may end up ripping this very ship to shreds.

"Danion, you need to control yourself." I hear Golon's voice as if from a great distance, my entire focus is on the male in front of me.

"I should have killed you back in the lost city," I growl to him.

"I would like to see you try." With his words, I decide he has signed his own death decree; the red before my vision darkens even further.

Just as I am about to step toward him, the haze begins to lift. Eleanor has grabbed my arm and I can feel peaceful warmth traveling from her to me. I turn my body and envelop her within my arms, greedily taking everything she has to give me.

Time ceases to exist to me; all I am aware of is the two of us wrapped around the other. Finally, I am able to release her without the rage descending upon me again.

My control still feels tenuous, so I move both Eleanor and myself back to her seat and sit down, pulling her onto my lap and wrapping my arms around her.

Eleanor rubs my arm comfortingly. "Jaeson, perhaps I did not make myself clear. Danion is my mate." My body glows hot at her words. "Unlike you, he has shown me how much I mean to him." Her words cause a look of pain to reflect in Jaeson's eyes, and even though I did not think it possible, I find myself feeling a little sympathy for him. Eleanor's next words, however, wipe any thoughts of her father out of my mind. Instead, I am filled with joy.

"I will always, always choose Danion over you in a battle. Stop baiting him or I will tell him to send you packing. You are on thin ice with me as it is."

I watch Jaeson, curious as to how he will respond to his daughter. He appears to genuinely care for her. But that is often overlooked when a warrior is challenged in front of adversaries. From Jaeson's behavior, it is clear that is what he considers us.

"Eleanor...try to understand that this is not easy for me." They seem to share a silent communication, some private thought only they know. "I know that Danion is important to you. You are important to me, and therefore I will attempt to be more civil toward him." Eleanor seems to accept this with a nod.

I, however, have had enough. "Oh, she is important to you when it is convenient, you mean." I gently lift Eleanor and stand. I place her in the chair and take up position between her and her father.

"What does that mean, youngling?" Jaeson fires back at me, power in his words.

"It means that you seem to care for her but think nothing of that concern when you need something from her. This is dangerous and you know it. If you truly cared for her, you would not be suggesting that we send her there, to a place that she very well might not return from," I throw at him, the rage the thought of my mate in danger causes me is almost too much.

Jaeson, however, is oddly silent. He seems contemplative. "I think you are confused about something," he finally says. "I do not relish the idea of sending her there, but it is unavoidable. Eleanor and I are the only two beings who could go there successfully, and I cannot think of a way I can achieve this if I were to go on my own. I understand and accept what you refuse to, that she is an immensely powerful woman and she is destined for greatness. I would never hold her back just because I was frightened for her well-being."

"Why do you think that you two could go there unaffected?" I ask him, curiosity temporarily negating the rage I am still battling.

"Because of the way this poison is interacting in the warriors here," he says as he walks to the monitors again, pausing before Rale's bed. "This male here wove *simul*, and this is why he is in the worst shape of the three."

Golon steps forward. "Explain."

"The lineages that you know of all descended from the original line of *lacieu*, my lineage. Eleanor's too. This poison is specifically affecting the pathways within the body that each lineage uses. That means it was designed specifically for each power. Our power is so ancient, no one even believes it still exists. They would not be prepared for it and would have no knowledge on how to design a poison for it."

"How can you be so sure that the poison is custom designed for each lineage?" I ask, searching for a reason, any reason, that I can argue to stop this mission. It goes against everything within me to allow my mate to take such a risk.

"There is no other way that these results would be seen. Each molecule of *tatio* has been poisoned to affect the lineages differently. There is no knowledge of the line that Eleanor and I share." Jaeson seems confident, but I am not so easily convinced. Neither is Golon, as his next words prove.

"But the *tatio* is still poison. There is no telling how it will affect the rest of your bodies," Golon comments, "or your natural healing abilities. The risk is too great."

"We will bring our own supply of *tatio* with us and will make sure that we only bring the untainted mineral into our bodies..." Jaeson trails off as the door opens and Amell enters with Etan following closely on his heels.

The two newcomers come to stand before my mate and I and give a slight bow of their heads. "Greetings, Dane, Eleanor. We need to discuss something with you that we discovered in our evaluation of the lost city," Amell says.

"This is not the time, Amell. Jaeson is trying to convince us that Eleanor should travel into enemy territory and try to collect poison." I spit out the last word. I am in no mind to listen to Amell, and I need to settle the matter of my mate's safety first.

"Why?" Amell looks to Jaeson. "Why do you want her to do that?" Amell seems more contemplative than angry at the plan.

Jaeson is belligerent in his reply. "Because we are the only ones who can, and I cannot do it alone. If we have a hope of defeating this enemy we need a sample of this poison and we are the only two who can get it."

Amell thinks over his words for a moment. "You are sure that you and she will not be affected by the poison that plagues our warrior brethren?"

Golon's temper seems to snap. "You cannot be serious, Amell! We do not send babes into the fire!"

Amell's stoic face reveals no emotion. "You need to not underestimate our queen. She has already proved that she possesses great power."

Golon and Amell face off against each other, the anger is pulsing between these two warriors. I can feel the tension in the air, and by the way that Eleanor sits up straighter and grips my hand I can tell she does as well.

Etan strolls over to us with a small, amused smile on his face. He stops on the other side of Eleanor, rests a hip against her chair, and folds his arms over his chest. For all intents and purposes, he seems to be relaxed and enjoying the sight of these two warriors.

"Seems we may finally get an answer to the age-old question, huh, Dane?" Etan asks with a smile. I shoot him a look of disgust and say nothing in response.

I am shocked that Amell seems perfectly fine with the idea of sending Eleanor to an enemy stronghold.

"What do you mean, Etan?" my mate asks him.

"I mean that no one knows who would win in an all-out battle between those two. They are so close in power it would be interesting, that is for sure. Golon is older, but Amell has seen more battles. So, if you lean toward experience Amell would have the upper hand." He leans down to talk more directly with Eleanor. "But if you consider the fact that there is no single being in existence that has as much knowledge as Golon holds within his mind, the scales begin to tip in his favor."

Eleanor manages to pull her gaze away from the two males who are still in a silent battle. Golon may be angry, but I know Amell well enough to know he is as calm as he was when he walked in here. Once he makes up his mind he is implacable. Like his lineage power, he is as steadfast as a boulder.

"You mean we don't know who is stronger? But their class rank puts Golon higher than Amell, I thought. Wouldn't that mean he is stronger? I thought that is how rank was decided," she asks Etan.

"In most cases you would be right, but these two's position is a somewhat unique situation. Right, Dane?" He does not allow me to answer, not that I was planning to. "When it came time for Danion to pick a second in command everyone knew it would be either Golon or Amell, but which one is truly stronger? For every advantage one has over the other, they have an equally compelling disadvantage. Amell graciously refused the position, stating that Golon would be an infinitely better choice due to his 'relationship with King Danion, and specific skill set,' but to this day no one knows who is stronger."

"I see," Eleanor murmurs to herself.

"Enough, Etan," I snap at him, then with a squeeze to Eleanor's shoulder I walk toward the two males. "You will both stand down. Immediately."

Slowly, both males turn to me and give a slow nod of acceptance. "It is not for you to decide. In fact, it is no one in this room's choice but Eleanor's and mine." I direct this last part at Jaeson in particular.

I hold out my hand for my mate and she comes forward to take it. I begin to lead her from this room. I know enough about her to know that she will not like me informing her that she cannot go in front of a crowd.

I am sure she is not considering this folly; she must understand that she is not a warrior and has had no training to prepare her for such a mission.

I will take her to the privacy of our chambers before I tell her that she is not going anywhere near that base. This way she will feel comforted by the notion that the team will think we both came to a rational decision together, not that she had her choices taken away.

But regardless of her wishes, this is something I cannot give in on. She will not be going, not if I have to chain her to my bed to stop her.

Chapter Twenty-Two

Ellie

Danion leads me through the ship back toward our chambers. My heart is feeling so full, my mind reaching out to his through the bond. He is finally beginning to trust my opinion.

He's allowing me to make decisions in my own life. I know it will be hard for him to accept, but wars cannot be won without sacrifice and risk. It will be dangerous but I must go. I know I must. I cannot simply stand by and watch more warriors fall to this horrible poison.

The door closes behind us. Danion turns toward me with a fiery expression. Just as I am about to thank him for his consideration, he speaks in a tone so low and filled with steel that it sends ice down my spine.

"If I hear one word about how you plan to go through with that *fiefling* idiotic idea, I will lock you up for the next fifty years," he growls. "You are not to even consider this. It is an asinine, foolish, ridiculous notion to even think of sending you there."

My spine stiffens. "Excuse me?"

"You heard me, mate. Don't pretend otherwise. You are not going. And that is the last I want to hear of this stupidity," Danion snarls and walks away.

"Why are you so angry? What happened to this being our decision? Last I checked it took two people to make something be 'our' decision," I ask him calmly, trying to remain rational.

"It was until I heard through the bond your plan! You want to go through with this! You have no training! No experience! You don't even know how to weave your power on command, and yet you want me..." He pauses and takes a deep breath. He is visibly trying to maintain control of the emotions that are raging through him. "You want me to allow you to travel to a base that is heavily enforced by our greatest enemy and that is quite literally covered in poison. You want me to sit idly by and watch you risk your life."

I can feel his worry and despair through our bond, and I can feel his concern for me. It helps me remain calm and not act out in anger, knowing that it is not a lack of faith in me that causes his harsh words. It does not make his words hurt any less, but it does help me look past them.

"Danion, the things you mention we can fix." I walk to him and place both my hands on his biceps, forcing him to face me. "I don't mean to go this instant, I can have some training. I can't make up for the experience, but I can plan for this. We won't go in half-cocked."

"You are asking me to let you risk your life, going somewhere that I very well may not be able to follow if you do get captured," he whispers to me, his hands coming up to cup my face. "I cannot lose you, *aninare*."

"And you won't. But we have to discuss this. You are always saying that it is your duty as king to do whatever is necessary for our people. Well? This is my duty as queen. We have three warriors in that medical wing in extreme pain. Another missing. Potentially the entire race will die off if we cannot get our *tatio* supply back. I must do this." I speak fervently to him.

I have to make him see that this is not a choice. "Am I frightened? Of course, I am terrified. But that does not make this any less necessary or any less important. The fate of our people depends on this."

Danion closes his eyes, lowering his forehead to mine and pulling me close. We are entwined together, standing silently while Danion works through everything I told him.

"I know you are right," he finally whispers. "But I am not sure that I can let you take such a risk. Eleanor, it is so dangerous..." Danion trails off. He breaks our embrace and begins pacing the room in long, angry strides. "If we do this you will need to receive training in all the disciplines. Each lineage. I will train you."

"Danion, I don't think that it is a good idea for you to train me," I whisper tentatively.

"Why not?" he snarls.

"Because you are barely maintaining control while we are merely discussing my mission. Do you really think you could maintain your calm while we are training?" I ask him succinctly.

Danion stares at me for a hard moment. "Fine. You are right, I would not be able to concentrate with the thought of the danger you are going into in the front of my mind. You will study under your *praesidium* warriors then, since they each represent the strongest of their lines. And you will have to allow me to be the final judge to decide if you are ready. I will be the final say on if you can handle this mission. It cannot be rushed."

"Time is a concern, Dane," I remind him.

"If you go off without proper training it is no different than if I were to send you off to your death," he snarls at me.

"A compromise then? How about I train with each warrior plus Jaeson until they say that I am ready to move on to the next discipline. Then you can be present for the final training and observe me?" I ask him.

He considers me for a long, tense moment. "I will agree to that, on the condition that you also train with Golon. I will be the one who decides if you are capable of moving on to the next lineage though. I will speak to each of them, be present if I need to be, and I will make the final decision."

"I agree, with the understanding that I cannot be waiting for months. These warriors need help now. I will not be here in training for more than two weeks."

"Two weeks! That is absurd. You can achieve next to nothing in two weeks."

"But I must. I will learn enough to manage a quick, stealthy mission to the moon." I lock eyes with Danion and stare at him intently. "Two weeks is the absolute maximum amount of time we can delay. You know that." I speak directly and firmly, making it clear that I refuse to back down in this instance.

I know that the bond is making this all the more difficult for him, but that does not mean that I can delay any longer. Three warriors are in immense pain while they wait for us to get a sample of the poisoned mineral. Sylva is captured, being tortured on that moon. I refuse to let these warriors suffer any more than is absolutely necessary.

I can actually see Danion stiffen, his eyes going hot. Instantly I know that he has been pushed too far. I brace myself, unsure of where Danion is going now. "You will command me? Is that it, mate?" he growls at me as he approaches. He moves like a lethal predator. He controls his body with the utmost precision. He appears to glide to me, stopping a hairsbreadth from me.

"I will accept your conditions. I will give you your two weeks." His hand moves faster than my eyes can follow and burrows into the hair at my nape. "I will give you your time because as you say our people need us. Need you." His head descends and pauses with his lips grazing mine. They are so close I can feel his hot breath on my skin. "But you will have to accept that I will *never* be alright with this. Never accept you walking into danger. The bond madness is ripping into me, and you will have to accept the consequences of your actions."

The growl of his words sends a ripple of desire coursing through my body, settling deep in my core. I can feel my body readying for his, my nipples growing hard, my core heating.

"Consequences?" I gasp, barely able to concentrate.

"Yes, consequences. You know that without the completed bond my sanity is constantly being tested, constantly being ripped apart by worry and thoughts of you. The thought of you in danger is enough to push me over the edge. The only thing that is grounding me is touching you right now, and even that is beginning to fail. I am losing control as we speak."

"What are you going to do?" I ask with a desperate, needy whimper that I am unsuccessful at hiding.

"I am going to bury myself within you so deeply and so completely that we will forever be one. You will always know what it feels like to have my body within yours. I am going to take you, Eleanor, and it will be a savage affair. I have no control left to make it a civilized mating."

With those last words, Danion's other hand comes up to join the one buried deep in my hair and his mouth plunders mine. His mouth is so violent that there is no word for it except *savage*. I understand what he meant.

I am unable to match his ardor, merely submit to it. When he realizes that I am not resisting him, his hands relax their grip on my head. Both hands travel down my body, each one gripping the globes of my bottom and lifting me wholly against him.

His firm, muscular arms begin to rhythmically move my body against his, mimicking the act we are about to engage in.

"*Aninare*," Danion murmurs thickly against my mouth. "Why do you fight me?" His words are filled with anguish.

"I...don't." I gasp my reply into his ravaging mouth.

His mouth lifts away from mine and begins to travel along my jaw to my ear. His tongue does magic over my sensitive skin.

"So close, yet so far. Never letting me in." Danion's words are distracting, taut, and angry. His mouth takes on a more forceful journey down my neck. "Refusing me. Rejecting the bond." I can feel his teeth nibble and bite along my collarbone.

I cry out in rapture. He can inspire such overwhelming responses with little effort. He has only touched me with his mouth and hands and I feel myself nearing orgasm.

"You are never to fight me again," he growls, and his mouth drops and engulfs my nipple right through the thin silk of the X-shaped band that covers my breasts.

"Danion!" I gasp his name, my hands moving to his head to hold him steady to my breast.

He pulls back, his gray eyes glowing with heat. "*Animare,*" he growls at me.

I frantically pull at his head, anxious for him to continue what he started. He holds himself rigid, not moving one inch. All my struggles are for naught; he is like steel before me. Immoveable.

"Call me *animare*, not Danion," he growls at me. "I am your mate, and you will *fiefing* say it."

"*Animare! Animare!* Please, your mouth..." I plead to him. He still resists though. I stifle a scream of frustration.

"You are to call me *animare* from this point on. I am your other *fiefling* half, and you will call me as such. Do you understand?" he growls, his body moving even farther from mine.

His aggression and dominant attitude are stoking the fire within me even higher. I am sorry that my actions are punishing this male that I love. I know every day that I fail to complete this bond is torture for him. But it is not something that I can change. I cannot make my soul open to him. But this? This I can give him, and I want to give it to him so badly.

"Yes, yes, I understand." His eyes slant down into a heated glare.

"Yes, what?"

"*Animare! Animare! Animare!* Is that enough? Now continue!" I bellow at him, frustration obliterating the control I have over myself.

He gives me a wicked smile, and I see his hands glow briefly before the edges of my clothing are suddenly torn asunder, forcefully being thrown from my body.

I am left fully naked, and I know he just used his power to rip all my clothing off. I find the act as arousing as the way his mouth is suckling at my breast. I love when he loses all control, literally ripping the material from my body. Desperate to reach the skin it conceals. I smile to myself as the feelings his hands and mouth evoke consume me.

I let my head roll back and allow sensation to rule me. As my mind is succumbing to the pleasure he is giving me, my final thoughts ring in my ears. *He really is the most virile male I have ever met, and I could never love him more.*

Danion

My control is gone. I doubt even an attack on this ship would be enough to pull me away from my mate. The bond madness is a heavy burden on my shoulders.

The madness is skating up my spine and mocking my decision to allow her to go on the mission. The instinctual desire to protect our mates is hardwired into us. The thought of sending her out there is driving me mad, beating at my sanity with every passing moment. I know that the only hope I have is to join with her; I have no other options.

I know there is no choice about this mission. She must go. But I also know that the only way to prevent myself from snapping and locking her up so that she cannot leave is to give myself over to the carnal urges of the bond.

She is so much smaller than I am. Due to worry of hurting her I have always held the bulk of my desire back. There is no option this time, as I shred her clothing I collapse into her breasts like a male possessed. I open my mouth wide and suck hard, attempting to fit as much as I possibly can inside.

I move between each of her breasts indiscriminately, rapidly, hungrily. My hands are still holding her body by the beautiful, round, and full cheeks of her bottom. I squeeze them firmly, just enough to hear her gasp, but not enough to bruise. I use the hold I have to open her legs wide and fit myself between them.

I notice the sitting area to our left and move to the chair, sitting down and keeping her astride me.

"Ride me, *aninare*." I tore my clothing away when I rid her of hers as well, and I can feel nothing but the wet heat coming from the haven between her thighs. I desire nothing more than to dive deep into her depths, to seek the pleasure I know I can find there.

My *aninare* moves against me sensually, rubbing her core against my shaft erotically. But she never takes me within her body. Never sheaths my shaft like I so desperately need her to do. Her eyes are closed in ecstasy and her movements become jerkier and less controlled. Suddenly her entire body tightens and she cries out, panting out for me repeatedly.

I rock her against me, refusing to let her come down from her climax but keeping her trapped in a world of pleasure. My soul is being soothed with every breathy moan she utters, every wild and ecstatic cry.

"Dane, it is too much!" she cries out finally, attempting to pull away and I feel my body stiffen.

"What did you call me?" I ask her sharply, moving my hand to massage the bud in her folds. I am rewarded with an answering cry of pleasure from my mate. "I told you what you are to call me. What was it?" I move the fingers of my hand quickly on her, demanding she answer me.

"*Animare!*" she screams as another orgasm crashes through her body. "*Animare!*" She chants my name in increasing volume as the waves of pleasure crash against her unforgivingly.

"That's *fiefling* right," I growl as I stand up and lay her down on the closest surface. I am beyond caring about where we are or the need for a bed. All I know is I need her body as much as I need air. Her arms and legs fall open as I place her before me on the low table in the center of the sitting area.

Her position gives me an uninterrupted view of my favorite part of her anatomy. She is positioned before me as if she is a meal for me to devour. My mouth waters at the thought and I cannot hold off any longer. I have to taste her.

I place my hands on her inner thighs and push them open. I fall onto her, enjoying her as if she is the sweetest delicacy. Because she is. Nothing in the galaxy tastes as good as she does. I let my lips devour her tender flesh, determined to bring her to another screaming orgasm. I will not rest until she is as crazy as I am for her.

"*Animare!* I cannot...not another... Oh!" my mate cries again with yet another orgasm. Watching her find her pleasure once more is my final undoing.

I rise over her, and with one deep thrust I am buried to the hilt within her. I cannot control my movements. I am thrusting and twisting and riding her like an animal; rotating my hips with no conscious thought, driven only by the pleasure I am feeling.

I have no idea how long we continue or how long I plunder her, but finally, I can feel the bond madness abate. With a final, hard, deep thrust I empty myself inside her and collapse on top of my glorious mate.

Chapter Twenty-Three

Ellie

I wake up to a hard pressure on my back, as if something is poking me. I open my eyes and notice Danion and I are both lying on the coffee table in our antechamber.

I reach beneath me and pull out a small serving spoon. Once I am lying comfortably again, I look over at Danion and notice his eyes are closed and he is breathing deeply.

I have so rarely gotten to study him while he sleeps since he awakens before me most days. I gently caress his face, pushing the hair back from his forehead. He stirs, his eyes opening and immediately focusing on me.

A look of distaste comes over his features. "Did I hurt you?"

His words confuse me. "Why would you ask that? You would never hurt me."

"I mean during our joining? I know I am large for you and I was not gentle. I lost all control and I took you for hours. *Aninare*, I am so sorry if I was too rough for you." His words cause my face to flush scarlet.

"I am fine. You were...exuberant...but I enjoyed it. I was not in any pain." After everything that we have shared, it seems silly that discussing this would be a source of embarrassment for me.

"Are you sure? I have never taken you so hard or so long. Do you have any tenderness down there? Do you want me to run a bath or get a warm cloth?"

"Yes, yes, I am sure. It was fine, can we please move on?" I ask desperately. But he does not seem to pick up on the hints.

"Fine is not acceptable, what did you not like—"

"Fine! If you won't drop it, I will tell you. It was unbelievable. I never knew the body could survive that much pleasure. I would love to do that again, all of it, because it was so perfect. If we did not have a war to deal with, I would tell you we would do nothing but that for the next year. Happy? Now please, drop it!" I stand up quickly and move toward our bedroom.

I can hear Danion following close behind me. Just as I open the door I hear a knock at the outer door from the hall. I look at Danion with panic in my face. We are both naked and smelling distinctly like sex. It is heavy in the air around us too. There will be no mistaking what we have been doing in here.

"Don't worry, they will not enter uninvited. I will meet with our guest. You go to the bath chamber and clean up and get dressed. Join us when you are ready," he tells me with a quick kiss to the lips.

"I will hurry." I move quickly across the room toward the shower stall. I cast a longing look at the bathtub but I know there is no time.

I take a fast shower and dress once again in the casual wear of the Gelder women: a pair of loose pants that are tight at the hips and ankles, and a top that is little more than a wrap of material that crosses into an X across my breasts, then wrapped once around my waist.

I decide to don the matching black set since I have not worn anything in this color before. I slip into a pair of the matching slippers as I open the door.

I pause at the scene that is before me. Danion, Golon, and Jaeson are sitting around the table we just made love on. Danion is sitting with no more than a sheet wrapped around himself, the sheet riding low on his hips leaving his entire top half naked to my gaze.

I finally manage to tear my eyes away from admiring his sculpted muscles as I join the threesome. I sit beside Danion on the sofa and avoid the knowing gaze of Golon.

It cannot be a mystery to either of our guests what was occurring before they arrived, though I doubt they know how close they are sitting to the location of said activities.

"*Aninare*, Golon and Jaeson have some ideas about the training you need," Danion tells me as he wraps his arm around me and pulls me close to his side. He rests his chin on my head and I can't help but feel cherished.

I smile up at him before turning my attention to our guests. "Oh? What is it?"

"Daughter mine, first know I am deeply sorry for my actions upon your birth that have damaged your trust in me. I know you will not wish to train with me, but it is imperative that you do so." He takes a deep breath.

"Why?" I cut in before he can continue.

"Because no one else here can train you in how to weave all the lineages through *lacieu*. Since it is the founding power line it is possible for you to weave all the powers through it. This is the only way you will be able to travel to the moon and be unaffected by the tainted *tatio*," Jaeson explains.

"Why do I need to weave everything through *lacieu*?"

"Because this poison is specifically designed for each specific pathway." At my bewildered expression, Jaeson continues. "The way that each lineage is controlled uses distinct pathways in the body. This is why Rale is in so much worse shape than the other two. He used *simul*, and by doing so, opened himself up to the most damaging threads to weave. *Simul*, uniquely, allows for the weaver to thread all the major lines together. It is an impressive feat, but it also is the most damaging."

"What does *lacieu* have to do with this?" I ask him.

"It has everything to do with it. Because it is the dead lineage." Jaeson enunciates these last two words, implying that there is some great importance to them.

"What does...?" I trail off as his meaning finally occurs to me. "They will have never seen it. There can't be a poison for it because they do not know it exists."

Jaeson nods at me, a pleased expression on his face.

"We must begin training at once. There is no time to waste." Jaeson stands up and offers a hand to help me stand.

"Not yet, old one. We are not done here." Golon speaks to the room in a deep monotone. I am not sure what, but something has put him in a dark mood. "We still need to decide the order for Eleanor's training."

I can tell by the mulish look on Jaeson's face that he wants to argue. A tense moment stretches uncomfortably long while he battles with himself. Finally, his more intelligent half wins the fight, and with a terse nod he sits down.

"After her training with me I would think that the first line for her to attempt should be *ignis*. It requires a completely different skill set than *lacieu* and, therefore, is a good place for her to move on to," Jaeson advises.

"No," Golon disagrees. "I will be her second trainer and her first. Eleanor"—Golon fixes his stare at me—"you need to learn how to master your aura sight as well as begin unlocking your true power. Without learning how to manipulate your *chakkas* you never will be able to do that."

"What do you mean her first trainer?" Jaeson asks belligerently.

From his behavior, you would think he was the child in this room and not the most ancient warrior ever known.

I have to agree with you there. I was beginning to think that you had forgotten me. It has been a while since you spoke to me.

It was just a lot to take in, learning that you are not just a figment of my imagination.

I understand. One day soon you will reunite us and we will not have to have these kinds of conversations.

Do you think I can trust him? He is the reason that we were torn apart.

In this matter, I see no other alternative. You have to learn to use my power, and he is the only one who can teach you.

I was afraid you would say that.

"I will train her every morning in her aura sight and her *chakkas*. I am confident that I can have her ready for this mission in seven Earth days."

Danion rockets up from his seated position next to me, his sheet dangling precariously. "That is a bold claim, Golon. I would have thought I could trust you not to be so eager to feed my mate to the enemy!"

"Danion, calm yourself. I, like you, would prefer her nowhere near the moon. However, if we are set on this path, as it appears we are, I am not going to send her there unprepared, and I am the best trainer we have. Regardless of the opinions some absentee father has, I am the best male for this job."

Jaeson opens his mouth, but Danion stops him with a glare. "No, Golon is right. With his ability to see a person's aura he can more accurately guide any trainee." Danion lets out a harsh sigh. "But seven days, Golon? That seems like an ambitious goal."

"Ambitious? Perhaps. Achievable? Absolutely. I will have Eleanor ready in seven days." Golon turns to me. "We will train every day, all day. You will start with me then continue in the afternoon with a lineage master. First will be Jaeson, that will be this afternoon. Next, I agree should be *ignis* with Arsenio."

I give him a nod of my agreement. Danion, however, is less pleased. I can tell by the tensing of his body. "No, I will train her in *ignis*. Arsenio is not to be alone with her."

"Excuse me?" I object. "He is good enough to protect me but not to train me?"

"His skill level is not what is in question, it is his intentions. There is no one stronger than me in any lineage, so I will train you in everything except *lacieu* since I have no ability there."

I am about to protest, to remind him that we already had this argument, when another voice speaks up for me.

"I am sorry, *cognata*, that is not an option," Golon says firmly.

"Why not?" my mate all but growls at him.

"Because you would not be able to focus on her training. All you would think about is the potential danger she will be in, and that will not do. You would endanger her if you train her."

I can see Danion is about to argue, so I intervene. "He is right. I won't train under you. Not this time. I will use my *praesidium* like we discussed."

"I do not like this," Danion tells me, fire in his eyes. I will not be intimidated. I meet his stare head-on. With a grunt of frustration, he storms away to pace the length of the chamber. His sheet is barely maintaining its fragile position on his hips. It is hung so low that little is left to the imagination.

His rippling muscles are fully displayed, and a familiar warming sensation begins to enter my body. I have to force myself to turn away from the temptation that is Danion.

"Who will I train with after Arsenio?" I ask Golon.

"After Arsenio, you will work with Malin. Then it will be Etan, Griffith, Amell, and finally Kowan. At the end of each training session you will meet with Jaeson briefly to have him inspect your weaves and ensure they are indeed safe from the poison." Golon's gaze flicks to the other two males. "Agreed?"

Jaeson nods. "Yes, except she also needs to be trained on how to direct her *tatio* intake. We will be bringing our own supply of *tatio*, so we have to be sure that we don't accidentally take in any poison."

"Agreed. Once she has mastery of her *chakkas* it should be an easy lesson. I will cover that," Golon says. "Anything else? Danion?"

All Danion does is give a brief nod.

"Alright. Eleanor, if you will join me. We need to get started right away." I rise to follow him when Danion reaches out and grabs my upper arms, bringing our bodies into close contact.

"You still need to pass my inspection at the end, so train hard, *aninare*. I will be waiting for you."

Danion

I wince as I see Eleanor collapse to the floor in front of Golon. *Chakkas* are incredibly delicate, and learning how to use them is draining on a body. Seeing her crumpled on the floor stirs every protective instinct I have. Golon is pushing her too far. I warned him. I move to step into the room when a hand falls on my shoulder.

"Danion, she is in good hands. Golon knows what he is doing," Amell tells me, which is little comfort to me even though I know he is right.

"It does not make this easier," I tell him shortly.

"I know, Dane. I know." Amell sighs. "But she needs to do this, you know that, or else you would not have agreed to her training for this mission."

I smile without humor. "She called us 'her people' and demanded she do her duty as queen. For the first time, she showed me that she thinks of us as her people, her family, not the humans." I inhale deeply, letting the emotions rush through me and taking the time to gather my thoughts. "I have waited so long for her, *twenty* years I have waited for her. It was so difficult, to know she was out there but not being able to claim her. To watch out for her, protect her as she needed me to. Since I have claimed her, since the very moment that she joined with me, all I have wanted was to know she thinks of us as her family. Thinks of me as her family."

Amell gives me a look of morose understanding. "Mating is never easy, Danion. No gift is given freely and a mate is the most precious gift of them all. It will happen soon, do not worry. Her trust is worth the wait. You have her love; she will allow you into her mind. Soon you will be joined in all the ways there are and you will finally know happiness." He shoots me a brief smirk. "And then I am sure I will complain that you are too cheerful. You know I am never pleased." He chuckles and I join him.

"I know that all too well." The grin quickly fades from my face. "It is only that everything is wrong. I feel like I failed her, completely and utterly failed her. How did I let myself be fooled by the humans?"

"Because we never suspected they would deceive us. We have always tried to focus on the Erain threat, allowing the mortal worlds to live their own lives. Since the crimes of the ambassador have come to light, I am making plans to investigate all the mortal worlds and see if any others took such advantage of our situation."

"Good plan," I murmur distractedly. My eyes focus on the beautiful creature that is my mate as Golon once again instructs her to enter some kind of trance.

What could he possibly be doing?

Ellie

"Again." I grimace at the barked command from Golon. My entire body is shaking, every part of me aching, crying out for mercy but finding none.

"I said again, Eleanor." I slowly start to pick my exhausted body from the floor.

Hands grip me under the shoulders, yanking me suddenly up from my position of kneeling. "Golon, I do not know if I can do anymore," I gasp to my merciless taskmaster.

"You can, and you will. You have a stronger gift in aura sight than even I do, meaning that you can manipulate your *chakkas* at will. You will be able to master a lineage a day if you follow my teachings."

I stare at him in disbelief. "No." I gasp. "There is no way that I could master the lines so quickly. No one could."

"No one except for you. You already are a master, we just have to get that side of you out in the open. I can sense the control from deep inside you. You already know on a subconscious level how to use your power. Now all you need to do is learn how to harness your power on your command."

I stare at Golon, dumbfounded. I never suspected that he knew about my power being separated from myself, that it is more like its own person locked deep inside me. Golon must have read on my face how confused I was.

"Yes, I know about your inner self. I also know that it is a greater issue than you are aware of. Jaeson believes that he just bound your powers away, but that is because the Gelders of his time did not realize the true danger of abusing the dark lines."

"Dark lines?" I ask hesitantly, not sure I like where this is headed.

"Yes, the dark lines. Some things in this existence are better left alone, even if we can manipulate them. Your father used deadly dark energy to strip your body of your power, to incarcerate it deep within you. Except he did not possess the strength that was needed to confine your power. Your power fought back; it found a way to hide in your mind. Taking a little piece of your conscious self with it."

"Why would it do that?" I ask Golon.

"Because that way you're still controlling your power. Not physically, but mentally and metaphysically your body already knows how to use your power. In a way, he made you stronger. The power that resides within you displays signs of a deeper understanding of our world." Golon's eyes glisten with excitement. "It is evidence for a theory I have looked to prove for quite some time."

With no small amount of trepidation, I ask, "What theory?"

"That the power we can wield is more than just the excess energy found in the cosmos. It is…" Golon pauses, struggling to find a word to construe his meaning. "Sentient, in some ways. Your power was able to learn and grow while locked within you. That is so remarkable it borders on the inconceivable. Add to that the fact that there are times that you innately control your power and it shows that it can think for itself."

"But how are you so sure? If my power is able to think for itself, wouldn't I be a lot stronger than I am?" I question him. Internally, I recognize that my power *is* sentient. I actually converse with it regularly.

"The proof is in how well you are handling my beating. Most warriors cannot survive what I have just put you through until their sixtieth year, and you are nowhere near your breaking point yet."

"Sixtieth year?" There is no way, just no possible way that I could be performing as well as a warrior three times my age.

"Yes, well beyond that actually. If I did not know your age, based on just your skill level and mastery of *chakkas*, I would place you just before your hundredth year. Very impressive, young queen."

I open my mouth but no sound comes out. I am left speechless and confused by his revelations.

"And none of this is going to get you out of another meditation so stop stalling. Now, again."

With his words, I step back and close my eyes.

I clear my mind and focus on the instructions Golon gave me.

This meditation will not only strengthen your chakkas, *but also allow you to tap into the subconscious control you have of your power.*

Picture the colors you see when you look upon a warrior. Picture each and every color right now and pull from deep within yourself.

You have each of them within you, and you have the ability to call them forth simultaneously.

Soon my arms, legs, abdomen, and head are pounding. I can feel the power pulsating through the *chakkas* points all throughout my body. Every fiber of my body is screaming, begging for relief.

I open my eyes and I see the room before me, ablaze with a multitude of colors. You cannot distinguish where one color stops and another begins. It is a perfect compilation of the auras swirling around each other.

"Wonderful, Eleanor. Your power is still flowing while you have your eyes open, which means your focus and control have already strengthened."

I look at Golon and realize that he is right. I had no idea that I could feel so much stronger in just a few hours of training.

"Now take it up a notch. Pour more power into the weaves." I look at him in desperation, hoping he will grant me a reprieve. His eyes are unwavering. I will find no leniency with him.

Genuinely doubting I have more to give, I pour more into the weave. I funnel everything that I possibly can into the weaves I am threading. I keep pushing until I feel like I am pressing my very life energy out.

I am so focused on Golon's implacable face that I do not realize that my vision is fading until it has narrowed so far all I can see is Golon. Faintly, I hear an angry shout near the door, but I have no energy to give it any thought.

The last thing I think as the darkness takes me is that I hope Danion is not watching, or he is about to be very angry with me. And no doubt Golon.

Chapter Twenty-Four

Danion

"Ellie!" I yell as I race across the room and catch her moments before her head crashes on the ground. I gather her close and glare at the male across from me who, up until now, I considered family.

"Golon!" I snarl. "You are supposed to be training her, not killing her!"

"Do not come in here all belligerent and question my technique. I knew exactly what we were doing. She will be fine in no more than a couple of hours. She will rest, eat a meal, and then train with Jaeson."

I stare at him, furious anger coursing throughout my body. "How can you even think that she will be ready for more training?!"

"Because she will be. She is stronger than any of us think. She already shows mastery of her lineages that would rival a warrior five times her age."

His words shock me. "Five times?"

"Yes, and one who has seen battle even. She is a descendant of a great and powerful Gelder line. She will be our greatest warrior, I have no doubt about that."

"Even so, you still took her body too far. You know how much time it takes a warrior to heal from overusing their *chakkas*," I remind him. We will be lucky if she rises from her bed by morning.

"For a warrior lacking in aura sight, yes. But, those few who have it, have enormous control of their *chakkas*. Ours are more flexible and grow abnormally quickly. I assure you, two hours is the most she will need."

I stand with my mate curled safely in my arms, staring at my cousin that I trust with my life. Torn between my rage that my mate was harmed and my belief in Golon's competency and ability.

"Listen to me carefully, *cognata*. You may have trained hundreds of warriors, but this is my mate. I will give you leave this time while I wait to see if she heals as quickly as you claim. If she does not, I will have you demoted and thrown off this ship. Never doubt that for a second. Now, perhaps we both will be hoping for a speedy recovery."

I turn and begin striding from the room with my precious cargo. I hear Golon speak, but I do not stop.

"I do not need hope, I have knowledge. She will be fine, Dane, trust me." The door slams on the last word of Golon's plea.

I lengthen my stride and send a message through Jedde to have Jarlin in my chambers. In very little time I am able to cross the massive ship and deposit my mate safely in our bed.

I stare down at my beautiful mate and marvel again at the gift that was given to me. There is nothing I want more than her happiness. I value her peace of mind over all things, and it is ripping me apart that I have to send her to this moon rather than go myself.

I reach out and brush the hair from her forehead. Golon better be right, and all she needs is rest. The sight of my mate lying unconscious is becoming too familiar by far.

A faint knock at the door precedes Jarlin entering the room. The healer rushes over to my mate's bedside and places one hand on her forehead and one on her abdomen. He glances at me then diverts his gaze back to my mate.

"What happened?" he asks me briskly. "I have to admit that our queen is becoming one of my most frequent patients." His face is grim, but nothing compared to the grimace on my face I am sure. I need no reminder how many times my mate has been injured while under my protection.

"Golon was training her and he pushed her too far. Her *chakkas* are overworked, he claims. He is confident she will only need a few hours' rest," I say with a snort of derision.

Jarlin nods his head in acknowledgment and then focuses his entire attention on diagnosing my mate. The bond madness rides me hard to fling the hands of this unattached male from my mate, but I fight the impulse. I know that he needs the contact to correctly diagnose a patient.

Finally, after what feels like ages, he raises his head and turns to me. "She will be fine, Golon's assessment is correct. Her *chakkas* are strained, but they are already healed and doubling in size. A few hours should be all she needs. I will send down a supplement that will help her body heal even faster, but there is nothing wrong with her."

I nod at the healer before me, torn by conflicting emotions. While I am pleased that she is unharmed, ecstatic really, I am disappointed that I will have no reason to forbid her from training again. Eventually, the relief wins out and I lie down beside her, curling my body around hers. I stroke her hair as I wait for her to awaken.

I am woken by a gentle stirring in my arms. I open my eyes and see my mate's brilliant blue eyes peering at me.

"How did I get here?" she asks me, an adorable furrow on her brow. Because I can't help myself, I place a gentle kiss onto that furrow.

"I carried you after you collapsed while working with Golon," I tell her while keeping my lips on her brow, moving them slowly across her furrow until it smooths out.

"Oh." She tries to avert her gaze, but she cannot escape me. "I suppose you are going to forbid me from training again," she says with a little pout on her lips.

Despite my concern for her welfare and my desperation to stop her from going on this mission, I chuckle at her behavior.

"Why are you laughing?" Her voice is indignant. Which only increases my merriment with her.

"Because there is no one like you, *aninare*. No one at all, and there is no one I would rather have as a mate." I claim her lips in a ferocious kiss, rolling us over until I am nestled between her thighs and she is panting from arousal. "You are right that the desire to prevent you from training is burning strong in me, but I also know that it is important to you and to our people. So, I will not forbid you from doing what you feel you must. As you said, it is your duty. Not mine. I never want to stifle your ambitions, love."

My restraint is rewarded by a brilliant smile that she bestows upon me.

"Really? You will allow me to continue training?"

"Yes, I am assured that it was a normal part of your *chakkas* training and that you are ready to continue your training with Jaeson as planned. Unless you feel too weak to train now?" If she indicates that she is even a tad too weak to train I will postpone until tomorrow.

"No," she insists quickly. "I am fine. I can train."

I hide my disappointment, guarding my facial expressions so that she is not aware of how fervently I wish she would relent. I paste a smile onto my face and distract myself with her delectable body.

I let my hands roam freely up her chest and take several moments to reacquaint myself with her glorious breasts. Soon, Ellie is writhing and moaning, begging me for more. I am only too happy to appease her.

Ellie

"Your training with Golon was very successful. I can sense your power within you now. However, I can sense all your threads independently. We will need to show you how to weave each one through your *lacieu* lines." Jaeson stands before me, legs braced apart and hands clasped behind his back.

For the last hour I have been holding a *lacieu* weave in front of me. A simple weave, one that would have challenged me even just yesterday, but after one session with Golon I am barely feeling winded. Yesterday I still doubted my ability to control lineages, but it has come to me with surprising ease.

Golon's explanation is the only possible answer: my inner self has already mastered these on a subconscious level. I am merely learning to bring the skills out to the front of my mind.

"You are doing well with holding that weave. Now I want you to increase it slowly. Just a little bit."

I nod at him and open my internal barriers just a little bit...

The blast sends me flying backward and slamming into a wall over fifty feet away. I sit up and look around dazed. I see Jaeson sprawled out on the opposite wall.

He stands and stares at me in disbelief. "That is what you call a little?" he asks me with a small smile.

I look away sheepishly. "I tried to do just a little bit," I defend myself. "It came so quickly and so strongly that I couldn't stop the power..." I trail off since I have no real defense. Shame sinks heavily in my stomach. Apparently I can't do this right. Maybe my mother was right and I will never accomplish anything worthwhile...

My self-deprecating thoughts are interrupted when, to my surprise, he laughs! "I knew you were strong, daughter mine, but even I did not think you would have such power so young. I was braced for an energy burst and I still went flying across the room." Jaeson is shaking his head.

"You are not...angry?" I ask him tentatively.

"Angry? No! I am so proud of the woman you have become, the female that you already are. You are all that I ever hoped you would be," he says with a genuine smile.

His words cause a strange warm sensation in my chest. My whole life I have wondered why my family hated me, and now I can barely accept the truth that is obviously before me.

My father loves me, he really does. He is not a perfect man, he is flawed in many ways, but then again so am I. He has not seemed disappointed in a single thing that he has discovered about me, and I can't even manage to trust him.

I return his warm, open smile with a small one of my own. "Thanks," I murmur.

"You are most welcome." He strides over to me and offers his hand to help pull me to my feet. "Now that we know what we are dealing with, let's see if you can manage to control more of your power without it sending you flying across the room," he says with a smirk.

I throw a playful glare his way, which causes him to laugh all the more. "I am sure now that I know what to expect that I will be more than able to control it," I say with misplaced confidence.

After several hours and more bruises than I care to admit to, it becomes apparent that I cannot handle the power that is inside me. I can contain the simple weaves that are shown to me, but those are for defense; they can block an attack or shield an area from an assault.

The larger, more complicated weaves, those used for offense, come barreling out of me with such magnitude that I am forcefully thrown across the room. I have been thrown clear across the room dozens upon dozens of times and still have made little progress on controlling the power.

"How is training? You look exhausted!" an angry voice intrudes into our solitude. "I thought I could at least trust you to train her safely this time." Danion is striding angrily across the room.

"It's not his fault, Danion," I interrupt, causing that red-hot glare to focus on me instead.

"Do not speak on his behalf! He knows better than to work you this hard. Your *chakkas* have barely recovered from the session with Golon this morn.".

"It is not her *chakkas* that are tired, young king, it is her body. She possesses such strength inside her...such an abundance of power that she cannot brace herself against the outpouring of energy."

Danion's gaze swings to me. "Is this true?"

I glance away sheepishly. "Yes, whenever I open myself up for any real weave the power feels like it explodes out of me and I can't control it."

My words are met with silence. I risk a glance up at him and see him studying me with interest.

Finally, I hear his response, spoken so quietly it is as if he is talking to himself, not me. "Hmm, now that is interesting. Very interesting."

"I hear you are having some trouble controlling your power?" Golon asks me as we meet the next morning to begin our second day of training.

"Yes, I am."

"Show me. Do what you were doing yesterday with Jaeson," Golon commands.

I take a step back and look over at him. "You might want to brace yourself or give me some space."

"I will be fine," he answers with a cocky grin.

"Fine, don't get angry at me when you are lying across the room." I close my eyes and do the same thing I was doing last time, slowly opening myself up to the energy that I now can feel inside me.

This time, however, the power feels even more explosive. It blasts out of me so violently that even I am surprised by its ferocity. My back and head snap back against a wall.

I had spaced myself out so that there was not a wall anywhere near me for over one hundred feet. There is no way that I threw myself that far by merely weaving my power.

I look up and see Golon hurrying toward me. He seems to be unharmed which is a relief. I would not relish the idea of harming any of these warriors who have done so much for me.

"Eleanor, that was...remarkable!" Golon says with disbelief.

"Eleanor! Are you alright?" Danion is rushing toward me. I should have known that he would not let my training go unsupervised now that he knows what happens when I weave my powers. I am actually more surprised that he was not there yesterday, if I am honest.

"Yes, I am fine. Just a little banged up. It will clear up soon."

"You just flew over one hundred feet! That is not something to take lightly," Danion growls. He turns to Golon. "What happened?"

"Her weave was executed with perfection; the threads were formed precisely as they should have been. Honestly, I have never seen such beautiful weaves. They were even better than yours. The power behind it though was enormous. More substantial than any I have ever seen before, and it was simply more than the weave could handle. It exceeded the weave and blew out, causing a small explosion of energy."

"Small?" Danion counters.

"Comparatively, yes."

"Compared to what?"

"To the full force of power that I sense within her." Golon says the words deadpan and they drop like a weight in the room. I am stunned, and apparently so is Danion.

"Explain," Danion demands.

"The power I sense within her is at least the same level as yours, but her body is still young. Even though she is advanced for her age, she is still a young warrior trying to contain the power of an ancient one."

"Wait, you are saying that I am as strong as Danion?" I ask, baffled. "That is impossible."

"No, we see the proof before us, it obviously is not impossible. You have power, so much in fact that you cannot actually contain the power within you."

"So, what do I do now?"

"Now we work on the control. From what I heard from Jaeson, you are fine with defensive power. It comes to you innately, as if you have been weaving it your whole life. So we will be focusing on having you be able to weave an offensive weave without being flung across the room."

"Alright..." I agree tentatively.

"Golon, I do *not* like this."

"I will make sure she is fine, Dane. Now go, you are interrupting our work."

After several arguments Danion finally agrees to leave, and we begin again.

This training is disconcertingly similar to the session I had with Jaeson. With every attempt my body becomes increasingly sore, but there is no measurable improvement in my control.

"It is remarkable, truly, that you can weave so much and are not reaching the end of your ability yet. I can sense your aura and it seems to be growing not dimming."

"What does that mean?" I ask him from my position on the floor. I am so exhausted that I am lying prone before him while he studies me pensively.

"Only time will tell. I should know more tomorrow." Golon leans down and takes my hands and pulls me up. He places two small capsules in my hand. "Take these to help you heal so that you are ready for Arsenio in two hours' time. That is all for today."

I am so relieved to be done for now that I do not even question him. I take the pills and slowly begin my trek across the ship to my chamber.

"I am really sorry..." I say again to Arsenio, who is busy putting out yet another fire that is destroying the walls in front of us. "I thought everything on the ship was fireproof?"

Arsenio levels a stare at me that causes me to flush in embarrassment. "Yes, it is. It seems that your fire is in a class all its own and can burn that which should not be able to burn. And do not worry, it is not your fault that you cannot control your fire. I hear it is not just this lineage, it is all of them."

"Yes, you are right. But before I was just throwing myself against the walls, not burning them down," I mutter.

Arsenio laughs. "Yes, well every power has its own challenges." He walks over to me and crouches down so that we are at eye level, quite a feat seeing that we are over a foot apart in height. "Do not concern yourself with this. We are only just beginning, you will get the hang of this."

But he was wrong. After hours upon hours of Arsenio and I working together I could not control even a simple weave without the fire bursting free of my threads and inevitably catching something on fire.

"This is hopeless! What was I thinking to believe that I could help anyone?" I scream out in frustration, trying valiantly to stem the tears threatening to fall.

"Ellie, *ignis* is the most volatile of all the lines. The first few moments of the weaves are promising, but then the fire rages and it escapes. It is not the weave you struggle with, it is the control of your power."

His words are of little comfort. I know that I cannot control my power.

"How about we stop for the night? I honestly feel that once we get you able to control the amount of power exploding out of you, you will be fine."

Chapter Twenty-Five

Ellie

"How did this happen?"

"Will she be alright?"

"Can no one manage to train my mate without her collapsing!?"

Words are swirling above me. I fight my way out of the fog surrounding me.

I open my eyes and see Jarlin, Amell, Golon, and Danion. They are all standing on golden rocks. Wait, no, they are not rocks. Are they pieces of the...wall?

It all comes back to me. I was working with Golon again and he had me try to weave just as I did yesterday, but this time the power was so abundant that I was not just flung at the wall, I crasked right through it.

Danion stops glaring at the males around him and makes eye contact with me. "Are you hurt?"

"No, I think I am OK." I look at Golon. "Why is it getting worse?"

"It is as I wondered yestermorn. Your power is growing with each use rather than being diminished. Every time you use your power your body is making room for even more power to take its place. I have no idea where the power that fuels *lacieu* originates from, but something inside of you is providing you an almost infinite amount of power."

Jaeson looks contemplative. "Yes, that would make sense."

Danion's gaze flicks to his. "Why would that makes sense?"

"There are things you do not know, young one, things that I am not able to tell you yet. But it explains why she would have so much power. Eleanor, I told you about the origins of our powers. If you think on it, you will understand." I stare at him in confusion, then my mind grasps what he is saying. Soul power. The only power that is not drawn from the universe around us, but from the power you have inherently deep inside.

"I think I know what you mean." I nod. His gaze turns back to Danion.

"And because of her almost limitless power in *lacieu*, she is seeing a limitless power in all the lineages. I have been wondering why she is not struggling with weaving the actual threads of all the lineages when she has never used her power before. I believe it is because her subconscious has learned to manifest all the weaves through *lacieu* already."

Golon nods gravely. "I too have concluded that."

"What does that mean?" Danion asks while kneeling beside me and wrapping his arm around my shoulders.

"It means that she has all the training she needs in how to use her power, it is actually containing her power that she struggles with. Each one of us is going to have to work on showing her how to control her power, not how to use it," Golon answers, looking contemplatively at me as he speaks.

"You train with Malin this afternoon. I will speak with him about some techniques to try."

"Do you think he will be able to help me?" I ask doubtfully, a feeling of overwhelming hopelessness surrounding me.

"I believe he will help you contain your current power level, but how effective that will be tomorrow and every future day will need to be seen."

"What do you mean?" I ask him.

"Remember our discussion about *chakkas* and aura sight? They can grow exponentially with every blast of power through them. Your power doubled overnight, and I expect to see it grow like that every evening. Until you can learn to harness the energy and not let it rule you, you will never be able to weave like we do."

"Oh," I respond despondently.

"*Aninare*, do not look so sad. There are worse things in this world than being too powerful," Danion says while he places a kiss to my forehead. "Now come on, let's go share a meal and I will escort you to Malin."

"Is this how it is supposed to look?" I ask Malin as we stand side by side looking at the now empty pool. This is the pool that Danion had installed briefly after I first came here.

Due to my own stubbornness, I refused to speak to him when all he wanted was to bridge the gap between us. I was so terrified to lose my newfound independence I pushed him away. This pool was a symbol of the concern he held for me; once filled with water, it now lies empty in the room.

"No, this weave normally allows you to pull water from the air around you so that you can harness its healing abilities. Normally only a microscopic amount is used." He shakes his head ruefully. "But on the bright side I have never felt better. You have healed quite a bit more than just the little cut I gave myself."

Malin holds up his hand and indicates the thin line of blood left behind from the blade he sliced it with only moments ago.

"What do you mean I healed more than that?" I ask hesitantly, not sure I want to know the answer.

"I mean that I feel as if I am a new warrior, fresh from the training field. Even my *chakkas* are wide open and ready to go. I would bet that you added decades onto my power level."

"I did?" I ask in horror. It seems there is nothing that I can do right.

"Eleanor, this is a good thing. I promise. We are a people of warriors, why would we be unhappy that our queen is powerful?"

"Powerful is one thing. I am out of control. Nothing I try goes as it should." I walk over to the empty pool and sit, allowing my feet to hang over the side. I feel Malin approach and sit beside me.

"Now, young *piin*, that is not true. You just go to extremes. You aimed to heal me and heal me you did."

"I suppose," I murmur, in no mood to be comforted.

Malin looks at the empty pool thoughtfully. "You know that this pool holds over one thousand of your gallons?"

"OK." He may be a mighty warrior, but his distraction technique needs some work.

"On my best day I would only be able to fill this half full in one weave. How about you try to fill this pool, instantly, using nothing else but your power?"

"Are you kidding? I would probably drown the ship."

"No, I don't think so. And if you do, I am here to siphon off the excess. Manifesting water is quite different than the other lineages; it is fluid and heavy. It takes an incredible toll on the body. I believe that you have so much power in you that it needs to escape. That is where your lack of control comes from. If we can manage to have you get rid of some of that power, you might be able to weave more efficiently. This is a safe way to drain some of that power."

I glance at him with disbelief, desperate to have him tell me this is all a joke, but he stares back at me with determination and a little bit of challenge.

"Fine, but when Danion is yelling because his ship is flooded with water, I am sending him to you." I stand up and focus my mind on my new task.

I know the weaves to thread to fill the pool; the knowledge is there in my mind even though I have never used this skill before. It is disconcerting to know these things, but that apparently is from my subconscious and she was an avid learner.

I begin pulling the atoms all around me into myself, beginning to manipulate them within my body. Once that is done, I start pouring them out of my body. The explosion is expected this time and, for the first time, I am able to remain standing up.

I do stumble as the power releases from me so suddenly. I hear a mighty splash and then water is creeping over the cloth flats I am wearing for footwear. I don't want to look at the disaster that I have made, so I keep my eyes closed.

I am distracted from my worry by masculine laughter. "Wonderful! See, I knew you could do it," Malin exclaims while grabbing my arms in his hands and picking me up to spin me around the room.

I open my eyes and stare in amazement around me. The pool is full and there is only a small smattering of puddles around the deck area. The pools of water reflect the golden material rather brilliantly, and the whole room seems to shimmer. The oasis in the back that Danion designed to mimic my river back on Earth glistens in a gorgeous, golden hue.

"I did it?" I gasp in disbelief, then louder. "I did it!"

"You did. I knew you could. How do you feel?" Malin asks me.

I open my mouth to respond automatically that I am fine, but then I realize that I genuinely do feel great. Lighter, as if all the tension in my body has faded away.

"I feel good, like really, really good. Lighter, as if all my stress has faded away. How did you know that would work?"

"Power has a way of backing up and causing strain on the body. One way to help is releasing a massive amount of power suddenly. Now, let's try the healing weave once again."

I open the door to the training room where Etan is waiting for me. After my training with Malin, I felt very confident going in to train with Golon this morning and I think that I proved myself well.

With Malin, I was able to handle several of the weaves he gave me without the expected explosion of power. But with Golon? Same issues again. The power had grown so much overnight that I was flung into a wall once again, fortunately Golon was ready to catch me this time.

After explaining Malin's technique, Golon had me siphon off power as well and then meditate for hours. The entire purpose of the meditation was to focus on strengthening my inner walls so I could weave without first draining myself of power.

Now I am ready to see Etan and nervous about how he will try to handle my power excess.

As I enter the room I see Etan floating several feet off the ground, his hands out-stretched and every item in the room is levitating. Upon my arrival, his eyes open and he smiles in my direction.

I feel myself smiling back at him. I have missed the cheerfulness that Etan brings me. He is such a joyous person. I suppose that has something to do with his power. He embodies the lightness of the air around him.

"Ellie! Wonderful! I am so looking forward to spending some time with you again." Without a sound all the objects drop lightly and Etan lowers himself to the floor.

"Me too, Etan," I answer with a smile. "What are we doing today?" I ask with a glance around, nervous that he is going to ask me to levitate something. I will most likely throw it through a wall.

"Come with me and I will show you." He leads me to a door along the far wall and opens it. There are stairs, and we begin to descend down several flights.

After what feels like forever we reach the bottom; I am confident we are at the bottom of the ship by now. We walk over to yet another door and he opens it. Inside, I find a room that looks like an elevator shaft, but it is empty.

"What is this place?"

"This is where all young masters of *caeli* come to demonstrate their strength. We are going to see how far you can throw yourself in the air using only *caeli* to carry you. It is heavily reinforced, so if you let out a tornado it will not damage the ship."

"Really! I can't hurt anyone here?"

"Nope, not a soul. The only person who will be in here with you is me, and *caeli* could never harm me. Eventually, I would like to get to a point where you are able to control the air so delicately that only you move. For this first time, however, I expect that there will be tremendous gusts of wind emerging from you. So, for now, release everything you have and try to move upward and centered in the shaft. Let's see how high you can fly," he says with a sparkle in his eyes.

"Of course, I am sure you will not even touch my record high," he adds with a devilish gleam in his eye.

"What is your record?" I ask him.

"I can throw myself over a mile in height, but I am the best in the entire fleet so no worries if you fail miserably compared to my greatness," he adds with a slight chuckle.

With his laughter at my back I let loose everything I have in me, fully expecting to demolish his record. It seems the one thing I can do here is let out unbelievable amounts of power.

I am rocketed upward; the air that explodes out of me is violent and uncontrolled. I have to throw out a constant stream of air to keep me from hitting the walls.

I look up and see Etan laughing while he follows my ascent. "You look like a leaf, floating one way then the next. You will have to do much better than that if you wish to beat me."

My ascent has slowed to a mere crawl up the shaft. "How high am I?"

"About one hundred and fifty feet. Nowhere close to me." He laughs delightedly, and I grumble. "Here, I will help you go back down safely."

"Why did I go so little distance? Everything else I have done I have overshot my goal."

"Because this requires more than power. You released a torrent of wind in this tunnel but only managed to direct a fraction of it where it needed to go."

As my feet touch the ground again, I smile at Etan. I understand why he wants me to do this. It is an exercise in learning how to release massive amounts of power and also control it precisely. I smile and throw myself upward again, determined to beat him.

We continue for hours until, finally, Etan calls it a day. We walk together up the never-ending stairs and part ways in the hall. I slowly trudge my way back to my chamber to share a private meal with Danion.

"How did the training go with Etan?" Danion asks me as we sit down for dinner that evening.

"I don't want to talk about it," I grumble to him, chagrined to admit that after all my efforts I fell drastically short of his record.

Danion throws his head back and laughs. "How high did you get?"

"How did you know what we were doing? You aren't supposed to be watching my training anymore," I ask suspiciously.

"I did not spy on you, I swear. I merely know that Etan is a master at *caeli* flight and not even I can beat him in it."

"How high can you go?" I ask him curiously.

"I am able to attain a kilometer in one bound or roughly three thousand three hundred and thirty feet. Quite a bit shorter than his mile in height."

I sit back, amazed at the heights these warriors can achieve.

"Come on, I told you mine. Now, tell me how high you got."

"Ugh, what does it even matter? I am learning how to control my powers, isn't that what counts?" I ask mulishly. Not actually hesitant to share my height but appreciating the joy in Danion's eyes as we banter.

"Tell me." Danion chuckles.

"Alright fine," I say with an exaggerated sigh. "I was able to hit three hundred forty-eight feet. But I will beat him one day, you wait and see!" I add with a laugh.

Danion joins in, and for the first time since we joined I feel like we're an ordinary couple. We are two people, eating a meal together, and sharing stories with one another.

"After Golon's training you meet with Griffith tomorrow, correct?" he asks me.

"Yes, that is right."

"Don't let him overwork you. Of all the lineages, his power is the most deadly."

"I won't, trust me."

Danion nods his head and we continue eating our meal in comfortable silence. Afterward, Danion comes around the table and offers me his hand. The fire in his eyes tells me what he intends for us.

He leads me into our bedchamber and suddenly presses me violently against the door, slamming it closed with the weight of our bodies. Lust flares bright and hot inside me, and I lose focus on anything that does not involve our two bodies.

Our lips are crashing together, our hands desperately peeling off clothing, heedless of the tears we are leaving in the material. We fall ravenously onto the bed, and I am surprised by his ferocity.

It is as if he is desperate for me and I am just as desperate for him. As I drift off to sleep that night, I smile in the darkness, happy for the first time in a very long time.

Chapter Twenty-Six

Danion

I look up and see Golon stride into the room; his body language is projecting an air of casualness that the look in his eyes contradicts.

"How did she do today?" I ask him.

He looks deep in thought and makes no move to respond. "Golon?" I ask again, this time seeing his gaze swing to me.

"Yes?"

"How did she do today?"

"Marilee? How did she do what?" His words astound me. I have no idea what he is referring to.

"What do you mean Marilee? I am asking about Eleanor. Her training, remember?" I prompt him.

"Oh, yes. She did well. She is still struggling to contain her power, but she is doing much better with the blasts. I would say she only flew thirty feet on her largest power release. She is learning how to hold some of her power in."

"Do you truly think she will be able to handle this mission on the Paire Moon?" My stomach is thick with dread whenever I think of this upcoming mission. She has had so little time to prepare. Most warriors train for years before ever going into the field, and yet we are going to be sending her out on a perilous mission after only a few days of training.

"I do, and you know that I would not send her if I felt she was not. As I see it, there are two main concerns about her going on this mission. Her ability to defend herself and the poison itself. The poison should not affect her since she innately weaves everything through her *lacieu* power. She also has easily picked up how to direct the flow of her *tatio* consumption. As for her defensive skills, if she got into trouble she would merely need to explode her power outward. The amount of power that she outpours is enough to level a battlefield. Her not being able to contain it should not hinder her ability to defend herself. Rather it will make her very difficult to defend against."

Golon's words provide me with some relief, but the tightening in my gut still remains. "I would do anything to keep her safe, Golon. Even make her hate me. If I feel she is not ready for this, I will not allow her to go there."

"I understand, but trust in me, *cognata*. She will be ready."

Anger burns inside me at his words. "Can you guarantee that my mate will come to no harm?" I growl at him. "No, you cannot. Do not stand there and expect me to handle this well when I am being asked to let my mate go into danger without me there to protect her."

"I understand your difficulties. Believe me, I understand more than you know. But she is a capable female and the training she undergoes will help her be even more capable."

"Do you know what Griffith has planned for her?" I ask him, desperate for a change in topic.

"I believe he plans on having her work on anchoring herself to another life. It requires tremendous power, so it will help relieve her power excesses while also helping her learn how to control herself in an emergency."

I nod mutely, lips pressed tight, anger locking my body rigid. No mate would sit idly by while their female rushes into danger, but that is precisely what is being required of me.

Ellie

I stare at Griffith through a gold filter; my entire body is sweating. I can feel immense pain in both of my hands and my chest. It started as a dull throb and now is an incessant, pulsating burn that I cannot ignore.

It feels as if there is something inside me that is threatening to burst free, and I fear I will die if it happens.

"Eleanor, stop now." Griffith's urgent words cause me to jerk back, breaking the connection I was holding between our life forces.

"What is wrong?" I ask him dazedly.

"I can feel your life flickering. You are near death. I can feel that you are in great pain. Pain so great your life is in danger. Or at least you were. It has stopped now."

I realize that he is right. The pain in my hands and chest are already fading. They are still throbbing, but it is much more manageable now.

"Yes, my hands and my chest were burning through the last part of that exercise." Griffith's face pales. His reaction causes me to sit straight up and stop breathing for a moment. "Griffith? Why do you look so terrified right now?"

"You were experiencing the pain that accompanies *chakkas defel*, or death of your *chakkas* points. Generally, it will heal itself naturally, except the ones in your heart and brain. You can never utilize either of those two to such extremes. If they die, they will take out the organs around it and they will never heal. It is one of the few ways that we can kill ourselves."

I inhale sharply, my mind jolting back to realize that I was so close to my own death. If Griffith had not alerted me I would have ignored the pain, determined to train all the harder.

"We can't tell Danion. Promise me, Griffith," I say in desperation, my words tumbling over one another. "He will forbid me from the mission and then we all will perish."

"Eleanor, you ask a great deal of me. This is a colossal secret you wish me to keep. From my king no less—"

"And I am your queen, and I am asking you to not tell anyone. You will keep it," I interrupt harshly. I despise abusing my position so blatantly, but it is necessary.

He studies me for several tense moments, and then he nods his head.

"Very well. But if I feel that the concealment of this information will be detrimental to you or the mission at any time, I will tell him."

I nod my gratitude. "Agreed."

"I agree only because I know the risk that you take is great but necessary. I also know that you are right; if King Danion were to hear of this he would never allow you to go forward with the mission." Griffith stares at me for several more seconds, his eyes glowing faintly golden in color. "Now, we must continue training. If we stop early they will suspect why. We will take the remainder of the time working on your ability to direct which *chakkas* you are using so that you will know how to prevent overloading either the heart or the brain again."

I nod and we sit on the floor, cross-legged and facing one another. For the next several hours he directs me on how to close off my heart and brain *chakkas* when I am weaving power.

It is exhausting work, and I now understand what Danion meant by saying that this is the deadliest of lineages. To channel *vim* throughout your body feels as if you have syrup running through your veins. My arms are heavy and my body feels sluggish.

It takes a massive amount of concentration to weave *vim*, and we have been working on it for hours. I am now able to move between the various *chakkas* points with ease. Griffith says this is so if I am in battle and one of my *chakkas* becomes strained I can quickly move between them.

At the end of this session, I feel more competent both with my ability to weave the *vim* lineage and with my control of my *chakkas.*

After five days of training, I am shocked to discover how capable I feel. These warriors are more than battle smart, they are magnificent trainers. Even so, I am nervous for the next stage...when my training is done. I know that I will be entering into dangerous territory with only Jaeson to help me.

As much as I may want to, I still do not trust Jaeson fully. He has done nothing since he has come on board to make me trust him fully. The idea of going into enemy territory with only him as my backup is causing me some anxiety. I school my face to conceal my concern so that no one can see it.

These moments are why I cannot bring myself to open myself up to Danion complete-ly. I know that it pains him to have me withhold my mind from him, but if Danion knew of my thoughts it would only provide him more fuel for his argument not to let me go.

I turn and exit the room after a brief wave to Griffith. I am too tired to do more than head straight to my bed. As I walk to my chamber my body is sluggish and weak, exhaustion pulling at my limbs. I enter our chambers and see Danion is not here yet, which is rather strange since he has been here to meet me every other time.

I have no energy to go find him. I approach the bed and lazily kick off my shoes before collapsing. Without even removing my clothes I curl up right where I land and fall instantly into a dreamless sleep.

Danion

I enter our rooms and see my mate in a deep sleep, lying atop the covers and still wearing the clothes she donned this morning. The slippers are kicked carelessly off at the foot of the bed.

I cannot help but smile at the picture she presents. Training is difficult no matter who you are, let alone for a powerful queen who is being forced through all seven lineages within a week. She looks so small and precious curled up on the bed.

I gently lift her and place her under the covers, quickly remove my clothing, and lie down beside her. Peacefully, my mind quiets with her in my arms.

My worry over her going on this mission is finally able to be set aside while she is lying beside me wrapped in my arms. I have no idea how I am going to be able to function while she is on the moon base with only the unknown, and not wholly trustworthy, Jaeson for protection.

Golon's words come back to me in the darkness, reminding me that she is so powerful that even she can barely contain her power. It is true that she will be tough to defend against. If she gets cornered, she could level a battlefield with one blast of her power.

Beside me, Eleanor curls closer and tucks her head firmly beneath my chin. Her arms and legs come to tangle with mine. I can't fight the smile from taking over my face, and I pull her closer still. I put my concerns aside and just relish this moment right now.

I run my fingers through her hair and allow her even and deep breaths to lull me to sleep.

Chapter Twenty-Seven

Eleanor

The room is spinning. It is the only explanation for the wild movements I am seeing as I stare up at the ceiling. I am lying on my back in the training room after this morning's session.

Slowly the ceiling comes into focus and I can breathe normally once again. I have been training with Golon, and for the first time over the last six days we have trained together I managed to keep my footing while weaving power.

I was forced to stumble a few feet backward, but I never went airborne. It seems the work with Griffith yesterday has helped me even more than I first realized. I asked Golon to leave me alone once our training was complete. I wanted some time to myself to process everything I am feeling.

The toll that these powers take on me is concerning. Managing to maintain my footing today has left me so exhausted that the room has been spinning since Golon left over half an hour ago. I know that this mission is necessary, but I am concerned that I am rushing into this.

If I cannot even weave power without being blown backward or having dizziness consume me, how helpful will I be?

Golon assures me that I will be ready after tomorrow, that I am making all the steps he wants me to be making. I resolve myself to waiting until tomorrow and seeing how I feel then.

I also have to pass a check from Danion himself after I meet with Kowan tomorrow. I know that Danion will not let me go if he feels that I am not prepared.

I know that if I rush this I am doing no one any good. If he says I am not ready I will have to accept that.

I desperately want to be prepared though. Every day my thoughts turn to Sylva and the atrocities she may be facing.

The door opens and I tilt my head up to look behind me. I watch as Amell enters the room.

"There you are. I have been looking for you. You weren't at our agreed meeting place," Amell says with a gentle, if slightly severe, smile.

The hard look to his smile is not his fault, it is merely how he is. He is such a large and bulky male, he has an almost boulder-like appearance. I suppose it makes sense, as he is a master of the rock lineage.

"I am sorry, I did not realize that so much time had passed. I have just been enjoying the peace here," I murmur as I sit up and twist my upper body around so that I can see him. "It has been a little...tiring these last five days."

Out of all of my *praesidium*, Amell is the one I am the most comfortable around. From our very first meeting, he has proved himself to be an honest, compassionate, and trustworthy male. He was the first warrior who truly made me feel welcome when I started this new life.

I study the male before me, pondering everything I know about him. I do not trust easily, but with him I have always felt at ease. Welcomed. Cared for. Even when Danion himself made me feel isolated, Amell has been there for me.

"What is it, *myo breva*? You look so serious. What troubles you?" Amell crosses the room and kneels in front of me.

"What does that mean?" I ask, only in part as an excuse to avoid answering. I do genuinely want to know what it is he called me.

"It means my brave one. No, do not shake your head, you are brave. You are so young, so innocent, and yet you did not hesitate at all to enter into this battle. To risk yourself to save all of us. You are brave, my queen. Do not let anyone tell you otherwise. Not even yourself," he adds admonishingly.

I nod my agreement. "I will work on it. It is hard, Amell. So hard." My voice quavers as I fight tears. I hate to cry. It is such a useless activity, solving nothing except making my face blotchy. In most cases, it only caused me more pain, since tears infuriated my stepfather.

Amell is like my rock, pun intended. He makes me feel safe and secure. Danion does as well, but Amell offers me a silent acceptance as opposed to Danion's quite often violent reaction to my past and the effects I still live with today.

"Is this what is troubling you?"

"Yes. No," I add with a sniffle, determined not to let the tears fall. "I just feel like all of this is for nothing. I keep hearing my mother's voice telling me I am useless, that I will never accomplish anything. It is so hard to trust in myself, and I am so worried that I will let you all down tomorrow and that I won't have learned what you all need me to learn."

I say the words in a rush with barely even any air between. Until I started, I did not realize how badly I needed to talk through this. Amell is the one person here with whom I feel comfortable doing so.

"Eleanor, never feel as if any one of us will think poorly of you for what you are doing. You astound us all with the progress you have made already. To discover that your own subconscious has been learning the weaves independently is remarkable."

"I know, even I have to admit that is a pretty neat trick my mind did." I smile at him, but soon it drops from my face.

"Eleanor, you must learn to move past the things your mother did to you. You must find a way to move on, to exorcise these feelings of inadequacy she instilled in you."

"How do I do that?"

"Only you can answer that. How do you feel when you think of her now? Especially knowing that she is not your true mother, merely her sister?"

"I feel..." I stop and force myself to truly examine my emotions. The feelings that the thought of my mother brings to me are a jumble, scattered all over the place. "I feel betrayed by both my birth mother and the one who raised me. And I feel guilty for feeling that way about my birth mother. I know she most likely had no choice."

"It is normal to feel betrayed. You were a little girl who ended up being raised in horrific conditions. Being resentful that she did not protect you is natural. Do not feel guilty about this. What would make you feel better? Punishing them?"

His words jolt through me. "No." My reaction is lightning fast. I may not know what I want to do about this, but revenge is not the answer in my mind. "No, causing pain and suffering to another person seems abhorrent to me, no matter the cause."

"You will have to forgive me, but I must say that speaks more about your youth than anything else." I look over at him, unsure of his meaning. "Only the very young can excuse horrendous crimes with no desire to see a just punishment given to the perpetrators. It shows you have not yet witnessed the true depravity that is out there in the universe."

"I have seen horrific—" Amell cuts me off.

"No, not firsthand. You have not heard the screams of innocent lives being indiscriminately murdered with no mercy. You have not walked on the scarred ground, with nothing but mutilated bodies surrounding you. One day, probably sooner than you would like, you will come to understand why sometimes death is the only answer. Why revenge must be taken."

"I hope not, Amell," I whisper.

"For your sake, I too will hope that you are spared that particular lesson." His tone informs me precisely how unlikely he thinks that is.

Danion

"Kowan, welcome." I look over at the warrior who enters the training room with us. Eleanor and Golon are over on the far side of the room.

Her control of the power inside her is truly remarkable. Only two days ago she was still being thrown in the air, and now she can pulverize everything Golon puts in front of her without so much as taking a step back.

"I have seen everything now," Kowan remarks with a grin on his face. "I truly doubted Golon's claim that he would have her ready in seven days and yet here we are, and she is knocking down obstacles that a warrior ten times her age would struggle with."

As much as I dislike the fact that she will be endangering her life, I have to admit, at least to myself, how proud I am of her. She was raised as a mortal and she is more powerful than the majority of the warriors on this ship. Warriors who have seen countless battles.

"Yes, she is a magnificent female."

"Yes, yes she is. I would expect nothing less for our king."

"I offer you gratitude, *simul massa*," I thank him formally, in the old ways.

"I accept your gratitude and offer you respect in return, *dulief massa*." I nod my acknowledgment, marveling at the title I have not heard in ages. Master Defender.

Since Joy came to live with us, we have all adopted the universal language as our predominant language. It has been quite some time since we have spoken in the old tongue. Our native tongue.

"Do you think she will pass your test?" I ask him.

"I have little doubt. From what I have seen and heard, she is a remarkable warrior already."

"We shall see" is my murmured response. While I want her to succeed, since I know she has worked so hard for this, I also realize that I would be able to refuse to let her go on the mission if she failed.

A part of me wishes I could let that part win, to sabotage her test and keep her here with me. Safe.

Could I do that? I would know just how to do it. No one would ever know I did anything...

No. I cannot deceive my Eleanor in this way.

I know that I cannot do that to her, not when she has tried so hard to master these lines. I will have to stand on the sidelines and force myself not to interfere. No matter how difficult that is going to be

"Enough, you can stop now, Eleanor," Kowan calls out as she completes the final test. Eleanor drops her arms and then drops to her knees, her entire body shaking from the tremendous power she just channeled through her cells.

She has just demonstrated her skill in each line individually and then used them all at once. She did phenomenally. Even I was skeptical until just this moment. Witnessing everything she has accomplished is remarkable. She still has a long way to go before she is actually a master, but her power is unbelievable in someone so young.

I stride across the room and kneel beside my mate, bringing her under my arm.

"How did I do?" she asks Kowan, her eyes briefly glancing over at first me, and then Golon. I give her a subtle nod.

Kowan answers her first. "You demonstrated immense power and the ability to withstand channeling truly staggering levels of power through your *chakkas* without imploding them."

"Why do I feel like there is a 'but' coming along?" I hear the worry beneath my mate's carefully neutral tone.

"Because you are quite bright," Kowan replies with a small twitch at his lips. For Kowan that is the same as a full smile on his normally stoic face. "You have almost no ability to weave a small or stealthy weave. For you, it is all or nothing. I see no reason that this should stop you from completing the mission, but you need to be aware. Do not weave unless you are ready to expose yourself."

Eleanor nods. "I won't. If it is delicate, Jaeson will do it."

"I don't like this." I cannot stop myself from saying. I tried as hard as I could to not voice my concern, but in the end it was inevitable.

"I know, but there is nothing that can be done. I must do this."

I feel impotent, useless. I should be the one going to this moon, not my mate. I snap my jaw closed tightly and try to calm myself before responding.

Suddenly the door explodes inward and Amell comes barreling into the room. "Danion, you need to come quick!"

Both Eleanor and I are on our feet and moving toward him before his words are done echoing off the walls. I can hear both Golon and Kowan following behind us.

"What has happened?" I ask Amell as we follow him out of the room and begin walking toward the new grid room at a brisk pace.

"The new grid that Eleanor designed is complete," Amell answers, but his words are grim. I can hear Eleanor inhale sharply.

"Isn't that a good thing?" Eleanor asks.

My words are cold. "Depends on what it showed us."

"Quite right," Amell comments. "What it showed us... There are no words. You have to see this." There is grave concern in Amell's tone and dread is traveling along my spine.

I begin increasing my pace with every breath I take. I can feel fear seeping into my body with each possibility racing through my mind.

Is a mortal world lost?

Is an emmortal world lost?

Have we lost ships?

I reach the door and weave faster than any of us thought possible to bypass the threads guarding the entrance. Once the final thread is unraveled I stride inside the large room with the floating model of the galaxy open in the center.

What I see is...impossible. I stop dead in my tracks in the doorway. No, no it is not possible. Just not possible. I blink my eyes slowly, convinced that it will change the image I see before me. However, it does not.

How can this be?

Chapter Twenty-Eight

Ellie

"Dane, what is it?" I ask urgently. I am not sure what he is seeing that is so concerning. From what I see in front of us, we have not suffered any significant losses since the last time we were informed of the status of our bases.

Golon and Kowan skirt around us, and then they too stop dead when they get their first glimpse of the screen. Both warriors literally drain of color.

"Will someone PLEASE tell me what is going on?" I scream, terrified of what I do not yet know, but from the reactions of these ancient warriors I know it is going to be bad.

"Their army...it is impossible," Danion whispers, more to himself than to me. Then he turns to me and clears his throat. "Eleanor, remember I told you that the Erains outnumber us, but that we are stronger, so it balances out?"

I nod at him, too terrified to speak.

"Somehow, they managed to hide their true size from us. They found a way to avoid our old system, something I did not believe possible, but they obviously did. They do not bother with it now since they beliebe they have crashed our system. They have revealed their true numbers."

"What are you saying, Danion?" I ask urgently. "Tell me. How big is their army?"

"Their forces are three times the size we expected, with numbers like that we cannot hope to beat them. It is simply impossible."

"No! There must be some mistake," I cry out.

"No mistake. The size we expected was going to be tricky enough, but now this? I do not see a way we can win a war against such a vast enemy. There are simply not enough of us. They already outnumbered us five to one. Now it is fifteen to one. Those are impossible to beat odds, especially with our powers being limited." Danion's hands slowly begin to clench so hard that the whites of his knuckles begin to stand out.

"Not alone." Golon speaks up. Danion does not even acknowledge his words, but through the bond, I can tell that the words anger him even further.

"What do you mean, Golon?" I turn to him, curious as to both his meaning and Danion's reaction to it.

"There are other races, emmortal ones, that are not inexperienced on the battlefield. Many of them also have ships of their own who are also our allies. We could ask them to join with us."

"It is not our way!" Danion snaps. "We are supposed to protect all life, not bring them into the battle."

"Danion, we need them," Golon replies quietly, so quietly that I have to strain my ears to catch what he is saying. "You know this."

Danion sighs with resignation. "I know. I wish there was another way. We took an oath. *I* took an oath to protect life in this galaxy. I abhor the idea of risking that life in a battle that should be ours." I walk over to him and place my hand on his arm.

"What are the other options?"

"The loss of all life. I know that it is necessary, mate. I just dislike the necessity of it. For three thousand years I have been guarding the life of everything in our galaxy, and now I have to accept that I am no longer capable of doing that."

"Do not think of it that way, Dane, think of it as rising to the challenge. The Erains are counting on the fact that you have never used outside help. If we want to beat them, we are going to have to change. Just like they did. They have surprised us at every turn. We never expected the factions to join together or for them to poison the *tatio*. It is our turn to surprise them," I say with determination.

Danion studies me for several moments, then nods his head. "You are right. The Gelders will not survive this fight without us evolving. We have already lost millions of souls to these *infers*." He swoops down and places a quick, fierce kiss to my lips. Inside my head I can feel his gratitude, his love for me flowing through the still-tentative bond.

Danion turns to Golon. "What races were you considering?"

Golon looks pensive for a moment. After my training, my aura sight has become much more defined. For the first time, I can actually see the extremely fine threads of Golon's power. I used to believe they were not there, now I can see that they are just so precise they are barely visible to the naked eye. There are thin threads of power swirling around

Golon's head, indicating the weaves he is using to sort through the information he has stored in his mind.

"I believe there are two races that are both capable and likely willing to join the battle: the Robarians and the Sliets. They both are active in their quadrants protecting their lands against Erain attack. They both have ships already and both have petitioned us to let them join in our defense of mortal worlds."

"Who are these people? I mean beings?" I quickly correct myself. I still struggle with correctly using the universal adjectives when discussing multiple races.

Danion is the one who answers. "The Robarians are a race of warriors, similar to us actually, except they have no metaphysical powers of any kind. However, they possess extended life, increased strength, and nearly impenetrable skin. They excel at hand to hand combat, but they also have an adequately sized fleet of ships. Robarians are well known for delivering goods across the galaxy, in an effort to protect against piracy. They have learned how to defend themselves in a space battle by necessity. They would be very skilled allies."

"They sound like perfect allies! How can we contact them?" I ask.

Kowan is the one who speaks up this time. "I will be able to handle the communications with the Robarians. When Sylva and I were serving missions in our youth, we often crossed paths with them. I know a few that I will be able to discuss a possible alliance with."

"Very good. Once we are done here I want you to contact them, then report back to me with their response as soon as you have it."

"And the Sliets? Who are they?" I ask Danion once again.

"The Sliets are a clever bunch. Extremely technological, they rival even our advances. There are few races in existence that can challenge their understanding of the physical world, and they utilize this knowledge to achieve teleportation, matter deconstruction, and various stealth practices."

"Stealth practices?"

"They can make things invisible for one thing, and they enjoy using this ability to make mischief," Danion grumbles. "It is beyond irritating."

Golon surprises me by laughing. "Danion, you are only mad because they hid your ship and you searched the entire planet for over a full rotation. You did not find it until they decided to let you find it."

I glance at Kowan and see he too is fighting a grin. My lips twitch as well as I get a glimpse of the small pout on Danion's face. It is not every day that you see an ancient warrior pout like a child.

"You may find it amusing, but I assure you I did not." At this, Kowan loses the battle and begins chuckling, as do Golon and I over Danion's behavior. With one final glare at all of us, Danion continues. "As I was saying, they also possess sophisticated battle strategy, they are active in predicting where the Erains and other hostile races will attack next, and they are integral to designing our plan of defense and the location of safe bases. I agree that they too will be an excellent ally."

"What makes them emmortal? You said the Robarians have extended life, what about these beings?"

"Sliets do not possess any natural longevity, but they are able to extend their lives by several hundred years due to their advanced medicinal capabilities."

"I see. Who will be reaching out to this race?" I ask the group.

Danion and Golon exchange a glance, then simultaneously say, "Etan."

I can't help but smile. There is no one else I think who would enjoy this race more. Etan has much in common with a people who once dared to play a prank on Danion himself. I would not be surprised to find out Etan put them up to it. I smile with a shake of my head.

"Enough, all of you," Danion barks but I can do nothing to stop my laughter now. Danion finally shakes his head with a small smile of his own. "Fine, fine. Have your fun. That is enough for tonight. We will see what they say and, depending on their response, we will plan our attack in the morn. We will talk with Jaeson, and the whole team will be present. For now, let us rest."

As we are leaving the room, Kowan goes to contact the Robarians and Golon is heading to speak with Etan about his new duty.

Danion and I head toward our chambers. It is late and after my final training day I am anxious to find our bed. My body is in desperate need of sleep.

Tomorrow we will be meeting with Jaeson and designing our mission for the Paire Moon.

Chapter Twenty-Nine

Danion

I lean my shoulder against the hard gold archway that leads from our sleeping chamber into the bathing and dressing rooms. I let my eyes wander slowly up the exquisite creature before me who is wearing only a thin, silk cloth draped precariously low on her body.

My eyes stop to take a moment to enjoy the view as she bends low to choose a pair of slippers to accompany the clothing she has for today.

As she turns, she gasps softly and laughs to herself in embarrassment.

"Danion! You're too quiet for your own good," she says with a soft shake of her head. "How long have you been there?"

"Long enough to know you are the most perfect female ever to be born," I tell her. Her blush lets me know she thinks I am merely flattering her, but it is the truth.

She calms me. She allows me to see the world from a new perspective, which is something I have always desperately needed. I just didn't know that I needed it until I met her.

I glance at the clothes she has laid out over her dressing table. "I love that color on you. It makes you shine, *aninare*."

She has a set of casual wear in the deepest purple laid out before her. Her fair skin seems all the fairer in the dark purple coloring. My skin is darker, rougher than hers.

I walk behind her and turn us toward the reflection screen and admire the contrast we possess. Me, tall, dark-haired, and with dark bronze skin. Her, small, hair so blonde it is almost white, and fair skin. We are opposites, but complementary in every way.

"Thank you," Eleanor murmurs. She reaches for her outfit, and then one hand goes to the sash holding her thin cover closed. She stares at me as if she is waiting for something. "Aren't you going to leave?"

"Why would I do something like that?"

"Because I am going to change."

"Yes, and I am quite looking forward to the show, I assure you," I add with a smile. When she still hesitates, I can't help but scoff at her in disbelief. "Ellie, I know every inch of your delectable body, have spent intimate time with each curve." I make a big show of leaning comfortably back against the wall again. I cock my eyebrow and smile at her in challenge.

"I know, you are right. This just feels more...intimate, in some way. It just does."

"Perhaps it is, but I crave intimacy with you. I crave it more than the very air I breathe." Somehow the conversation has shifted, transforming from the light and airy flirting we were participating in earlier.

With a small nod, Eleanor slowly unties the sash, letting her cover drape open. I am granted a tantalizing view of naked flesh from her neck to her toes. A teasing glimpse of the body that I have found pleasure in countless times.

The material has become hooked on to her hard and pointed nipple, shielding her luscious breasts from my view. Absently, I am very pleased she is as aroused as I am.

Slowly, with a teasing glint in her eye, she shrugs her shoulders delicately and lets the material fall from her body in a silken heap at her feet. She is naked before me, and I allow my eyes to leisurely climb up her body, pausing in all my favorite places.

"If we had time...if anything except a war was waiting for us, I would say to fire with the meeting and ravish you where you stand. I would not stop until you were screaming in climax no less than five times," I growl at her, desire racing through my veins, pooling in my shaft and causing a painful ache. "But it is a war, and there is no time. So dress quickly *aninare*, and then we will head to plot our victory."

Ellie

I can barely believe how close Danion and I seem to be now. Not long ago I was hiding from him in my sisters' chambers, and now look where we are. We have come a long way in our relationship, and compromises have had to be made on both sides.

I was feeling nauseous this morning when I awoke, and I am delighted that it seems to have passed already. Stress must have been the cause. Or maybe it was just the constant state of uncertainty that I have been in that caused my queasiness. Every day I am plagued incessantly with fears of what the future will bring. I constantly worry over this war, Sylva,

Joy, my lost mother, and a never-ending list of problems. I am so relieved that I feel fine now. If I was coming down with something it would be the worst possible timing.

We are walking through the passageways, heading toward the new grid room. Golon, Jaeson, and my entire *praesidium* will be meeting us there.

We are going to plot how to conquer both our enormous enemy and formulate a plan so we can be successful on the moon. Idly, I sneak a glance at the gold-covered walls. I still struggle with accepting the fact that one of the most treasured metals on Earth is used as little more than paint on these ships.

As we enter the chamber that houses the new grid, I notice that we are the last to arrive. All heads in the room turn toward us. All the warriors are leaning casually against a surface somewhere in the room, except for Jaeson. He is sitting at the lone table to my left. The center of the room is one large holographic display of the galaxy. Thousands of objects are moving within it: real-time tracking of every object that falls into our scanners' paths.

I am surprised by the smiles that are staring back at me. The situation we find ourselves in is a dangerous one, not a time for smiles. At least, I feel that way, but it is evident that these warriors do not share my sentiments. These warriors always take the time to ensure I know that I am welcome here. It is something that I appreciate so much about these males.

Out of the corner of my eye, I notice a strange blink on the edge of the grid. I turn my head, but I have lost track of it. Perhaps it was merely a trick of the light. I move to take a step closer and examine it further when a voice distracts me.

"Congratulations, Eleanor. I hear you passed with flying colors," Malin tells me with a smile on his face.

"That is not exactly how I heard it. Apparently someone likes to show off," a wry, teasing voice cuts in. Etan is leaning against the wall to my right and not even attempting to disguise his mirth in the situation. "Only weaving massive amounts of power that put all of us to shame? In all my years I have never heard of that before."

"Etan, you better watch yourself or you are going to find yourself through the wall. Again." I smile back at him. "You know you will. After all, I can't do a little weave. I only know how to blast you at full power. So back off." I can't stop the little bubble of laughter that comes out.

The whole room lights up with masculine laughter, and I am amazed at the levity we can all feel even in these dark times. These are the moments that we fight for. These are the moments that define us as the heroes of the story and not the villains. These moments remind us of the beauty of life.

As the chuckles slowly die down, the seriousness of the situation settles on each of us. Danion runs his hand down my arm and gives me a smile. Through the bond I can feel his determination, but also his fear. He does not want me in this war, but he is committed to letting me fight my fight.

"Kowan, Etan? What were the responses from our potential allies?"

Kowan pushes himself off of the table he is perched against. "The Robarians accepted wholeheartedly. They said that they have been attempting to contact us for several rotations to share some important intel they have come across, but with our grid down they had no way to reach us. They will be joining us remotely to contribute to the strategizing."

"Thank you, Kowan. I am pleased we can count on them for the fight." Danion nods his head, then he settles his intense gaze on Etan, who clears his throat and stands taller under the scrutiny. "And our mischievous friends?"

"The Sliets have committed themselves to the cause and their exuberance was barely containable. The Erain threat they face in their quadrants is only recently getting worse. They are eager to end this war once and for all. They too will be joining us through a communication array."

"Excellent. I believe that with the help of these allies, despite it being against our traditions, we can rid these *vermiens* from the galaxy." The warriors in the room all nod, except for one.

Jaeson is studying Danion intently, but he is not nodding. While he smiled upon my entrance, I also don't recall hearing his laughter with the others earlier. I raise my eyebrow inquiringly at him, but he only gives me a small shake of his head in response.

I turn away from him, deciding to pursue it more when we are alone. "When are we expecting our new allies?" I ask Kowan.

The words are barely gone from the air when two displays along the far wall light up and alert us to incoming communication. Kowan approaches both and accepts the connection. Soon the large, square screens are displaying beings I have never seen before in my life.

The screen on the right is filled with large, insanely large, males. Their skin is a deep, brilliant gray and their eyes are a bright purple. They look...magnificent. Even after being around these warriors so much I am taken aback by the size of these males.

They appear to be similar in height to Danion, but their muscle mass is enormous. Nearly double the width of Danion if I had to bet. My eyes trace over their uniqueness; I have never seen anything more beautiful. The diversity of life is so beautiful, so extraordinary, and so breathtaking. Their eyes are remarkable, filled with strength.

I do not need an introduction to know that these are the Robarians.

I turn my gaze to the next display and see one lone male. He is as night is to day compared to the males on the other screen.

He is small—well, not compared to humans or me in general—but to the other males he is. His frame appears lean and muscular, but he gives off the sense that his body is meant for stealth and speed as opposed to brute strength.

The small, lean male has bright red hair, which complements his muted dark green skin color. His eyes are a deep ocean blue, hidden behind thick spectacles he wears perched on his nose.

Danion rises and walks over to the screens. "Greetings and gratitude, my *ferins*. The road ahead of us is fraught with danger. Many may very well perish before we can claim victory. I will not insult you and insinuate that you were not aware of this risk to you and your people, so I will merely thank you for your willingness to lay down your lives for those who cannot fight this enemy themselves."

The Robarians nod their heads. "Thank you, King Danion. We have long been anxious to be allowed into this war."

"King Danion, these stars are already fraught with danger and will continue to be so until we put an end to their tyranny. Anything the Sliets can do to be of service, we will do."

"Many thanks to you both." Danion turns and extends his hand to me. "I would like to introduce to you your new queen. Queen Eleanor Belator. Eleanor?" I walk forward as calmly as I can.

I am determined to make a good impression on these allies. I may be small, but I recently discovered I am powerful. I will not let myself be intimidated.

"Before you on the left is Kilso Gerril, ruler of the Sliets. Master of deception and strategy." The lean, red-haired male nods at me respectfully.

"It is a great pleasure to meet you at long last, Your Queenship."

"And to you as well...Kilso Gerril. I am very pleased to meet you and to fight alongside you," I say with a slight pause. I do not know if there is a title I should have added before his name, but no one acts as if I committed a faux pau at all, so I suppose I did well.

"And these noble fighters are Merkan Foeslask—" The male on the left of the screen nods his head. With the movement, the light catches a deep scar that runs down his face, from temple to chin. "And Sorle Berkel. These males are the reigning overlords of the United Robarian Council." The second male gives me a deep nod.

"We are both pleased to meet the female strong enough to match King Danion. It is an honor, noble female," Merkan states in a deep, gravelly voice.

"And I am pleased to meet such strong and capable warriors as yourselves," I say smoothly, if not a little awkwardly. These social niceties are more difficult than the training hell that Golon put me through.

"Let us begin. We have much to discuss." The communication displays are floating along one side of the table with Jaeson. We all sit together. The tension in the air is palpable. We have barely taken a seat when Danion continues.

"Now Merkan, Sorle. Kowan informed me that there was an urgent matter you have been attempting to discuss with us?"

Merkan and Sorle share a look, then Merkan leans slightly forward. "Yes. Just over one pallie ago." I have to think for a quick moment before I remember that is just about a week in terms of Earth days. "We noticed a disturbing pattern in the trade routes. They are slowly becoming more and more filled with Erain-controlled ships. They are posing as traditional merchant class ships."

Golon raises one finger just slightly, but Merkan halts and offers him a nod of his head. "What about these ships identifies them as Erain?"

"Our warships have the ability to detect electromagnetic waves. Most beings' brainwaves are so weak that they do not appear on our scanners. But Erain brains? That is a whole different game. Their brains light up our scanners if they are even within a starmile of us."

"Why?" I blurt out, then quickly apologize. "Apologies, I did not mean to speak out."

"Do not worry, strong Eleanor, any questions you have are welcome." The warmth in this giant's face is surprising to me. They hardly know me, but they are so welcoming. "And in answer to your question, we do not know. Almost nothing is known about the Erain race for sure, with the exception that death and destruction follows in their wake."

Jaeson tilts his head slightly then turns to Merkan. "Have you engaged with any of these disguised ships?"

"No, we have let them pass with no questions. We felt that the benefit of concealing our knowledge outweighed the benefits of a quick confrontation. At least until we know more."

"Very wise of you," Jaeson murmurs, seemingly pleased with this information.

I lean to Danion and whisper, "What do they mean?"

I apparently was not quiet enough, because Merkan answers me. "With the collapse of the Geldan outposts and safe hideouts we knew that the Erains were planning something bigger than hiding their trade routes. By letting them move unnoticed, we have concealed from them that we can track their hidden ships."

Now I understand the importance, but with this knowledge another worry comes to me. "Did our accounting of their resources yesterday take into consideration these hidden ships?" I ask Danion, my tone betraying my fear. They were already too large a force to contend with, now they could be even larger.

"No," Danion bites off. "No, it did not. The merchant ships were counted as merchant ships. How have they grown so large so quickly?"

Griffith speaks up. "We are assuming we have ever been informed of their true size. It is possible they did *not* grow quickly, simply we have never known the extent of their resources."

"Griff is correct. They could easily have been concealing their numbers for centuries," Etan seconds, the lighthearted male replaced by the fierce warrior.

Danion looks to Merkan and Sorle. "How many of these Erain disguises have you seen?"

Their faces darken. Sorle's eyes travel the table slowly, making eye contact with each of us momentarily. "Hundreds. Hundreds of them have been observed crossing the galaxy."

I hear Danion curse under his breath. "This will not be an easy victory for us. Their numbers are too high. Greater than we ever imagined. Even with both of your resources added to ours, we still fall short. We are still desperately outnumbered."

Jaeson lets out a heavy sigh. "I may have a solution." All the heads turn to him. "I know of a race we can approach who will be more than able to stand against the Erains. Only I have not spoken to them in over five millennia, so it would be expected they no longer know me."

"Which race?" Golon asks him.

"The Draga."

A soft snort comes from Arsenio. "They died out over two millennia ago. No allies are to be found there."

"I assure you, the Draga are very much alive. We will have to travel to their homeworld for me to speak with them, however. They abhor technology, and if they are faking their extinction once again they will be hard to track."

"Faking their extinction?" Kilso asks, interest making his eyes brighter. I recall how Danion described him. Master of deception.

"Yes, the Draga dislike interacting in stellar politics and have an uncanny gift for predicting wars. They go to ground when they expect a major celestial war. Without extreme reason, they will not fight with us."

"Then why do you mention them as an ally?" Danion asks with no hostility. These may be the most civil words he has ever spoken to Jaeson.

"Because I plan to give them an extreme reason," he answers with a smirk that earns one in response from Danion. "Next, I have another possible solution to the issue before us. First, I preface this by saying that I was not hiding this from you, King Danion. I was merely waiting for the precise moment to reveal it. I swore an oath long before our kind locked us on this path to self-destruction to protect this secret. If I saw any other way, I would take this knowledge to my grave."

Wariness is now evident on not only Danion's face but every single being in this room. "Tell us what it is that you speak of."

"The *Carnifex*." The word causes stark fear to appear on the face of each warrior in the room. The three males on the screen share my expression of wary curiosity.

Danion leans forward suddenly. "The *Carnifex*? You have in your possession the weapon that was deemed the bringer of death? I thought it was destroyed long before even your time?"

"That is what the record shows, but it cannot be destroyed. Not without ripping a hole in the fabric of space and time. So it was made, it can never be unmade. I merely protect it, hide it, and long ago I deactivated it. Removing the power source so that no one could stumble upon it."

"What is this *Carnifex* thing that you are talking about?" I ask, not sure if I actually want to know the answer.

Jaeson is the one who speaks after a long and poignant pause between him and Danion. "Long before my time, before the Gelders matured into a race of noble warriors who defend life, we built the ultimate weapon of mass destruction. It can destroy an entire planet all at once. No fight and no loss of life. On our side at least. It would obliterate all life on the surface."

"Why would anyone make that?"

"Because we could. Or they could. They were a powerful race and they were divided. Factions fought for control, regimes changed rapidly. Our people enjoyed war, then and now. We always have excelled in war tactics, and our ancestors relished in it." I feel sick to my stomach at his words. "Eleanor. Our history is a bloody one, yes. But you cannot judge yourself on the actions of your ancestors. All you can do is know that you would not make the same choices as they did."

"But isn't that what we are doing now?"

"No, because they created this merely to prove they could and for the sole purpose to win a war they weren't actually fighting yet. Once the true might of this monstrosity was understood, this weapon was hidden away. Once it was decided that we were going to take to the stars we spread the rumor that it was destroyed, to ensure that it was never used to control the galaxy. It was created and used once and only once."

"Why only once?"

"Because once they knew how utterly destructive it was, they knew they had to destroy it. And when they could not do that, they hid it and made history think it was damaged beyond repair. On the day it was tested, the actual might of the weapon was discovered. The creators were eager to prove how destructive this weapon could be. It was theorized that on the lowest setting it could wipe out everything in a fifty-mile radius.

"As a precaution, since the creators were harnessing energy they truly did not understand, they decided to travel to an abandoned area of Geldon. They had a safety zone cleared out the size of Texas." Jaeson must see the look of confusion that sweeps over the room because he clarifies. "About eight hundred miles of completely abandoned safety zone. When they tested the weapon, a size eight times that simply ceased to exist. Everything within it was gone—trees, land, Gelders...everything just vanished. Millions dead in a mere blink of an eye."

"No! How can that be? How?" I cry.

"And that alone was not the only danger. The entire planet was at risk, suddenly a Russia-sized hole was there. The mass of our world was radically altered. Gravity began to weaken, the planet started to collapse, and it took the combined efforts of every single *terra*-weaving soul to save the planet. If they had not succeeded, we would not be here today.

"Finally, they were able to see what their path of war and destruction would lead them to. Everyone who worked on the weapon was destroyed in the test, and my ancestors decided to lock it away for study."

"And you want us to use it now!?" I demand, nausea rolling through me.

"Eleanor, if we do not we will fall. If we fall, the Erains will slowly and methodically attack every known inhabited planet. There would be no more life in this galaxy except for them. Do we have a choice?"

My stomach is rolling. "We have to find a way to destroy it afterward. It is too dangerous to keep."

"There is no—" I interrupt him, not interested in excuses.

"We will find one," I say with steel in my words. I will not budge on this. "If what you say is true and that was the lowest setting, that weapon could do a lot more than just dedstroy a planet. It would take out entire solar systems. It is too powerful."

Jaeson meets my stare and we hold each other's gaze for a long time, both refusing to back down. "You know I am right, Jaeson. You do not want this weapon, I can tell. We will find a way to destroy it. Together."

Finally, I get one brief movement of his head. A nod of acceptance. I give him one in return, but mine is one of thanks. Jaeson speaks up again. "Once we have…"

I do not hear the rest of what Jaeson says because once again I notice that odd blink out of the corner of my eye. I turn and I see a lone ship, an Erain ship at that, skating the outskirts of the new grid.

I stand up and walk to the grid, but just as I reach it the ship disappears. Outside the range of the scanners.

"What is it, Eleanor?" Danion asks me. I notice now that the rest of the room has fallen deathly silent.

"There was an Erain ship, alone and—there! It is back, see?" I point to the ship that is back on the scanners again.

"Well, I can't believe it," Danion murmurs. "There are no other ships around. If we can capture this one, it would be very effective to use as a means to make it onto the moon base undetected." He turns his gaze to Amell. "Quick, let's head to the shuttle. We are taking that ship. It should only take us a little over four hours to reach it."

Before I know it we have excused ourselves from our new allies and we are rushing to the shuttle dock with eight males trailing us, my hand in Danion's. "Shouldn't we think about this?" I demand. "Plan it out a bit more?"

"No, we have never had an opportunity like this. We need to capitalize before they disappear and we lose our chance. This ship could be our answer to the war. A hostage could provide valuable intel about their powers, resources, and plans."

"But we are going? Both of us?" I ask.

"Yes, I need to be the one to do this and I am not letting you out of my sight after all the near-death experiences we have had with you. We never have captured an Erain alive. They kill themselves before we can get them restrained."

"Alright, I suppose...ooph!" I exclaim as I am pushed down into a shuttle seat, strapped in, and within seconds the ship takes off. I suppose when Danion means now, he means *now*.

Chapter Thirty

Nix

I need to get up and check where we have drifted but I cannot leave Sylva now. Her ribs are becoming an increasing concern. It appears as if the poison has prevented her from healing in any way.

She needs to be resting. They do not seem to bother her very much when she is sitting on her own, but movement causes great pain. I can tell from both her expression and her mind that the pain is getting worse, not better. She is determined to walk on her own around the ship now, stubborn girl.

I can sense the pain coming off of her, one of the cursed abilities I get from my Erain heritage, and my concern is growing with each passing step she takes. Suddenly, I feel an immense wave of pain coming from her and I hear her cry out.

I am beside her in an instant, my arms catching her mere moments before she crashes to the floor.

"Sylva! What has happened?"

"Hurts..." She gasps, her eyes locked in pain.

"Where? Where does it hurt?" I ask her. I notice she is curled inside of herself, cradling her abdomen.

Gently, I ease her top garment out of the way and what is revealed causes my stomach to tighten and the color to drain from my face. Her ribs, stomach, and sides are a mess of purple, black, and yellow bruises.

"Sylva? When did this happen? They were not like this when we escaped; I examined you then. I also rewrapped your ribs two cycles ago and these bruises were not there."

"Just...now...so much...pain..." Sylva's body is racked with coughs so violent that they cause her battered form to contract painfully. After what feels like an eternity, Sylva calms and pulls her hand from her mouth.

Blood is all over her hand and cold slithers up my spine. No. This poison is doing more than just stopping her from weaving her power, it is killing her. I pick her up and carry her back to her bed, setting her on the surface gently. I am about to rise to get her some water and medicine for the pain when my scanners go off.

Diem! Not now! I have no time to fight off an enemy. I cannot risk my dear Sylva, not while she is in this condition. I place my hand on her head, lowering my lips to rest on her clammy, sweat-covered brow.

"Peace, *beb.* I will not let anyone harm you." I send calming waves into her to help her handle the pain that she is combatting.

I rise and head to the display in the front of the ship, leaving the door open between us so I can monitor her. I press the screen to bring up an image of a Gelder ship heading right for me, traveling faster than should be possible.

Seems the Erains aren't the only ones who have new technology that they have been hiding. I cannot risk that this is a trick of some kind, or that they intend to blow us away without knowing that Sylva is on board. I sneak a look back at the strong, muscular female moaning in pain behind me.

I did not want her to know the true extent of my powers, and I particularly do not want to let the Gelders know about them either, but I have no choice. If even a rumor of the actual power I wield gets out, I will be hunted by the Erains for more reasons than just my treason.

It cannot be helped. Sylva is in danger and her people may be able to help her. With one last look behind me, I open the locks I hold in my mind and cast it out toward the approaching ship. Preparing myself, I let it explode out of me. I keep the ship tightly within my grasp, halting it dead in its tracks, preventing it from moving forward. I also lock each individual onboard in invisible, unbreakable chains.

Last, I look into the minds of those on board and begin speaking to them.

Danion

We have almost reached the lone Erain ship when the shuttle suddenly lurches as if we hit an invisible wall. I look over to the automated guidance system and see that the engines are still running, but we are going nowhere.

I turn to Eleanor to assure myself she is unharmed when suddenly I cannot move, not a single muscle except for my eyes. By straining them I can see that Eleanor, Golon, and Amell are all similarly held unmoving.

Based off the lack of noise from the rest of the warriors on board this ship, I gather that everyone else is being held frozen in time. What kind of power is this?

"To those of you onboard this Gelder toy, identify yourself and state your intentions. Failure to do so will result in me pulling your ship apart and letting the emptiness of space end your lives."

The voice is a dark, floating sound in the air. By the startled look in Eleanor's eyes, she heard the voice as well. Telepathy, interesting. It is a rare gift, rumored more often than it is found.

Unfortunately for this mystery male, my newfound gift of *abiciant* allows me great control over mental powers. I grasp ahold of the fleeting threads of the mental link and follow them back to the source.

When I connect with him I can sense his surprise; he was clearly not expecting me to be able to link back. A mind as old as mine has learned a few tricks, as he is about to discover. *"Why do you hold us hostage? How are you stopping our ship?"*

"I ask the questions and you have yet to answer mine. Why would you think that I would answer yours?" His words are rich in humor, but I can detect an undercurrent of worry. He is very anxious about something, I just do not know what it is yet.

"And you will not know it! What I feel is my business, Gelder," he growls at me. The emotions I was detecting are now gone, locked behind a mind that is impenetrable. Mental powers have never been my strength; I never needed them. I studied with a master of the mental races, monks of the strongest spiritual control, but they knew only enough to teach me to defend myself against mental manipulation. This is a true master that I am connected with now. While my *abiciant* power levels the field a little bit, he is obviously stronger than I in this regard.

"Fine, I will answer your questions. I am Danion Belator of Old. High warrior king of the Gelder. With me are my top warriors." I omit Eleanor's presence for now.

"And your...mate. Your mate is here." His voice hesitates when he speaks of a mate.

"You will not harm her!" Anger is rushing through me. My arm moves slightly, anger causing my power to spike. With the rage within me, my power rises and begins to weaken the binds that this male has us in.

"The emotions you feel for her. This mate of yours, they are...interesting. It is a connection."

"What does that matter? Why do you focus on my mate? You will NOT touch her!" I growl at him. He is quiet for some time, and then his voice is back, slower this time. As if he is distracted by something.

"I rarely offer assurances, but I will this time. Your mate will be unharmed. Even if I kill you, I will make sure she is safe."

For a moment his words leave me speechless. Before I can respond though, a new presence is here with us. It seems this unknown individual is still speaking to the whole ship. I thought that I had blocked them out when I followed the link back to him.

"You will NOT harm my mate!" Eleanor's voice is blistering in its anger.

"You too care for your mate. You both belong to the other. I can sense that you both will do whatever is necessary for the other. This is...love." This male seems contemplative.

A brief but powerful echo of his emotions comes rushing down the link. It is a wave of longing so intense it causes me to cease breathing for a moment. This male, whoever he is, is desperate for something. Determination enters into his next words. *"Danion, I have someone on board you have no doubt been searching for. Your warrior Sylva, and her life is in danger."*

"Sylva!? You have her, how do you have her? Is she alright? Release me so I can go to her!" Eleanor begins to fight the control he has over us, but so far I can sense no budging of our chains.

"I rescued her from her cage on the moon base, but the poison that she absorbed is too much. She needs more help than I can give her."

"My mate is right, release us so that we can go to her. We can help her."

"I have no proof except for your word that you are the king. I will need you to give me more before I risk her by placing blind trust in you."

"What proof is it that you seek?"

"The king would have no trouble breaking free of me, as he is much stronger than I. Simply break free and I will bring you on board."

Nix

As I feel his power rise, I let him struggle for a brief moment and then release my power. I know it is him; I read his mind when he connected with me. He may think that he has strong defenses, but he has never had to face a mind like mine. My mind was shaped by unmentionable pain and suffering at the hands of the deadliest of torturers.

I only had him do this little act as a test, letting me see his strength, and more importantly making him think he is more powerful than I am. I have managed to survive all these years by never revealing my real power. Old habits, as they say, die hard. Idly I start pulling their ship closer to mine. I walk back toward Sylva.

"Do not worry, *beb*. Danion and his warriors are here. They are coming to get you and they can heal you. Soon the pain will be gone and you will be at full strength again." At least, I hope they can heal her.

"You?" she gasps out around the pain-filled moans she is releasing.

"I will be coming with you, I am sure. I doubt that they will be leaving me here to go on my merry way."

In fact, I know they won't. That is why I let them come. I heard in this king's mind that he is looking for a hostage Erain, someone that they can use as an informant. I now know how I am going to save Sylva, and at the same time have her willingly give herself to me. While in the mind of these bonded royal mates I recognized what I crave. Sylva bonded to me, in every possible way.

Chapter Thirty-One

Nix

I survey this shuttle with only mild curiosity. My real focus is on the strong, dark-haired female who has four males surrounding her. The blond male looks up and speaks with the tallest of the group. Danion. The king.

"She is not in as bad of shape as the others. Since she never wove it her body's ability to process her power has not been affected, merely the poison is staying in her body with nowhere to go. It needs to be flushed out." Interesting. The poison enters the body even when the weaver is unaware and then remains stagnant inside.

"How do we do that? Flush it out?" the small, almost frail-looking female asks. I suppose her looks are pleasing to her mate, but I much prefer my darker, taller, and stronger Sylva.

"It will take all of us who possess control of *hael*. Except for you, Eleanor. You, I am afraid, lack the control necessary to assist us," the blond warrior informs her.

"We need to begin now! Enough of this talking! Look at her, she may not make it until we return to the ship," the one who has hovered over my Sylva since she was transported here says. His possessive attitude angers me. It would not take much and I could have his head separated from his spine.

Except I can tell he is strong, and he seems to have control of this power that they need to save her. I will wait, then I will kill him.

"Kowan, I know that you are worried. We all are, but let Jaeson tell us what we need to do." Danion speaks, and when I hear the name, it is all I can do to contain my fury. This is the male who has lain with my Sylva.

He will die, simple as that. He does not get to live with memories of my female in his mind. As soon as he has done his part to save my *beb*, I will kill him. And then...and then

Sylva will be hurt. I sigh inwardly, annoyed that I must spare this male's worthless life to save her feelings. This mating business will take some getting used to.

"I have done all I can do. I agree with Kowan, we cannot wait." He looks around the room. "Golon, Danion, Kowan, Griffith, and Etan, you will weave with me. I will weave the first *hael* threads and you will only add to mine, *not* weave your own powers into her body. My power is immune to the poison, yours are not."

Those words pique my interest. That is fascinating to hear, certain powers are immune to it. I wonder how that is. Fenke was convinced that it would be a universal toxin. From what I saw of Sylva and her team, he delivered on that promise.

No matter, as long as they are able to heal her, I have no concern. I have no desire to see the Erains triumphant, or the Gelders either for that matter. My only concern is for the raven-haired beauty who is on the floor fighting for her life.

The one they call Jaeson speaks again.

"I need every last scrap of *tatio* that you have. I need to flush out the poison from her body and replace it with the undamaged mineral so her body will be able to begin healing."

Soon they have the *tatio* next to him and his hands are glowing. One by one the surrounding males add their power to his, and for hour after excruciating hour, they work on saving my Sylva.

Just as we are docking onto their main ship, Sylva shows signs that she is beginning to improve. I can see the bruises rapidly disappearing. Finally, the tension starts to fade from me. She will be alright.

The thought of her face without the familiar grimace of pain makes all of this worth it. I relax, even as I am escorted into a cell. I know that she is going to heal now, and I know that she is going to be mine soon. I lean back against my empty cell wall and smile.

Danion

"How is she?" Golon asks me as he approaches from down the corridor outside the *hael* wing.

"She is doing very well. Now that the poison is out of her, her own body's healing abilities are taking over. Jarlin says he expects a full recovery. Eleanor is with her now while she is being examined."

"That is good," Golon murmurs. I can tell that there is something more he wishes to say.

"It is not like you, *cognata*, to evade. What is it?" I ask him.

"The prisoner, the male who had Sylva, refuses to speak to anyone until Sylva is present and he is assured of her wellbeing."

"Who is this male? What is this fixation he has with Sylva? How did he come to have rescued her? Why did he?" I ask more myself than Golon. His behavior does not make sense. I have never before met or heard of him. He is immensely powerful, not many can stop and hold a ship with nothing but their mind. "What is he? I have never seen any species that looks like him."

"We will not have those answers until we can speak with him. And he has not said a single word since he told us his demands," Golon explains.

Just then, the door to the wing opens and Eleanor beckons us to enter. We three cross the white floor and head toward the lone figure in the resting room across the wide open area before us.

Her teammates were moved into more private rooms when Sylva's arrival was imminent. It felt prudent to let Sylva heal without her hearing firsthand the pain they are all still in. We did inform the team of Sylva being found, which seemed to ease all of their minds, and they finally managed to rest comfortably, or as comfortably as they could in their conditions.

Sylva is sitting upright in the medical bed, her long and lean frame taking up much of the bed. Her hair, which almost always is confined when I see her, is loose and streaming down her back in shining black waves.

"Sylva, how do you feel?" I ask her, laying one hand on hers as it rests on the bed.

"Impatient to be out of here. I feel fine now. Perfectly fine."

"You just got here. Let us wait and hear what Jarlin has to say first."

"Jarlin agrees with her," a softly amused voice says from the side. Jarlin is standing ten feet away, studying the displays in front of him diligently. "Other than her body being mildly fatigued, she is perfectly healthy. No poison of any kind is present and she seems like her old self. Assuming she can be trusted to be on medical rest, she can leave the wing."

I look at the warrior in question. "Well, can you be trusted to be on medical rest? No training, no strenuous activity, just rest and relaxation until cleared by Jarlin?"

"If I must, but what am I supposed to do with my time? I am not used to being idle."

Golon is the one who speaks up this time. "Actually, there is something that needs your attention. The male who you were found with refuses to speak unless you are present and he can see you are well."

"Interesting..." Sylva says while she averts her gaze from us.

"Who is he, Sylva?" I ask her.

"His name is Nix. He is half-Erain, and I do not know the other half. He got me out after I was captured and then fled while I was unconscious. We have been in that shuttle since."

"Half-Erain? I did not know that they ever bred with other races," Golon comments while running his hand along his jaw. I too find this interesting. We know very little of the Erain race. If there is a more secretive race out there, I have never heard of them.

"They don't. Breed, I mean. Nix said that the Erains are not born like other races. They are reproduced by artificial means. He was born because his mother was a prisoner of war and he was a result of her torture." Sylva averts her gaze, seeming to be acutely uncomfortable discussing this topic.

"Are you willing to be there when we question him?" I ask her, conscious of the knowledge that we do not know everything that occurred between these two.

There is a brief pause before she says, "Yes. I will go."

Chapter Thirty-Two

Danion

The male in the cell is an interesting individual. He is leaning against the far wall, head lying back staring at the ceiling, one knee pulled up while the other is stretched in front of him. He is the perfect picture of casual leisure rather than of a male incarcerated.

His tall frame is just shy of matching my own, and his black hair is streaked with bright white sections. His body is obviously well built; muscle is easily displayed even in his reclined position. Strength is fairly rippling off of him. Whoever, whatever, this male is he has the potential to be a great enemy...or ally.

"I understand that you wanted to speak with me, unknown soldier?" I say to him, not revealing that I know his name.

He makes no physical reaction that he either heard me or even is aware of my presence, but he does reply; his gaze still locked above him. "You and someone else. If she is not in here then you are wasting your time. I know she is right outside, so you might as well have her come in. This concerns her."

Sylva, who was waiting just on the other side of the door, walks in. Nix's gaze focuses on Sylva with a single-minded intensity instantly. "You asked for me and now I am here. I decided to let you get your way one last time. But this will be the last time. What do you want, Nix?"

"What I have always wanted." Sylva stiffens upon hearing his words. There is a private meaning being shared between them.

"You won't have it!" Sylva retorts hotly.

An amused chuckle meets her outburst. "Don't be too sure now." Then his face clears, settles into a look of fierce determination and he stands in one fluid motion. "You are at war, a war that you will not win. Your enemy is more prepared than you can ever believe.

This battle has been in the making for over three hundred years. Every aspect designed solely to take your kind down.

"Your strengths? They have designed countermeasures for each one. Your weaknesses? Exploited. The things you love? Targeted. You do not know your enemy, but they know you."

His words spike my easily riled temper. "Your fear mongering is wearisome. We know this, all of it. That does not mean we will lose."

"That is where you are wrong. There are things that you do not know, and without them this war is hopeless. You will be sitting ducks. Much like Sylva and her team were, even when they were expecting a trap. Just like how your mate's life has been threatened twice, even though she was on the safest ship in the fleet. I can help you. I can tell you all their secrets, help you go on missions. I can win you this war before it even fully begins."

"And how exactly can you accomplish all of these feats?" I ask with scorn.

"Because I was one of them. I know them, how they think, how they fight, how they plan. With me? You will win this war, I promise you that."

I look to Sylva. "Do you believe him?"

"Yes," she answers begrudgingly. "I believe he speaks true, about all of it. They are stronger than we ever imagined. I do not know if we can beat them alone. Or with any known ally we have. I also believe he could lead us to a victory. His powers are very...impressive."

"Then what do you want, Nix?" I ask him. "What do you require that will have you come and fight on our side in this war?"

"I want Sylva. Willingly." He speaks directly to her, a smirk blatant on his face.

Stunned silence comes from behind me; no sound of breathing, or steps. Nothing. I glance at her, my shock evident on my face. Slowly, her face turns red.

I turn back to the male. "I do not know what you think you know about us, but we do not trade our females. Under any circumstances. I will not let you enslave any of my people. No deal."

"I do not mean I want her as a sexual slave. That is, unless she so desires it. No, it is a much deeper connection that I am after. I want her to bond with me." His gaze burrows into Sylva's, his eyes practically burning a hole in her. "We will perform the *cerum fuse* ceremony of your people, and you will be mine."

"My answer is as it was. We do not sell our females, especially not in the most permanent form of bondage we have. There is no way to break a *cerum fuse* bond," I snarl at him.

"Which is why I want it. It is not your permission I am asking, now is it?"

"Only mates can perform the ceremony. It is not successful with non-mates," I attempt to explain to him.

"I have been in your mind and your dear Eleanor's mind and I recognize what a matebond is. I also know how a bonding of the minds is achieved. My powers are more than capable of performing this feat."

Sylva has remained silent so far; she seemed to be in shock. She does not need to speak. I will never sacrifice one of my warriors. "Why do you think that I would agree to this? That I would agree to trade one of my people?"

"Because you need me. I know of the mission that you are planning. Your mate will die in this upcoming mission. No matter how they proceed, that moon has too many soldiers on it. Defenses you know nothing of, but I do. When she falls, so will you. Every single soul in this universe will perish. Without my help, you are all as good as dead."

His words send rage coursing through my blood. I am about to release my power and blast him, when a soft voice comes from behind me. "I will do it. I will give myself to you, willingly. But on one condition."

"What is that, *beb*?" His words are carefully blank, but I can still her the excitement in them. And the anxiety. He wants this, her, badly.

"I will not perform the permanent ceremony until we are successful. Once we have won this war, I will bind myself to you." Her words may be quiet, but her tone is laced with steel. "Not before."

"I will give you until once the moon mission is over, then we will join. I will not wait for this entire war to be over to bind us together." The black-and-white-haired male in the cell is utterly fixated on Sylva, sparing not even a glance toward me.

"No, I will not bind myself and then turn around and find you have decided to make me *dance* to your tune and we are gone, far away from the battle, and you leave all of my kind to die."

"I have apologized for my—"

"I do not care! I will give you my word, I will honor my vow, but only after the universe is safe. You can trust my word."

Nix stares at Sylva for several pregnant pauses, then finally nods his head slowly.

"Fine, but you will act as if we are bonded and will declare yourself mine. As far as anyone, and I mean *anyone*, aboard this ship is concerned, we are mated. We will share living space, take meals together, and for all intents and purposes will be bonded. We will merely hold off the formality of the ceremony until the end of the war."

"Sylva, you do not need to do this," I interrupt. "I will not let you do this."

"This is not up to you, Dane. It is my decision and mine alone." She turns to Nix. "We have a deal, but no physical joining unless I say so. I will be a whore for no male."

"I do not want a whore, so there is no complication. I am sure you will come to admit your feelings soon enough."

Sylva sighs slightly, then turns to me. "Lower the shield and let him out. We will need to debrief with him and learn what he intends for us to do to win this war."

Ellie

We are in a new war room, sitting around a table with a half Erain, discussing how best to destroy the Erains. Odd. We did not feel comfortable revealing to him our new grid schematics, so we decided to forgo meeting in the room the new grid is housed in at this time.

Jaeson sits beside me. "Once the mission on the moon is complete, we will need to begin searching for your mother. She may have information that could be helpful to us. We will have to use your power since Ambassador Lexen escaped."

Nix's ears seem to perk up. "Lexen? The human ambassador has left Earth?"

I turn to him, cautious, but Sylva gives me a brief nod. "Yes, we arrested him and had him in a cell, but he escaped during transport to this ship. How do you know him?"

"Because he is working with the Erains. He is a mole, and once he completed his mission, he was to return to the Erain king."

Danion curses and then leans forward with a jerk. "What was his mission?"

"Even I do not know the particulars, but I know that he was looking for some sort of proof. I believe about an old mythical weapon that many do not believe exists. One that actually can use the power of space and time to make matter disappear."

The room goes deathly quiet. Nix studies the faces around the table, and he slowly pulls his one arm from where it was resting with casual possessiveness on Sylva's shoulder to place both of them on the table in front of him. "Tell me it is not real."

Danion shares a brief look at Jaeson, then says, "Oh, it is real, and this just upped the stakes. They want more than to terrorize all living beings in this galaxy. They want to destroy the entire universe. All of it."

To Be Continued...

Author Notes

Thank you for reading Book Three in the True Immortals series. This is part of a four-book series that will feature Danion and Eleanor's journey to defeat the Erains and overcome their own faults to save one another. If you are enjoying them, think about joining my email subscriber lists by visiting www.emjaye.org

Other Works by E.M. Jaye

The True Immortals:
The Claimed Queen
The Hidden Queen
The Lost Queen
The Mated Queen

Golon's Story

His Mate coming winter 23/24!

Gelder Warrior Stories

Etan's Hidden Pain

Lovers of Beverly Tennessee

Hate At First Sight- Coming Oct 27th 2023

Kindle Vella Stories
Gelder Shorts:
Kowan's Anger
Etan's Hidden Pain

Gelder Warriors:
His Mate (Golon's story)

Lovers of Beverly, Tennessee:
Hate at First Sight

Blackmailed Series (Dark Romance):
Blackmailed Marriage

Printed in Great Britain
by Amazon

29824861R00148